Camera Shy

Camera Shy
An H. J. Russel Novel

H. J. Russel

Writers Club Press
San Jose New York Lincoln Shanghai

Camera Shy
An H. J. Russel Novel

All Rights Reserved © 2000 by H. J. Russel

No part of this book may be reproduced or transmitted in any form or by any means, graphic, electronic, or mechanical, including photocopying, recording, taping, or by any information storage retrieval system, without the permission in writing from the publisher.

Writers Club Press
an imprint of iUniverse.com, Inc.

For information address:
iUniverse.com, Inc.
5220 S 16th, Ste. 200
Lincoln, NE 68512
www.iuniverse.com

This book is a work of fiction. Names, characters, places, and incidents are products of the author's imagination or are used fictionally. Any resemblance to actual events or locals or persons living or dead, is entirely coincidental

ISBN: 0-595-16231-2

Printed in the United States of America

Disclaimer: If you are interested in exploring the dominant or submissive component of your sexuality, I would like to remind the readers that this is a work of fiction and some of the acts depicted in this book could result in serious injury. In view of this, *Camera Shy An H. J. Russel Novel* should not be viewed as an instruction manual. Before you explore your dominant or submissive side, please conduct an extensive WEB search of "Safe Sane and Consensual." Nonconsensual sex is **not** D/S. It is rape.

H.J.R.

Epigraph

They're around us all the time. Sometimes they will let you see them. Body play is a key to seeing their world.
Attributed to Fakir Musafar

Acknowledgements

Thanks to Mistress LL for her encouragement, for reading my short stories and saying I was ready for a book.

Special thanks to copyeditor parexcellance with the patience of a saint, S.L. Roberts (copyeditor451@ aol.com, there's the plug I promised after copy 5). If you find mistakes I'm sure they're my fault, always tinkering after giving her my "final copy."

Porke

Larson Donald Wood was listening to his last patient of the day. As a Clinical Social Worker at a private hospital, his long-term patients consisted mostly of the worried well, although some of the hospital's health plans required that their enrollees see him instead of one of the staff psychologists, regardless of their level of pathology. The sicker patients usually weren't as much fun to work with because no matter what you did with them, they rarely got better. These clients, the sicker ones, were only able to avail themselves of a private hospital because of their family's largess, wealth accumulated prior to their illness, or insurance. Most of them would never again be able to hold down jobs which would pay for their continuing inpatient care, barring a new miracle drug. Larson tried his best with them but sometimes found his mind wandering, focusing on their seemingly insurmountable problems, and thought working with them was futile. His current patient, the last one before he could go home, was not psychotic but was plenty worried. She had just realized that her pattern of withholding information from her husband, a habit which was threatening to cost her her marriage, had begun with her parents. The realization of this lifelong pattern of deception was making her re-evaluate who she was and what she thought of herself.

I've got a secret too, the therapist thought. If you knew my secret what would you do? Would you run to the administration and demand I leave the hospital? Would you feel betrayed that you had placed your trust in the likes of me? Would it be *that* therapeutically harmful? Larson knew what he was doing. This was countertransference; his patient had touched on an unresolved theme in his own life and it was making it difficult to focus on her.

He was focusing on himself, not her, and this was supposed to be her therapy session, not his.

"How do you see this playing out?" he asked. In his own mind he knew how he saw his "it" playing out—he had no idea. They had been happy for years, at least he had thought so—*he* certainly had been happy, even ecstatic. But lately heat had cooled, and he wondered if his role in their relationship was still exciting for her. There was still magic but even that insane sparkle had diminished somehow into an almost cursory ritual. A year ago, or was it two, or was it on their second year together? It had been six, had the heat faded that for that long, had it faded for four years without his even noticing? He always told himself, "she just has to get over this next hurdle, this next accomplishment at work," but there was always another and he didn't know who or what she was trying to live up to. He knew there was still a solid foundation. He knew it in his heart and his head. He had willingly and gladly sworn his allegiance to her; she had required that. She had been his first and he had never questioned the wisdom of that choice but still....Still there was that nagging question, what would it have been like to experience others before her, or after as far as that went? Now he knew what he was doing—typical guy stuff, if one's good two got to be better, right? Well, maybe, but he knew he had a good thing and didn't want to mess it up. Shit, he thought, more countertransference. He saw the picture of the room in his mind's eye: a wife who was hiding $15,000 in credit card debt from her husband, talking to a sexual submissive whose true desires were known only to his lover of six years.

Larson Wood, Clinical Social Worker primarily for the worried well, was performing his 'leaving ritual.' He placed unfinished paperwork in one pile, unread memos in another pile and stuff he just didn't have a file for and didn't know if it was worth making a file for in the third pile. To anyone else it was chaos—to him, organization, comfort, and a bit of laziness thrown in. If nothing else it was a style for work and study that had served him well. Always a conservative dresser with a limited wardrobe, he looked like any nondescript professional. exchanging good-byes with the staff.

"Good-bye, Mr. Wood," said Ms Green, one of the nurses. Larson made eye contact and nodded, smiling shyly. He knew that most staff here had him pegged wrong. When one of the patients had urinated on the carpeted floor as a means of protest he knew that the story between staff was usually, "Bill pissed on the floor," but to him it was "Mr. Miller urinated on the floor." On one hand this created a distance between him and his coworkers that made him more lonely at work; on the other hand it did protect him from too many questions into his home-life. What was he gonna say if someone asked him if he saw the game yesterday, say, "No I had to strip and make supper, then I was chained to the wall for the better part of the evening?" So he was polite, professional, and had a messy desk.

His isolation, he realized was taking its toll. Especially now that things were getting strange at home. This is why he was starting to countertransfer just a bit more than he should. "I'll either have to get some therapy or supervision if this keeps up," he thought. When one has problems and needs to talk them over with friends it becomes very difficult when there is a big chunk of one's life that is secret. That's why the use of therapy was seeming like more and more of an option. If he decided to go he'd see a Psychologist; as a Social Worker he knew all their tricks and would spend his time judging his therapist's effectiveness before getting to work on his stuff. Even if a Psychologist used the same tricks he hoped the title and setting would be enough to get him working his stuff. His stuff revolved around a relationship with the most exciting, intelligent, of course dominant, and lately preoccupied and increasingly distracted woman he had ever known.

He knew the problems had begun shortly after her father's death. Like him she had grown up an only child, like him this has made her self-sufficient, like him she was comfortable with her own company and therefore didn't usually seek out others, unlike him she was daddy's little girl. Her daddy, however, didn't want his little girl to be helpless or limited by her gender. He taught her how to use tools, taught her about boys and taught her that she was capable of dealing with problems that life threw at her, lessons that probably saved her life and sanity during what Alice refers to as the ordeal. Unknown to Larson, Lar to his friends, her father was the one who taught her how to cuss a blue streak when she was angry.

Alice's ordeal took place when she was in her mid-20's, attending grad school at Louisiana State University in Baton Rouge. She didn't fall to pieces then and had come out of it seeming more assured in her ability to survive despite adversity. Lar also didn't know about the scar that Alice hid so well. A scar that was composed of much thinner tissue than even she knew. She knew that her greatest fear was seeing it again, and having been seen, the scar would turn to an ugly, weeping gash. If that happened she feared she would be much different, much—weaker and probably not at all sane.

After her father's death Lar noticed a change. He had been dating Alice for almost 2 years when she got word of her father's stroke. Lar had been seeing Alice every weekend and at least once during the week but had not moved in yet. That would be the next step. People turning 40 who have been living on their own for some time do not take the idea of disrupting their comfortable routines and ways of living lightly. Though Larson had been thinking that she was the one, he was hardly capable of being the least bit objective, because for him she was the first one. The first dominant woman he had dated, and oh, how he took to his submissive role, like Beck singing "Loser" or Hendrix playing guitar with his teeth, strange to look at but *soo* natural. As long as they stayed apart he was living in both worlds comfortably but if they moved in together than harsh reality would necessitate how he was going to live, and be, with this other person. He was old enough to realize that playtime can't be 24/7—there was too much else to life. So for 2 years he had lived the blissful life of being her submissive part-time without having to deal with the depth of their mutual humanity.

Her father's CVA had left his left side paralyzed and interfered with his ability to speak. Articulation had become increasingly difficult for him and with great effort her father's last words to her sounded like "make your mark." He died the next day.

If he hadn't been so enamored with his submissive role, as he understood it, he would have discussed the possible meanings of her father's last words with her. In fact he had discussed this many times with her over the years, but he didn't then, right after she told him the first time, when she decided the meaning of her father's words. She decided that she would provide her father's death with meaning by making her mark in the business world. Larson's suggestions that there are many ways to make a mark in life were heard but not deeply considered. Alice decided that she could no longer be complacent; however, she had some real deficits when it came to business. Alice was basically an honest person who genuinely cared about people, so she was not one to manipulate others for her gain or succeed on the backs of others. This left only one alternative, productivity, and she had ever so slowly increased her commitment to work and success. Unnoticed to Alice but painfully obvious to Larson, they had more time together when they were dating for two years than they had now in their fourth year of living together. What Alice did realize was that the more she focused on her father's goal for her, the less aware she was of her terrible hidden scar. She had also become painfully aware that changes were needed in their relationship. She wanted a break but the only break she could imagine was one from Lar since there was no way to break with the wishes of a deceased father whose upbringing had saved her, and may have caused her to commit murder.

Alice was only marginally aware of the behavioral changes she had undergone in the past four years, and Lar's vision was so clouded by his new lifestyle the he was not able to provide her with the feedback that might have helped her keep herself before she lost it. However the once-assured laid-back female who was happy in her short haircut and comfortable clothes that took a minimum of care, had gradually developed a corporate look. She became more critical of what she saw in the mirror and though what she saw was less pleasing to her she spent more time looking and analyzing. Was she dressed like the people she wanted to be? Did she look professional? Was her hair businesslike yet feminine? Did her posture show assurance and competence? In short Alice had developed a rod-in-the-ass posture, businesslike insincerity, and migraines. Playing with Lar, once a joy of natural expression, had turned into a release that she needed and tried hard, but frequently failed, to schedule in.

She told herself that Lar noticed something was missing but like most men he followed his dick and that's why he stayed. However, she also knew there was something more as well. Like those few men, the kind that if you meet one you would be crazy to let go, Lar was loyal to his friends and considered his lover his best friend. He knew that Alice was going through some life changes and he was willing to see her through them...also the kinky sex kept him interested she was sure. Well, if her plan worked he could have the kinky sex and her, just not at the same time, at least for a while...if her plan worked. If it didn't she could find herself more isolated than she had been since...well, since graduate school, when she acted on her secret. She hoped it wouldn't come to that and she didn't want to be alone. However, things were up at work and worrying about her relationship was slowing her down, and she had to keep a promise with the dead.

One thing Alice was sure of—she could still conjure magic. She had done it with men before Lar but with him it had come easier and had been more natural. The intensity and glamour of their coupling was something she had no intention of giving up for either of their sakes, she hoped. Perhaps that is the way of life's circles. When one is nearing the end of a revolution, there is an almost irresistible urge to shed everything as though the completion brings an entirely new life instead of the same life viewed differently.

Her plan was already set in motion with a phone call. She drove home to her 6th floor downtown apartment. The advantages of her apartment were as follows: no deadly commute to work, easy access to city life, and rent control which in DC meant that at least the rent would not go up any faster than inflation. The disadvantages of her apartment were that: the older building required street parking, there was not enough space for anything, and it smelled like the city in the summer. As old apartments went she had a nice one—a large living room/dining room with coat closet next to the front door, kitchen with half wall so there could be conversation when one is cooking and the other is on the couch, small office area to the left of the kitchen, bedroom big enough for her King, chairs, his-and-her dressers, walk-in closet and wardrobe full of toys. One day she would get out and take Lar with her but even with her high 5-figure income and Lar's low 5-figure income their options were depressingly limited unless they endured the deadly commute so screw that; she was making her mark and once made, the deadly commute would no longer be an issue.

Lar was already home when Alice arrived—she heard him tapping on the computer. She entered the study, leaned over him, palmed his pecs and kissed him hard. He gave her his full attention, swiveling in his office chair to palm her back, each hand caressing a side of her backbone. He was sliding his hands to the front when she stepped back and looked him in the eye saying, "I want my slave naked except for his collar this evening; once you're stripped you may fix yourself some supper. I already ate."

Lar stood up immediately and without further eye contact scampered towards the bedroom. Alice realized that their sessions had become more of a novelty and less of a lifestyle by the relief and elation on Lar's face. She figured that his look of anticipation alone was worth the lie she had just told.

Alice followed Lar into the bedroom at her own pace, stopping to check the mail before entering the bedroom. Lar was already naked and looking at her expectantly, partially tumescent. He was trim, thicker than boys in their 20's but his stomach was flat, well defined pecs and muscular legs from biking and running and, fortunately, his hair wasn't thinning, though there was gray mixed in with the brown especially at the sides.

"You have your instructions, Spunky," Alice said.

With that Lar turned to get his dog collar, put it on with his back to her and left for the kitchen.

"Nice view from the back too," Alice mused to herself. Noticing the hair between his shoulder blades she thought, "maybe we should go for the hairless look again—but of course, no time for that now." When their relationship had been new and the heat a surprising joy for both of them, he in his eagerness to fulfill his fantasy had offered to shave himself completely. She had declined because she didn't want it growing in thicker. They had done periodic waxings to her amusement and his dismay but again the devil time had expunged that activity.

Alice looked at her watch then stripped and left the bedroom for the bathroom next to the hall closet. She imagined a modern townhouse with a master suite, bathroom off the front door and one just for the bedroom. That, however, would require a new building with less likelihood of rent control. No point in being apartment poor, she always said and now that she had been in a stable relationship a substantial down-payment for a real house with a real dungeon was in the works. Sometimes she realized she wasn't making sense, saving for a relationship she was halfheartedly invested in; maybe the saving was a way to pursue her true goal and make her mark.

Alice showered, then returned to the bedroom and dressed in Levis, walking shoes and a blue workshirt. She took her preppy blazer out of the walk-in closet and inspected it, thinking that the blazer would offset her otherwise casual attire. Still looking for lint she announced to Lar that he had 5 minutes to get the kitchen cleaned up.

The sound of dishes being rinsed and placed in the dishwasher occurred almost immediately. For the first time in a very long time Alice was feeling exhilarated. She smiled a wide, mischievous, joyful smile and put the blazer back in the closet, reaching inside again just as there was a knock on the front door.

"Spunky, into the closet, all fours now."

She heard the scrambling as Lar closed the dishwasher and padded to the closet next to the front door. Alice dug in the closet for just a minute till she found what she wanted. Pulling her black leather blazer off the rack she brushed at its sides and walked toward the front door.

"Let the games begin," she said under her breath, her mouth making a wide smile.

YoLynn Rebecca Johnson, JD, was born into what her family referred to as "comfortably middle class"; to most Americans her family would be considered rich. Both her mother and father were successful lawyers with different firms, and her 2 brothers and one sister had all entered either law or medical school. She had gone to private schools and colleges and was considered the brightest one in the family. Her only rebellion against her family's tradition of profession and comfortable incomes had been when she was an undergrad. Instead of pre-law or pre-med she had majored in philosophy and her mother worried that her bright daughter was merely going to get her "MRS" degree and be a bright housewife raising children but never really venturing on her own. Being the bright one however, she had no intention of being dependent on a spouse's income for her livelihood. She thought that majoring in philosophy and eventually becoming a professor would establish her independence while putting her brain to work. Then in her senior year it hit her. She realized that she was afraid. YoLynn was experiencing the same fear that keeps some of the best and brightest in small isolated communities instead of seeking their fortunes in the big city—the fear of a life that would be totally unfamiliar. Also like the best and brightest that fail to leave their communities, the fear led to self-understanding. She understood that in addition to the fear of change there was a deep appreciation for the life she had been living. She liked what she had and who she was within the parameters her life as it had been. Living on a philosophy professor's income would not only require an unfamiliar belt-tightening, it would require her to construct a new definition for the person who stared back at her in the mirror. She would be a person apart from the loving and supportive family she had known and the community in which she had grown up. She had to know herself before she could presume to know the world and the self she knew was one destined to be successful and "comfortably middle class." So just as people graduate from college with honors only to return home to their Appalachian community and work for the Post Office, YoLynn enrolled in law school in her senior year. This was a decision she had never regretted.

Unlike her family and most of her cohorts she had an appreciation for those who were not comfortable. This appreciation began in high school and blossomed during her stint as a philosophy major; one can't fully appreciate the motivation behind Karl Marx without appreciating the mindset of the disenfranchised. So though YoLynn had the presentation of the comfortable her friends, though highly selected, had been varied. She met Alice while doing some consulting work for DemLab. They had a friendly conversation which led to occasional lunches and more frequent talks on the phone. Alice was always somewhat closed off in discussing her home-life and her relationship with men past or present. Yo had attempted to enrich their discussions by providing details about men in *her* life, even sharing graphic confidences. Alice always smiled, always laughed and made Yo feel accepted and appreciated, but her intransigence about revealing her own likes and dislikes in the bedroom was solid. All YoLynn knew was that Alice had a live-in who worked part-time as a Social Worker and apparently he was not going to be home this evening because Alice had made a point of saying that the dinner was just for the two of them. Boys night out, she guessed, and Alice tired of being home alone. When she knocked on the door she had no idea that the games had already begun.

Lar was lying on his back in the small closet, knees bent up to accommodate his length. He was sharing the closet with cool, cold, and middle-of-winter coats, knock around in Rock Creek Park, out clubbing, and going to work coats, and an ironing board and vacuum cleaner. He could roll over carefully but presently was content on his back. The carpeted floor was soft and the apartment warm, he was beginning a scene with his love, his Mistress and all was right and calm. He had heard the knock—Alice was about to answer the door, no doubt a neighbor or salesperson who got in the building somehow. He was getting excited, and aroused, and erect.

"Yo, so good to see you," he heard Alice bubbling. "Come in."

"You too," an unfamiliar female voice said. "Thanks for inviting me."

Lar noticed that she spoke very clearly; he even heard the "t" in 'inviting'. "I figured your significant other wouldn't be here or we'd be a threesome for dinner. Boys night out?"

"Something like that."

"What is this?" he thought. "Is Alice planning a menage-a-toi?" Lar experienced more excitement, more arousal and became fully erect. Then he remembered—he and Alice had always talked over things they were going to do...well, usually—she was capable of surprises. If it's to be a menage he would have liked to know the person at least a little. What if he doesn't like her? What if she doesn't like him? What if Alice feels ignored because he gives the new woman too much attention? The other woman obviously did not know he was in the closet. What if she finds out and leaves hurt and embarrassed? What if she's offended or embarrassed because I'm hard? What if she feels rejected if I'm soft? Lar knew that one drawback of his profession was that he always analyzed motives and looked at contingencies. He realized that this habit was not at all helpful now, for he had what-iff'd himself out of a state of arousal and erection. Figuring that he should be on all fours if the door opened, he slowly and quietly began the task of rolling over in the crowded closet.

Alice, meanwhile, was showing her friend around. "God! I don't even know her name," Lar whined to himself.

"I was trying for as much of a Gothic look as you can do in an apartment without major renovations that you'd just have to change back when you move out anyway." Alice was explaining the heavy metal rings attached to the darkly stained wood borders—three and five feet, waist high, on one side of the living room. "But the project started getting out of hand—at least the top set of rings is good for hanging coats in the winter. Now the bedroom, I did that one up right." Her friend was making pleasant sounds, an "oh that's nice," here, a "well done," there, mostly noncommittal. Lar could tell they had circled the apartment and were again by the front door.

"After seeing your bedroom your blazer goes perfectly with the decor," the other woman was saying. "I never knew this side of you."

"That's why I thought it would be nice to have dinner—we could get to know each other."

Lar almost went into a panic when he heard those words. Were they going out? Was Alice going to lock him in the closet? She'd done it before but never for too long. He'd have to pee! How long would they be gone? He could hear a hand on the front doorknob.

"Oh, I forgot to tell you," Alice said. "I have a dog. Would you like to meet him?"

This is my cue, Lar thought, on all fours expecting the door to open immediately. Yo started nattering, her voice imitating the childish enthusiasm many people reserve for babies. "What kind of dog did you get? Aren't you afraid that he'll tear up your clothes? He's sure being quiet in there." All the while she was straining to see what was going to emerge from the closet.

Alice, her hand now on the doorknob, started her explanation. "You know how I've never really joined in on our bedroom preferences conversations? Well, Spunky here is the main reason."

"Alice you don't!!"

Alice turned to Yo looking both sheepish and fearful, as though she may lose a friend.

"Aren't you afraid of disease?"

"It's a habit I picked up in grad school," Alice interrupted, "and at this point in my life I need someone else to know."

Yo was both repulsed and touched—touched that Alice had chosen her to share her secret but at the same time unsure what to do with her secret.

"Alice, I'm really touched that you're telling me, but I have to be honest—I'm not sure what to make of this. I mean if you had a man shackled in there that's one thing but a dog, I'm not so...."

Feeling 30 pounds lighter Alice interrupted her friend and said that Yo should meet Spunky before she made any further judgments and with that, she opened the closet door.

Lar was still in the throes of a deep conversation with himself when he heard the doorknob turn. On one hand he could be embarking on every red-blooded male's dream, two women. On the other hand he was caught completely off guard and though he was very comfortable being naked around Alice, this was a total stranger. On the other hand, what should he care, like he'd never had a one night stand before meeting Alice? But he knew what was different. This woman was going to be seeing the real him, so rejection on her part for poor performance on his part was far more significant—far more personal, and integral to the person he was. Failure here was significant because it would reflect on the part of himself that he always had known was there but kept hidden—the part he didn't share with his buddies at the bar. The part that had finally become, no, had always been, so important that to live any more of his life without acknowledging it fully and acting on it, would be hiding from himself and therefore a waste of his life.

Lar's contemplation into his own analysis made him seem unresponsive and minimally affected by external stimuli. When the door opened he groggily crawled out on all fours, his back legs still in the closet. He saw Alice's friend, probably 5'10", almost a head taller than Alice. Like Alice she was all legs but had long curled black hair instead of light red-brown. She was more slender than Alice, Alice a little more thick in the middle. Both wore jeans and blue workshirts—the only difference was their blazers. He had nothing to say and just stared up at them stupidly.

Yo was quiet too, at first her eyes widening in alarm, then transforming to the look of mirth, her mouth's former O of surprise turning into a broad smile, her eyes squinting to reveal laugh-lines. Alice explained that the dog had never bitten except on command, and though he is sometimes good, he seems to go through bad spells. When he goes through bad spells, she explained, he responds well to a good swat. She also added that he never growled or bared his teeth, though he does tend to whine excessively.

While delivering her discourse Alice was trying to read her friend. Yo was smiling broadly, not saying a word. Was she trying to think of a way out of here? Was she going to laugh good naturedly then remember an appointment in a few minutes, or was she able to accept what was going on, thereby demonstrating a step toward accepting Alice?

Yo regained some of her composure and started to speak. "Does he do tricks?" she asked, before reverting to her broad smile.

"A few—roll over, beg, fetch with teeth or paws," Alice responded.

"Will he obey my commands or only yours?"

"That's difficult to say; he should obey yours but I haven't given him a talking-to, so he wasn't expecting you. Here's his leash, snap that on and I'm sure he'll do fine," Alice said in a tone reminiscent of explaining the workings of her stereo to a houseguest.

"Well, this is a first for me," Yo said, snapping the leash to Lar's dog collar.

"It's a first for him too." Then, as Alice ruffed Lar's hair, "I'm sure he wants to please."

Yo hadn't taken her eyes off of Lar since the door opened and she still didn't meet Alice's eyes when Alice spoke. She did give a slight tug on Lar's collar and he lumbered out of the closet.

She held the leash loose and told Lar to roll over—a game he and Alice had played countless times but somehow this was different, he was feeling more vulnerable and exposed, and he feared he looked silly. The picture he saw of himself was not that of a man submitting to a powerful domme with the air charged with eroticism but of a middle-aged man naked in front of two women about to perform an act that would be humiliating and embarrassing. What if they laughed? What if he wasn't being seen as a submissive sexual object under their control but as a clown? His preoccupation made him clumsy—he half-fell to his side then rolled to his back, his arms and legs in the air like paws.

Yo was rubbing his chest and stomach as she would a dog, stopping just short of his privates. Lar's preoccupation also interfered with the erection he was sure he would have had if he and Alice were alone and she was rubbing him. Was his flacidity going to add to his humiliation?

Yo was telling Alice that having a pet like this would be such fun. Then she said the words that Lar knew should thrill but instead terrorized: "I wish I had him at my command."

Lar felt himself sinking into confusion and uncertainty. Meanwhile Alice either didn't know or didn't care as she provided Lar with no reassurance. Though this was out of character for someone as naturally attuned to a submissive's psyche as she, Alice, too was preoccupied. She had her own agenda and things were going better than expected.

Alice put one hand on each side of Lar's head, looked him in the eye and said, "stay," then, straightening up looking at her friend, she explained that she didn't want Spunky following her when she went into the bedroom and that she would be back in a couple of minutes. Yo walked over to the sofa and sat half-sprawled, obviously relaxing into this foreign environment. Lar held his ground on all fours and stewed.

He was both worried, indignant and self-deprecating. Worried why Alice would do something like this out of the blue. He couldn't believe that their relationship was so much more important to him than her. He knew that the experiences that they shared were far more profound than the torture he had initially experienced with her. He was indignant towards the prospect of serving an interloper after having been blissfully serving Alice. He was worried because he wondered if it had all been self-delusion. He knew, though there was now a sliver of doubt, that Alice shared the transcendental experience once he was on the other side of the pain. His doubt grew, which in turn led to more doubt. Had he been kidding himself about their special bond? About her special form of intuition? About their sharing? Was he only a romantic, finding a way to make the unacceptable acceptable?

Yo called, "here boy," her voice full of enthusiasm.

Lar was still lost in his thoughts. What if he did attend to Yo as an interloper? She could be horribly sadistic, cause inadvertent damage, she could have no imagination.

Yo called to the other room, "Alice, he won't come."

Alice left her room wearing a black cotton shirt; she had been changing so that she and Yo wouldn't look like they were uniformed. Her shirt was fastened with only one button in the wrong hole—she had obviously been interrupted.

"What has gotten into you?" she asked calmly, as if her actual normally well-behaved dog had inexplicably overturned a planter.

She had removed her belt as she was walking. Then to her friend she said, "notice, only one," and brought it down hard on Lar's left ass cheek leaving a red stripe and welt. Lar yelped, lurched forward, breathed deeply, then padded over to Yo. Alice returned to her room. Yo wondered how far this would go, how far she wanted this to go, and if it would be she, or Alice who would finally put on the brakes.

It was time to ham it up, so when Lar padded over to Yo she started cooing while scratching lightly behind Lar's ears like she would an old hound that had sauntered over. "Who's the boy that's right who's the good boy? Are you a good boy?"

Lar was unsure how or if to answer. He decided it best to continue being a mute mutt. Alice again exited her bedroom, this time with her shirt properly buttoned and tucked. She snapped her fingers. Lar looked up and padded over to her and Alice knelt and held his head so that she was making eye contact with him. "You need to get focused, we'll be gone a few hours; you stay right here until we leave." She then stood up and took her car keys out of her jacket pocket. Hearing them, Yo stood up and walked toward Alice and the door.

That's when it dawned on Lar that he was in the direct line of sight of the front door. He looked at Alice questioningly, nervous and unsure if he should say something. The neighbors surely didn't know about their sexuality—they hadn't broadcast their orientation. If someone was walking in the hall when they opened the door they could be shocked, mortified, they could call the police. Things don't go well for Clinical Social Workers who commit moral turpitude. His panic showed on his face though he was trying to look impassive.

"You need to focus and you need to get accustomed to new things," Alice said as she opened the door and they left.

When the door closed Lar stood up, straightened up the room and in the process realized that the chances of his being seen were small indeed, and the chances that anything would come of it, aside from a strange look in the elevator, was even smaller. He realized he was not focused at all—not that there had been many opportunities lately—and that he was exaggerating the importance of his reactions, seeing himself as a failure because he wasn't adapting easily to a new situation. Cognitive therapists called this catastrophizing, an apt name for seeing events as a catastrophe when they probably aren't. He had almost been looking for terrible things to happen, when all that had really happened was that Alice had brought an attractive friend over and visually disclosed her sexual orientation. Lar thought one of the pluses of being a therapist was that many of the techniques that are helpful with clients are also helpful when he's working on a personal problem.

Lar decided that his present difficulty was that, from his present perspective, Alice was acting out of character and this, in turn, was making it difficult for him to stay in *his* character when the situation warranted. He had something to sort out and for that he needed emotional distance, for emotional distance he needed to be able to relax, and since no one was home one of his favorite ways of relaxing was a very long hot bath.

As he adjusted the water and steam filled the room he set his agenda. He thought that if he reviewed what he thought of as one of the defining periods in Alice's life he would understand her better and in so doing understand how he fit in with her life. Unspoken in his agenda was that by understanding Alice's life he would understand his own part in this strange and wonderful relationship. He knew of the critical time period in her life when she experienced a liberation of sorts, which may have led to murder.

As he slid into the tub, however, the warm relaxing feel of the water could only remind him of sex with his love.

Alice had always known she was dominant. On dates in high school she enjoyed the power that petting gave her and was thrilled that she could control her date's need with a touch to the crotch or allowing him to touch her. Some of her early experiments went more smoothly than others. She, too, was subject to the confusion brought on by the first introductions of the hormones which sustain adults and override their former interests. Feeling that she had to be something other than herself in order to attract a boy who suddenly appeared godlike to her, she acted indecisive and unable to perform acts requiring logic or brute strength. She acted as if she didn't know what she wanted from her target. It frequently worked, or it worked frequently enough. When she became a young woman instead of a girl she realized why she was never happy in a relationship. How could she expect to be happy in a relationship when she wasn't getting her needs met, and how could she expect to get her needs met if she wasn't expressing them, and most importantly how could she expect to get her needs met with the oafs who were so full of their own accomplishments and needs that they never even asked about hers? Regretfully and hesitantly, at first, she realized that a new phase of experimentation was necessary.

To this day she looks back on her first attempt with a shudder, knowing that she was really lucky, that it scared the shit out of her, and could have been much worse. She didn't make another attempt for two years, trying to sublimate her needs in vanilla relationships, some with really good guys—guys she could fall for and did fall for, for a while. Then, over time, she tired. She tired of having to fantasize one thing while doing something else. She loved how excited her lovers got when she had her mouth on them, she loved the increasing intensity in their breath, their movement and their desperation if she stopped. She was empathic, knew of her man's needs and frequently imagined what it would be like to have him tied and helpless before sucking him. She imagined having his urgency build then denying him completion, doing it again and again till he pleaded and begged, till he promised ever-increasing allegiance to her, promised unconditional allegiance, then she would stop and have him satisfy her and not permit him release, she would have him satisfy her again and would not permit him release. She would have him wait on her and would not permit him release. She would tease him and finally allow him release only if he swore continued allegiance to her as his cum flowed. These were her thoughts; her actions were perfunctory. She knew she was capable of being a great fuck. She knew also that she was not a great fuck. How could she be? Her heart, and mind, were elsewhere.

Finally, two years after her disastrous first attempt, she convinced her boyfriend to allow her to tie him up and whip him lightly with her belt. She repeatedly promised not to get carried away. In one way she felt she should apologize for her request but didn't, because deep down she knew she shouldn't have to apologize for being herself. The overture had been made offhandedly; she had read a letter in Penthouse and it seemed novel. She wondered if this would be something she would like; she had never thought of something like this before but in the letter it seemed like everyone was having fun and she wanted to give it a try. Or at least that is what she told *him*.

"And besides," she said, "it will give me a chance to model that outfit you always wanted me to wear." That had been the clincher. He might have gone for it anyway without the prelude, without the promise of finally seeing her in the outfit he had wanted her to buy. It may have been oversell but that wasn't important. What was important was that he agreed. She tied his wrists together over his head and fastened them to the base of the headboard, tied his ankles together and fastened them to the base of the footboard. He was already naked. She was still wearing jeans and a T-shirt. She took his cock in her mouth and got him hard, kept sucking until his hips began rocking, then she got up, unwrapped her belt, and smacked him across the stomach. He gasped in alarm, a pink welt forming a single stripe on his stomach. He was still hard.

"Be right back," she said and left the room to change into her outfit, trembling so much she could hardly unbutton her pants. Putting on the garters and stockings seemed to take an eternity, and she was clumsy on her high-heels. She gave up trying to get the garters right and lunged unsteadily into the room, stocking tops uneven, the left stocking sagging attached by only one garter, empty garters flopping, face flushed, panting, wet and dripping between her legs. She had dreamed of this for so long she wanted it to last. She would tease him and occasionally whip him for hours; finally she would let him cum. She picked up the belt and noticed that his hard-on had flagged but his eyes were on her. She again whipped his stomach—another pink stripe—she trembled, whipped his nipples, and his hardon grew even as he winced and this time cried in alarm. In one motion she was on top of him. She had him inside of her. She rode him furiously, cumming before him, which didn't take long. Her technique and ability to savor the moment with languor improved with time.

When she had finished riding him she realized that she had made two mistakes. First there was no safer sex and therefore no birth control. Shit.

She had gone on the pill when she first became sexually active. That made sex easy, as she didn't have to stop the natural progression of things and didn't have to worry about pregnancy. This had been with her first lover and, if he told the truth, she was his as well. Their sex had been full of exploration and newness, doing what had been forbidden at least by someone in theory. Her mom had gotten her the pills and said most folks wish they had waited till they were older but most folks didn't wait. Alice had been surprised at getting the pills—she thought it was going to be another safer sex lecture. She'd had them in school, at home, seen them on TV and heard them on the radio. Talking to friends who had herpes and knowing someone sick from an STD had made the lectures real.

"If I had it to do over again I'd wait till I was 21," her mom said. "Maybe later, I didn't even know myself well enough to appreciate it when I was a teenager." Then after a pause her mom said, "But then I would have missed out on college," and smiled. So whoever this unnamed someone was who forbade her to have sex, it wasn't her mom. She thought it must be the moral majority that she had to thank for giving her a forbidden pleasure.

She was uncomfortable hearing her mom talk this openly. On one hand she was glad for the communication, on the other she wanted her own life to be different from her mom, and she would never be able to separate from her mom and be different from her if they shared everything. If they knew everything about each other, she and her mom would just be going on as Siamese twins, inseparable and undifferentiated. By the time she and her mom had this talk, her friends and the lure of the outside world were enticing. It had enticed her away from wanting that type of symbiosis, and besides, there were her fantasies that she was sure were not shared by mom. Her fantasies made her different too. So, she liked being able to talk, she liked the acceptance, liked the ability to get pills since it really was time for her and Derek to do the deed, but sometimes knowing this much about her mom's past made her uneasy.

After she and Derek had done it just a few times they had gotten creative, or at least limber, and her legs had stretched in a lot of directions. They did it standing up, her leaned against a wall one leg over his pelvis, him leaning against a wall supporting her but she always liked it best when she was on top—she liked the control.

After Derek she was careful over 90% of the time and used safer sex along with the pill. She was also selective, and (she knew well), damn lucky. Later she quit it with the pill. She told herself that maybe if she got back into a long-term relationship she'd go back on, but she was making damn sure not to get sick, and in the process made damn sure she wouldn't get pregnant. Now this shit with Mark. What about her plan?

She was going to put a rubber in her mouth and lower her mouth on her trembling slave's desperate cock; he wouldn't even know it was on, and she was going to get on him for a long slow ride. He would be near delirious, having been brought from the brink so many times he wouldn't know what was going on when she deftly stopped and raised herself off of his aching cock, his balls throbbing with the need for release and frustration. She was going to be cool, in control, manipulating his cock like a hot dildo pleasuring herself for hours if she wished, her helpless slave begging and pleading, BUT NOOOOO, she had to jump on him like a horny chimpanzee, ride him to climax like a whore behind on her rent and she hadn't even used birth control.

"Shit, guess I'll douche, can't hurt, might help," she panted. How did she get so lucid so quickly? She was reasonably sure of his health—they'd been going out for a while and had shared their histories. They had always been careful in the past. Fuck!

He was in a state of relaxation; it had been a good one for him. He spastically tried to respond to her statement, first mumbling something that could have been intended as, "OK cool," or maybe, "How 'bout untying me first?" His arms and legs moved ineffectually. He wasn't straining by a long shot, he looked too relaxed. She got up and went into the bathroom, dripping on his thigh and stomach as she rose.

As she walked toward the bathroom her second mistake was more noticeable; the neighbors had their stereo up loud; she could make out the words to Freebird. This wasn't good news either. She had thought that problem had been taken care of.

She had moved to her new apartment because she had moved to a new town, was going to a new school and had a new job. When she moved into her apartment she had been full of the hope that accompanies such a move. Any tedium, aloneness, or shortcomings that existed in her old digs, would be the tedium, aloneness and shortcomings of the old apartment, not the new apartment. This place was new and full of possibilities. A new place was a place of growth. It was bigger, the neighborhood safe, with off-street parking in a small lot. It was a loft apartment—two whole floors, closets, actual space for her stuff and—dare she hope—even space for new stuff. Imagine that, just being able to buy new stuff without having to go through the puzzle process of what would have to be moved or thrown out to make room for a new purchase. Guiltless stuff, that was the ticket, a new job, new school, new town, new apartment and soon new stuff. This elation lasted until 10 that night when the neighbor's bass notes became noticeable, then the drums that went with the bass notes and finally even the words to the songs became noticeable. She waited, hoping it would stop; it didn't, and she had to work the next day. Well, time to meet the neighbors, she thought resignedly, hoping this could be finessed well. She wasn't accustomed to being assertive but she wasn't meek and mild either.

She went outside and knocked. "I hope this doesn't start some sort of neighbor war," she thought. The door opened; there were three guys inside. The guy answering the door smiled broadly.

"Come in, are you our new neighbor?" The other guys were looking too, and smiling. Behind the guys was a typical guy mess—nothing put away anywhere, papers, beer cans and clothes on everything. There was a sleeping bag on the floor and a long sofa against the wall with a blanket and pillow on it. Her lease had said no more than two to the apartment and that noise should be kept down after 10, so these guys shouldn't be too hard to convince, but it should be done diplomatically. In the neighborhood where she lived before this, getting on the wrong side of your neighbors could lead to lots of surprises like a broken windshield or broken bottles around your tires so that you had to check and be prepared to sweep every morning. "Low class sons-a-bitches anyway," she thought of her old digs.

"Shit!.... Jocks!" she thought; that's what I get for living near a college campus. They didn't look dangerous but looks could be deceiving, especially in groups. She didn't really have anything against jocks except that they were so prone to act like assholes around their buds, and from her limited experience and second-hand stories from her friends, they were more likely to prefer a woman who knew her proper place. She knew that wasn't universal for jocks, but it was more likely. Her main concern with them was that her first experiment with dominating her sexual partner had been with a jock, and though she thought of herself as damn lucky when it was over, the thought of what might have been, what could have happened, still made her shiver. She had sworn off jocks after that encounter, just because of what could have happened. And here she was staring at three of them. They looked like they were old enough to be grad students so they might not be active school jocks, but still, what man in his early 20's would live with 2 other guys, unless they were lovers, grad students or artists? These guys weren't artists, and didn't look gay.

"Hi, nice to meet you—thanks for the invitation, maybe another time," she began. "I've been moving in all day and I have to work tomorrow. Could you turn down the stereo please?"

The guy stared at her stupidly. He probably wanted to say no but knew he really couldn't and was wondering how his buds would take his acquiescence.

"There's a killer song coming up—I'll turn it down in about 10 minutes, OK?" he said.

"No problem, thanks," she said, hoping it wasn't, "I Want to Rock and Roll All Night."

"Sure you don't want to come in for a minute and have a beer?" he asked hopefully.

"Nah, new job, gotta make a good impression, get good sleep," she said, walking away.

"K," he said, disappointed.

"Hey, what's your name? I'm Rick," he shouted, but she was already closing her door.

They did turn the music down after the killer song. It wasn't Kiss, but she could still hear the music faintly and since she had been required to make an issue of it even the low, barely noticeable volume got on her nerves and hindered sleep. This ritual went on for several nights. Probably Rick or one of the other jocks thought that by continuing to play the music loud at night the new girl next door would come around and perhaps she could be enticed to come in and become more acquainted. She circumvented this strategy by coming over first at one-quarter then at a full one-half bitch when asking them to turn down the stereo. This was sufficiently off-putting to quell invitations.

The end of stereo wars occurred over the course of three weekends in which she got up early and cranked her stereo to listen to her morning music. After about 30 minutes an obviously hungover jock would come over and ask her if she would turn down the stereo. After the third weekend they got the hint; there was peace or at least detente.

Detente had lasted for over a year and now the stereo was blasting. She must have been yelling her head off while they were screwing, and, as she remembered it, so had he. "Well, fair is fair," she thought. She was embarrassed. She liked her sexuality and its excitement but she was a private person who wanted it to be shared with people of her choosing, not broadcast to the neighbors. Nothing to be done about it now, she guessed, they were either respecting her privacy with the stereo or just figured her noise made it OK to make other noise. At least it wasn't dead silent, neighbors with ears to the wall and their dicks in their hands, she smiled. Well, what's done is done. Her boyfriend could usually be encouraged into another round or two but it would take a more traditional role on her part. That was OK. "What an exciting evening," she thought, smiling to herself. Before leaving the bathroom she inserted her well-jellied diaphragm then climbed into bed and fondled him and untied his feet first so that she could cradle his balls and tease his anus before untying his hands.

Rif lived in the adjacent building. He was large—probably 6'4," lean with wavy golden blond hair that was always worn like a TV evangelist. It was always in place. He was typically seen wearing tight jeans with a large silver and turquoise belt buckle, alligator or sharkskin boots and a leather vest over a stone-washed workshirt. He drove a red Corvette, with a bumper sticker which read, "Welfare Makes America Weak Keep America Strong Repeal Social Security." Rif wasn't his real name but he liked it and had used it as his own since he was a teenager, and he figured "Claude" just didn't have the chick appeal. At 27 he had it made; he had developed the contacts he needed to dispose of his merchandise and they paid well. New merchandise was always easy to come by and his main problem was to put up a front so that he at least appeared to be living within modest means, except for the car. That's why he still lived in the apartment. He'd think of an angle soon enough to justify a lifestyle befitting his income and until that time he could stash it away, go on trips and pay cash wherever he went. He had a couple of false ID's for checking into hotels, though he knew hotel management wasn't worried about his identity anyway as long as he spent money, bills were paid, and he tipped well, and he always tipped well. He did a lot of his work on trips though he liked to work at home as well. Work was satisfying, enjoyable and lucrative. On his last trip he had flown a thousand miles, rented a car and driven for 2 hours. After checking into his hotel he had met a young lady at a bar and after buying drinks, chatting her up and, making sure she saw he was tipping well, he invited the young lady for a ride in his rented Vet with gimp tags on it. He always drove either a Vet or Jag; they made the best bird bait as far as he was concerned. They went bar-hopping and he left her for a few minutes at their first stop, then came back saying he had scored some ludes from a guy he met and did she want to take some. He always made the offer after obviously popping a few in his mouth and chasing them with a shot of Tequila.

"What the hell," she said. They laughed. They did more shots, he ate a few more, she did another, she started slurring her words saying things like, "Fuck me now let's party."

He helped her to her feet and to the car, helped her into the passenger seat. He got behind the wheel, checked for traffic and cautiously pulled into traffic. At this stage his only concern was that she not get sick—that made things more cumbersome. He put his placebo tablets back into their proper container and the real thing into its proper container. He always patted himself on the back for thinking of the psychedelic; it sometimes made them harder to knock down with 'ludes but it made up for that with its disorienting effects. Then it was to his second room at the Town View. After checking into the Sheraton, he left in his rented car and drove to the other part of town, to the Town View motel. The Town View had no town view, not even a view of its patrons' cars. The customers of the Town View thought it more expeditious to have the rooms of their two-story inn right next to the highway and their cars in back, out of view from those on the street or driving by. At the Town he stopped, then checked on his date.

"Hey, you OK?" he asked.

Her eyes hardly flickered, just the way he liked them.

"OK, Sweetheart," he said in a conversational tone as he lifted her, "but you owe me breakfast for a week," then muttered in a slightly lower voice, "I wish you'd learn your limits. I wanted to fool around tonight." The ever whining boyfriend or husband, no threat to anyone—just in case anyone was listening.

When he got her into the room he lay her on the bed, closed and locked the door, made sure that the curtains were closed and the special window shade he had brought was drawn. Then on came the lights; he changed her makeup, even tried a wig on her, and started the series of 35mm cameras clicking, each camera taking a shot when he pressed the trigger so that he could remove a bit of clothing and shoot, remove a bit of clothing and shoot. Loosen the blouse, click, show the bra with unbuttoned blouse, click, shirt off, click, bra unfastened, click, pants unbuttoned, click, panties pulled down just enough to show the top of her pubes, click, and so on until she was naked. Few of the shots even had her face; most of those who ultimately saw the pictures would think that faces in a picture merely took up too much picture room and made the good stuff harder to see. The shots that did show her face would have her face blurry, or her eyes blacked, and don't forget the wig, as if this was a private scene between exhibitionist lovers. "Hell, bet these bitches wouldn't even recognize themselves if they saw their pictures in a boyfriend's magazine," he frequently said to himself, admiring his work. Each camera a different angle, each angle a different picture, each picture money in the bank. After she was naked he set the cameras on automatic. He had good lenses and good film, all the angles were covered. He'd had a lot of practice—he could fuck this bitch every way to Sunday. The more experimental and dramatic the poses, the more money in the bank, and as a bonus he got his rocks off. "What a job," he thought jubilantly. His women were always limber ('ludes were muscle relaxants, after all), and he could do stuff with their legs and thighs that would cramp or tear the ligaments of any woman but a gymnast or contortionist, and the more they posed in supposed lust for his cock the more money went into the bank. It was a nuisance having to change film every few minutes but sometimes that gave him just the break he needed to come up with a new idea, a new pose, or new camera angle. Man, life was sweet. And of course there were the standard money shots: cock in mouth, cock in cunt, cum dripping out of cunt, cum on stomach, cum on tits, cum dripping out of mouth; when he didn't have enough cum to go around he could always use hair conditioner. When he was through he would wipe her face and pussy and put on the panties and shirt, leaving the pants and bra at the foot of the bed. He always left a letter, written with his left hand, though he was right-handed: *Like I said last night I had to leave early this morning. Thanks for being so understanding. I really enjoyed meeting you. Is it OK if I call you when I get back to town? I should be back in about 2 weeks. I'd like that a lot.*

Hope to see you soon
Mike

Of course he never called, didn't have her phone number and his name wasn't Mike, but that was enough of a mind-fuck for a hung-over bitch so she would think she'd done something stupid with a nice guy. Hell, he bet most of them were actually waiting for a call. And when he didn't and when after a few days they realized that their muscle soreness or torn ligaments may have been more than a night of wild abandon, hell, he was long gone. Always stick to medium-sized towns; they're big enough to get lost in, there are a million of them so you don't have to repeat often if you don't want to, the girls are easier to impress, and the cops are dumb as shit. That was Rif's motto.

He was developing his latest merchandise in his home lab and packaging it for his usual customers, not *Penthouse* or *Playboy*, but more like *Slut* and *Alley Girl*, and his bread and butter came from the private customers who wanted something exclusive, even if it was the same shit they could buy in *Alley Girl*, just from a different angle. Lately he had been getting requests for some way-out stuff. The money that was offered would be great but he was hesitant. There would be no way a bitch would get out of one of these sessions intact; she'd have some sort of injury, even if it was just a brand, but there'd be no way that a hungover bitch, no matter how stupid, would believe that she just happened to get fucked up and fuck a really nice guy who just happened to put a hole in her tit. Hell, he might have to kill her just to assure his anonymity. That would present a multitude of potential complications that he would just as soon avoid, but the offers did keep coming in and the amount offered kept rising.

When she noticed that the music was loud and realized that at least that meant the jocks weren't all listening and whacking-off, the new girl didn't realize that someone was doing a whole lot more than listening through the wall. Rif was congratulating himself on a good investment. He had purchased an expensive video camera that used a lens smaller than he thought possible, that could be connected to a television. On a lark he had installed it in the ceiling of the bedroom of the apartment that the new girl had moved into. She looked to be in her early 20's and was cute, though not beautiful, not enough of a Barbie figure and almost no makeup. As he watched her and her boyfriend he thought one word—Jackpot.

Lar's reverie, which started as a search for Alice's motivation for bringing her friend and his own motivation for not being as enthusiastic as he thought he should have been, had turned into a review about this critical period of Alice's life. His review was interrupted by a fate that befalls many who fall asleep in the tub. He slowly drifted down until water was just below his nose and with the vehemence and hatred spawned by Rif's memory he inhaled deeply, readying for a fight. Unfortunately he breathed in a mixture of water and air. He sat up quickly in a panic, spilling water on the floor, coughing, choking and sneezing at the same time.

"Are you alright?!" Alice was opening the bathroom door, the door to the apartment still open. She was kneeling beside him on the wet bathroom floor looking at his face, her friend Yo in the living room looking in, her face full of concern.

Lar sputtered, forced out an "OK" between coughs and sneezes, held his thumb up like the FBI agent in Twin Peaks, though he was coughing and dribbling horribly. Finally he regained enough composure to explain that he had drifted off in the tub. Alice left him to get himself together and clean up the bathroom.

Alice had changed into sweats and a baggy T-shirt. She and Yo were in the living room, bottles of mineral water in their hands. She saw Lar leave the bathroom and pointed up, indicating that Lar didn't have to be Spunky right now and he could stand. "I think formal introductions are in order," she said; "Larson Donald Wood, please allow me to introduce YoLynn Rebecca Johnson." Lar took her hand in a formal handshake, more fingers then palms.

"Pleased to meet you," he said.

Yo stared at Lar intently. Somehow the introduction of a name personalized what she would have formerly described merely as a male. With a name to put with the face Yo was able to put Lar in another box, a box in which more details could be noticed. Lar appeared trim with a slight middle-age spread. At first glance she would have guessed Lar's age to be in his early to mid 30's but he was showing small tufts of gray in his chest hair and temples and who knows what his pubes would look like. It occurred to her that this was why he was trimmed. So her guess was mid 30s to mid 40s. She knew Alice was in her late 40s, though she'd have thought 30's if Alice hadn't told her, so she figured either Alice had been able to catch a younger man or her man had aged like she did. "Lucky stiffs," she thought, "folks think we're the same age and I know Alice has at least 10 years on me."

Lar was increasingly aware of Yo's stare. It wasn't as if she hadn't had the opportunity to see his body before, but her eyeing him up and down without saying anything in this context was making him feel self-conscious, reminding him that he was naked and she wasn't. Lar shuffled on his feet.

Realizing it was her turn to speak, Yo said, "So you have two last names like Larson Larson?" Her laugh lines formed effortlessly as she continued, "Blue blood Larson Witherby, Wheatherspoon." She was warming up, launching into comments Lar had frequently heard about his name, that it sounded rich or pretentious."

"Hardly," Lar said, meeting her smile with his own. "Uncle Larson was a favorite uncle who helped my parents out during some real rough times. He never asked for anything in return and always had faith in my dad and mom, even when things looked bad for them, so my parents named their firstborn after him."

"Good for them," Yo said, "good family."

"I lucked out with a good family," Lar said.

"Lar," Alice began.

Lar didn't like the sound of this for three reasons. When they were alone and until now with Yo he had been referred to as "Spunky." Lar was reserved for outside in society or when relationship issues were being discussed. First, like most men, Lar found discussing relationship issues difficult. For him a relationship discussion resembled walking across a stream with all of the stepping stones submerged; the woman always knows what the trail looks like and where the stones are and the guy just stumbles around not knowing that a trail existed in the first place. Second, discussing relationship issues was serious business and he was awkward enough at it without having another female to witness his ineptitude. Third, if the subject was going to get serious, that really lowered the possibility that he was going to get to play with two women this evening.

Alice could always read him like a book, and she could tell that his mind was everywhere but the here-and-now. She thought of something that would surely help Lar focus and would probably be instructive to her friend.

"Slave, never mind for now," Alice said flatly. Standing up, she walked into the bedroom briefly, then returned, handing a thick, black, stretchy cloth about 3 feet long and 6 inches wide, to Yo.

"Yo, I think this will be instructive for you and it will help focus Lar here who is too torn between roles and desire to carry on a simple conversation." She was half smiling. "When I call you could you please wrap this around Lar's eyes, tie the knot to the side, then lead him into the bedroom and onto the bed?" Then in a stage whisper she said, "and don't talk to him after he's blindfolded; the lack of contact will help direct his attention elsewhere."

Alice then turned and walked into the bedroom closing the door. Yo and Lar stared at each other for a moment. Yo broke the silence.

"How long have you been together?" she asked.

"Almost 4 years. We moved in together about 2 and a half years ago," Lar answered, then in an effort to keep the conversation going said, "Do you work with Alice?"

"Our firm did some work with her company," Yo said. "We had lunch and found out we both liked Southern Gothic lit so we went to a book signing together then we just started hanging out."

"Don't like Southern Gothic," Lar said. "That stuff's too full of quiet desperation for me. Personally I like thrillers…"

"Figures, guy stuff," Yo said matter-of-factly.

"Well horror 'n mysteries too," Lar said in mock defense.

"You know I almost forgot I'm talking to a naked man who is my dear friend's sex slave," Yo laughed, surprised.

"I prefer submissive," Lar said, continuing to be silly.

"Oh, excuse me," Yo said with such deference that Lar thought he had made her uncomfortable.

"I hope you know I was just being silly, and overly dramatic. I took no offense," he said quickly. "There's a lot more to our relationship than sex, though."

"Like what?" Yo said.

Lar was momentarily at a loss for words, staring blankly and stupidly, from his estimation.

"Do you have any idea what she's doing in there?" Yo said, rescuing him while asking what had been on her mind from the moment that Alice left.

"Precisely what I don't know. I know that it will be a way in which she hopes to bring us into focus," Lar said, almost in teacher mode.

"You lost me," Yo said matter-of-factly, with no self-consciousness at all that she wasn't understanding.

"Oh," Lar paused. When he started speaking again he chose his words carefully, as if he was explaining a concept he did not fully understand or have words for. "I know that when we have it, it feels like we're…." He paused for several more seconds. When he started speaking again his eyes did not meet Yo's, as if he was summoning all of his faculties in order to make this explanation. "Someplace else, I know that wherever it is, it's important, but the memory fades. It's like a dream after you wake up. The dream was so vivid, you say to yourself, what a cool dream, I'm going to tell my friends, but by the time you've started your day so much of it has faded that all you can say is, I had a neat dream and you're lucky if you can remember just the barest details but forget the essence."

"You said 'we're'?" Yo asked, hoping for more information.

"Yes I did, and that's the correct way to say it but I really couldn't say why," Lar said, voice trailing, his face taking on a puzzled quality.

"Can I get you anything, spring water, beer, wine, lemonade?" Lar asked because he was at a complete loss for words on their former subject and his confusion was making him uncomfortable—besides, it never hurt to be a good host.

"Are you going to have a beer? If so I'll have one too," Yo said.

"Not just yet for me," Lar said, "but I'll get you one."

"Just bring me some lemonade then."

Lar retrieved two tumblers, got himself a short glass of spring water and his guest lemonade.

"How long do you think she'll be?" Yo asked.

Lar hoped she wasn't uncomfortable in his company. He didn't want an uncomfortable guest and preferred that people be at ease, enjoying themselves. Falling back on his habit of feeling responsible for everyone's comfort, he tried to come to the rescue. "There's no telling, if it's an elaborate set-up it could be a while because she usually has me do it and...hey are you uncomfortable because I'm here naked and all? I have some sweats in the closet." He was already walking towards the door.

"No, you're fine, Lar," Yo said quickly. "I'm enjoying this but you have to remember this whole thing is new to me. I'm going to have a lot of questions. In fact," she said with increasing confidence, "I prefer you naked. I can see how there can be power in both situations. On one hand there's the person who is not required to wear clothes, above social convention and whose predilections others must defer to; on the other hand there's power in wearing clothes when someone else is required not to. I believe that is your status, and I am becoming more and more accustomed to it." Now Yo was smiling, her eyes mischievous.

"Oh," Lar said, his voice quieter, his mind a step closer to subspace.

With Yo on the sofa and Lar sitting at her feet, a comfortable conversation about movies was begun and continued until the bedroom door opened a crack and Alice called to Yo telling her it was time to blindfold Lar. After he was blindfolded Alice opened the bedroom door fully and put her finger up to her lips indicating to Yo to be quiet, then motioned with the you-come-here finger movement for Yo to leave Lar standing while she went over to the bedroom door for a conference.

Quietly into Yo's ear Alice said, "No more talking, it will distract him. Would you like to guide him into the bedroom and help me cuff him to the bed?"

Yo nodded and smiled.

"OK, after he's on the bed I think you'll find it interesting to watch, but you'll have to remain quiet—is that OK?" Alice said the second OK in an even tone instead of phrasing it as a question, realizing that she was giving her friend a list of instructions.

Yo put her finger up to pursed lips forcing down a laugh. She felt like a naughty second-grader. She went out and retrieved Lar, leading him into the bedroom. As she entered and closed the door she noticed that the door, like the walls, were thick with soundproofing.

Yo opted for a nice red table wine. Alice had directed her towards the wine before stepping into the shower. Lar, she assumed, would be showering after he was again capable of volition so she had some time to reflect. Her most pressing question was, how long had it lasted? She wished she had glanced at her watch before entering the bedroom with Lar or even when they arrived back from dinner, but she hadn't. Was she in there, or more importantly, had they been at it for 15 minutes or 2 hours? She didn't know. The disorientation of lost time was disquieting to Yo, who was accustomed to being in control or at least having a firm grasp on the here-and-now. Sitting on a sofa amidst the familiar in a well-lit room and having a nice glass of wine was helping immensely. She felt herself beginning to relax into her seat as if she had become heavier, now content to sit doing nothing. Perhaps in a few minutes she'd pick up a magazine or turn on the tube. Now, however, sitting was all that was necessary.

Alice entered, wearing the same tee and shorts combination she had on before she undertook to focus Lar, her hair wet and combed back. "How are you doing?" she asked.

"I'm very relaxed, but a little confused," Yo said.

"What did you see?"

"At first I saw an S&M scene. Classically dressed Mistress; Alice you have a lot of leather," Yo answered, her mind not yet thinking or not letting her think in linear terms.

"Yes, I do, a lot more than you saw today." Then Alice was silent, indicating it was Yo's turn to continue.

"You had him hooked up to that...what was that, Alice, did you buy that?" Yo's mind was still jumping around avoiding what it had seen, avoiding having to admit she had seen it because admitting the existence of what she had seen would mean that it did exist and if it did exist it would have to be explained, and Yo could imagine no explanation.

"I made it; the whole thing cost about ten bucks. I usually have Lar construct our toys but this brainstorm, well, I knew it would be much more effective on him if he didn't know it existed," Alice said pleasantly.

"So you make some stuff and buy others," Yo said. "Where do you like to shop?"

The door to the bedroom opened. Lar walked like a drunk to the bathroom and closed the door. A minute later water could be heard running in the shower. Both Alice and Yo watched him cross to the bathroom, Alice's face beaming at him. After the door closed they looked at each other again.

"There's stores in town and on the internet," Alice said, then repeated, "Yo, what did you see? I've never asked anyone before—I only know what it's like for me and Lar. What did you see?" Her voice took on an almost pleading tone.

This time Yo understood. There was more to this than Alice forcing a recalcitrant pupil to come to grips with a difficult concept. There were parts of this that Alice hadn't come to grips with. She was hoping that the perspective of an outside observer would help her to understand what was obviously a big part of her life.

"I saw an S & M scene, leather-clad Mistress administering increasingly unbearable torment to her helpless slave. At first it was interesting, entertaining, then I started getting uncomfortable. I was thinking that something wasn't right about this."

Alice's face betrayed dismay behind an attempt at an expressionless mask.

"Then that changed, right when you took off your bra and his blindfold; you looked him straight in the eye and he didn't take his eyes away from yours. By then he was covered in sweat, trembling and twitching, his breath coming in gasps that he was obviously trying to control, but there was a phase shift. Your breathing became more and more like his, you were glistening, by the time you had straddled his waist you were both breathing, trembling and twitching in unison. It almost looked like it wasn't two people." Yo's story had begun with enthusiasm but ended quietly more questions than answers. Yo continued quietly, "then you said, 'we're not going to see them'." She paused, then added, "who weren't you going to see?"

"Ask Lar," Alice said, getting up and going to the fridge. From her movements Yo realized that like Lar, Alice too was dazed, whether from her experience with Lar or its memory she wasn't sure. Alice meanwhile was lost in her own thoughts and revelations.

Lar got out of the bathroom looking chipper, almost radiant. Though his movements betrayed some stiffness he appeared to be looking for an excuse to smile.

"Can I get anybody anything?" he said, briskly walking towards the kitchen, opening the fridge and getting himself a Sammies.

"You didn't want to dull your senses before your ritual, that's why you didn't have a beer earlier," Yo observed.

"That's the idea," Lar said. "All senses in full operation, very perceptive."

"So Lar tell me something—where did you go and who weren't you going to see?"

"That's a tall order…"

"What happened?" Yo persisted.

Lar went over and unselfconsciously sat on the floor at the feet of the two women. "Well, at first I was just focusing on my breathing because it distracted me from the pain, then Mistress increased it." Lar's face became more and more expressionless as he told the story, becoming lost in his memories. "I couldn't ignore it, no matter what I did, then I started to get these brief glimpses of a purple body floating in blackness. The purple body had red sparks that radiated through it. The base of each spark on the purple body coincided with each point on me that was suffering. The sparks sometimes meet and bounce off of each other, sometimes meet and form currents that ripple through the body.

For each fleeting moment that I saw the body I felt like I was floating and watching." Lar's speech was becoming more deliberate and strained as he tried to articulate things he didn't have words for. "When I wasn't floating I was in agony, my voice hoarse, but the cycle continued, the fleeting moments of peace and observation increasing. I remember Mistress increasing the intensity of my pain again and all of my awareness being focused on my tortured body. I remember breathing so quickly that I thought I might hyperventilate and pass out, trying to do so, breathing deeply and rhythmically trying to remember the brief sight of the floating purple body coursing with red lightning, then the deep memory awakened and I again knew the purpose of the journey and the reason for my suffering." By now Lar was so entranced by his memory that it no longer seemed past tense to him He was reliving the moment, reliving the fleeting dream. "The memory of the silent ones who sometimes allow me to see them through a thick mist of light...I remembered that when I saw them I always felt detached, no horror, no fear, just wonder, relaxation, and peace. Why is that? They are certainly not human, they're hardly humanoid and still if I get to see them there is only wonder and peace. I was remembering that when I could see them the closest turns towards me ever so slightly as if acknowledging my presence, acknowledging that I could see them and that they were aware of the moment it happened, then they would go back to their business of being and awareness. I remember thinking that they were always aware of me, waiting for me to be able to see them. I don't know if they are my personal watchers or just endorphin-induced hallucinations. I didn't know. I do know that if I am able to see them, both Alice and I will experience an indescribable calm and fascination. I hoped to see them this time, just a glimpse, but something changed my focus, maybe because I want it so badly. I don't know, I think it's been over a year, but this time we seemed so close. Then I was back in the room, ravaged, my heart beating wildly, almost delirious. Alice said we weren't going to see them today and released me. She was very soothing towards me, then said I could lay until I wanted to get up."

Lar's faraway look of recollection faded as he joined the present. "I think that's the most I have ever been able to remember; usually the memory just continues to fade and I just know that the experience was important without remembering the details."

He looked directly into Yo's eyes and said, "What did you see?"

"I already discussed it with your Mistress," Yo said using 'your Mistress' to add credibility and hopefully finality to her answer.

It didn't work. "What do you remember, since I've told the story that you didn't remember before?" Lar asked, making it a question of *what* she remembered, not *if* she remembered.

Yo sat quietly then said in a soft voice, "It was like you were both looking for something that was awe-inspiring and fascinating, yet at the same time you both looked so relaxed, like what you were doing was natural as rain."

"It's her magic," Lar said.

Alice rolled her eyes. "I'm not really sure what it is; I had hints of it with other submissives before I met Lar, but we clicked almost at once. I mean I've seen subs in subspace...."

"Subspace?" Yo asked.

"Kinda, almost like a new personality that takes over—the sub gets so into his role that just performing the role is exciting for him, like he gets off serving and being punished, almost like he's someone else. I always enjoyed getting men into subspace—it always made me feel powerful to get them to where they wanted more and more punishment and humiliation from me and you know what they say—power is an aphrodisiac. So I had no problem with controlling men, getting them to the place where their primary focus was my pleasure. Well, guess I'm starting to go on and on. Sorry."

Yo expressed her surprise at Alice's hidden life, especially since Alice had never shared in any bedroom-preference conversations or can't-find-a-good-man conversations. She wondered if Alice considered her activities a hobby or lifestyle, to which Alice answered that it was her orientation because she could not imagine herself being otherwise.

"Well you sure as hell don't look *that* part," Yo laughed. Yo was clearly having difficulties matching her ideas of a dominatrix with the person in front of her.

"I guess some folks like to wear their sexuality all the time; I like comfort," Alice explained with a shrug. "In fairness, when I first got into it, especially when I wasn't attached, I liked to slut myself up but it attracted too many creeps. That got real boring real quick."

Yo had a eureka expression, "So all those people who wear all the studs and have rings through their bodies and all the folks at the B&D places...they all do what you do?"

"Hate to burst your bubble," Lar joined in from his place on the floor. "Life ain't that easy."

Alice started again. "I can say equivocally that you are wrong on that count."

"How do you know?" Yo asked, confused, wanting a simpler answer, a bit of knowledge that she could put in her hip pocket and carry around with her. A bit of knowledge that would not require further thought or judgment. The kind of knowledge sold by politicians, TV evangelists and Madison Avenue.

"Well," Alice answered, "if you're in a scene where there is some expected power exchange with either the man or woman in charge, you've got to weed out the misogynists, men-haters and true sadists, you know, folks that could give a shit about how their partner feels as long as they feel bad. Then you've got people who don't really know how to connect with another person or even really carry on a conversation. Those folks find it very comforting to be in a relationship in which their role, either dominant or submissive, is already established, that way they aren't required to speak except in stereotyped phrases or they only have to speak when they are told. It's a perfect setting for the can't-connectors, but they can create no sexual energy since their primary desire is to glom onto something to make up for what they see themselves as lacking."

"That's pathetic," Yo scoffed.

Lar joined in, "Well, I don't think that people in the D/S community have a lock on those who fervently enlist in its ranks in order to escape having to look at themselves."

Yo nodded. "Alice, how did you find acceptable partners?"

"Trial and a lot of error and wasted time," Alice said, realizing instinctively that the time was right. For her, Lar's account of their experience had mirrored her own except that this time, there had been something different. Their experience had always been mutual deep sharing, but not this time. This had been her revelation. This time at least part of the experience had been just for her, and her part of the experience had enabled her to make a decision that had been bothering her like a ripe blister on the sole of her foot. She didn't know if her decision was based on self-delusion, but if it wasn't self-delusion she would know once and for all if the place that she and Lar went, the place she had based so much of her life on finding, was good or evil. She said "Why are you asking—thinking of exploring another facet of your sexuality?"

Yo paused, then explained that it had always been in the back of her mind. She'd had boyfriends tie her up but suspected that the males' motivation had been more for an avoidance of foreplay than eroticism. She had also experimented with tying up one of her lovers, but he had been so concerned with the correctness of her knots and the placement of the rope that both his erection and her interest subsided. Lar wanted to know if Yo imagined a role for herself when she masturbated, but Yo indicated that was personal information. Lar started laughing, Alice started laughing and finally Yo got the joke and laughed as well.

"Guess I can't really say I don't know you that well," Yo laughed, then flatly recounted that she had used both roles during masturbation and found them both satisfactory to her.

The conversation seemed to be placed on hold; Alice seemed to withdraw, as though thinking something over. She was thinking that she was about to do one of those things in life that, for good or bad, cannot ever be undone. This could potentially be a short-term solution for a short-term problem (or just an attempt at one) that could leave two lives bruised and lonely. However the more she thought it over the more right it felt. She decided to go with her gut, not knowing if her gut was only telling her what she wanted to hear at this moment or if her gut actually possessed some knowledge that the rest of her could not reach.

Everyone sat and drank their drinks, not making eye-contact, then Alice in as matter-of-fact a voice as she could muster, suggested that Yo borrow Lar for one month if she wanted to see if being a Mistress would be to her liking. There were discussions of safer sex, which were resolved by Yo's until-now-6-month hiatus and recent physical; safe play, resolved by Yo's growing up around doctors, visitation if initiated by Alice, and Lar's responsibility to stay in touch with periodic reports. Both Lar and Alice had an uneasiness that this could ultimately harm their relationship but also having powerful reasons for continuing on their path. So with Alice going with her gut, Lar going with his balls, and Yo going with her curiosity, the deal was made and the new path irrevocably taken for the three of them.

Yo started making time-to-leave motions, the prospect of ending her 6 month hiatus foremost on her mind. Alice sensed her eagerness to leave and was fretting over Lar's safety.

"You know the difference between discipline—between what we do and sadism?" she asked.

Yo assured her she did but Alice still worried, so she made Yo promise to look over the contents of a floppy she got from her room before getting into anything serious.

"Alice, I have a question," Yo said with another brainstorm. "Have you ever tried to push further? I mean, I saw you in the bedroom—he was the picture of agony but you stopped it. You said you wouldn't be seeing them tonight. How did you know? How do you know that if you just didn't push him a little farther you'd get where you wanted to go?"

"We tried that—didn't work," Lar answered. "We tried pushing it. Mistress had that feeling that we were as far as we're gonna get, but we had planned to try to force the issue to see what would happen so she had a hair pin and just when she got that feeling, that 'nope it ain't-a-gonna-happen this time,' she ...." Lar made a face. "I about passed out, there was blood everywhere, I almost threw up, had bloodclots, couldn't get it up forever."

"About a month," Alice joined in.

"Yeah and it hurt and..." Lar started.

"We were out of focus for a few months," Alice finished.

"Did you see anything?" Yo asked. "Before it all went to hell?"

"I saw white, then gray—screamed myself hoarse—we were going for it, but nothing," Lar recounted.

"Nada," said Alice. "Whatever it is we see or wherever it is, it requires a balance of pain, submission, and control. I think going overboard sacrifices the control. It wasn't even sexy." Alice looked away with finality, indicating the end of this conversation.

Yo was looking for a way to ease the conversation elsewhere, hoping for a break in the heavy atmosphere that had suddenly formed.

"Lar, what was going on when we got back? Asleep in the tub?"

"Almost asleep, was remembering Alice in her younger days, then I remembered Rif, got pissed, took a big breath and inhaled water."

Alice's eyes lost their focus, she shivered and looked at the floor, her color draining.

Yo, obviously not paying attention, asked, "Who's Rif?" She did not realize that the line between tenuous control of traumatic events and full blown PTSD is thin. Lar had encouraged Alice to tell her story and tell it again in an effort to "integrate" her memories so that she wouldn't have to hide from them. She had tried and was better; the thing was, she was never sure if she was hiding from the memories or hiding from him.

Lar saw Alice getting herself together and decided on a diversion to give her time. "A creep, a fucking creep," he started. "Goddam psychopath; today he'd be using Rohypnol and GHB, but he had to be creative. Those came after his time." Lar was looking directly at Alice. He had an angry edge to his voice, a dangerous edge mixed with fear and determination, showing a side of himself that Yo would not have attributed to a submissive

"A, what's Rohypnol and GHB, they sound familiar, B, who is this again?" Yo asked.

"Date rape drugs. Scum put them in women's drinks. They're tasteless, odorless, and knock 'em out and produce amnesia," Lar instructed.

"Well, why doesn't Rif have them?" Yo asked

"This was years ago when I was starting grad school," Alice said, suddenly emotional, her eyes full of hate. She checked herself. "You want to hear the story?" She looked at Yo.

Yo nodded, realizing this was deadly serious and may take some time.

Deciding to do the therapeutically correct thing, Alice did not instruct Lar in the telling. She began with what she knew; what she had found out, and what she guessed. She explained what she understood of Rif's business, how he envisioned a windfall from the video camera he had put in his neighbor's apartment. He surely had some great shots from the scene he had just witnessed. These were shots he could sell to the buyers who had been asking him for something that was a little more on the wild side than he could easily produce with a passed-out naked woman. He wouldn't use hookers to model for him; that could destroy his anonymity. Up to the point where he photographed the grad student next door, no one knew for sure what he looked like. Rif had some very good reasons to hide his identity, the least of which was the law. These were the things that Alice knew or guessed. What she didn't know were his thoughts. For example, aside from self-preservation, the thing that kept him in the business even more than the money, was power—power he felt when he was able to cash in on an unknowing victim. He always thought of taking and selling his pictures as a double fuck. She also didn't know how Rif got into his business. If Alice had known these things she might have reacted quite differently, which would make her quite a different person now. Even with her eccentric sexual predilections, she would still have been able to be like most everyone else. She would be able to live her life without meeting evil like a toddler running toward an open-mouthed crocodile.

Rif's business had been built slowly. He started when he was young with a post office box and a Polaroid camera that paid for itself many times over. His big break came in seventh grade; he was bigger than most of the other kids, a combination of genes and the fact that he had been held back twice, not because he couldn't do the work but he just didn't feel like doing the work. He didn't give a shit. Even in grade school he knew that getting over was better than getting by. Because of his size and that fact that he was a badass he had a lot of suitors smaller, and younger kids who wanted to be him. They were good for stealing him cigarettes and their parents' beers but he didn't want to get too close, one, because he didn't give a shit about them, two (and more importantly), people were baggage if they weren't useful. They were nothing and having some young kid getting into trouble and potentially mentioning his name was definitely not useful. So he bestowed his presence on those who brought the occasional pack of cigs or pilfered beer, but not with regularity. They always had that hurt little expression when, after stealing daddy's six-pack, which would probably net them a whoopin, and delivering it to their idol, they were told to leave and not come near him again—no particular reason, "I just don't want you around me anymore." He thought it was always such a joke—and there were always more kids wanting to hang out with the badass because they couldn't be a badass themselves. He never ran out of supplicants.

That's what happened in seventh grade. Pathetic little shit was trying to use his knowledge of a hole that you could look through to the girls' locker room, as currency with which he could buy friends. Rif had shown a great interest in the hole and befriended the little shit just long enough to be shown the closet, the airduct and the opening. Once he saw it and they were in the hallway he feigned outrage.

"That's my fucking next door neighbor in there man!!!!" he had screamed as he broke the smaller kid's nose. Blood was flying everywhere. Rif loved it. The kid was screaming and crying. "That girl's like a sister to me, you shit, you fuck!!!" he said as he continued to pummel the helpless child. "If I ever, and I mean EVER, see you anywhere near here I'll kick your ass. You shit, I mean it, I'll fucking break you." By now the kid was balled up on the floor. Rif kicked him a good one in the stomach as the kid had started to unwind, just for emphasis. "If you say anything about this beatin' you know I will find you and I will tell them why I gave it to you, because you were looking into the girls' locker room. That's sick, you little pervert." The kid was regaining his breath, still crying but starting to fade into sobs, as Rif waited. He wanted to make sure he was understood, so he waited till he was sure the kid could hear. "I'm gonna guard this place every spare moment I have. Nancy don't deserve to be spied on, she's like family man!!!!" Rif punctuated each word with a finger in the kid's sternum. "I better not see you or any other little fuck like you near here. If I see anyone else I'm going after them and then I'm going after you."

Rif continued, his voice mellowing. He stopped poking the kid in the chest with his finger. "Tell the nurse you fell down the stairs. If you mention me, you know what'll happen to you, not only will I kick your ass much worse than you can imagine, but you will be expelled for spying on the girls." Rif waited until the kid was up and preparing to leave, head down, then said sternly, "Now

GET," as he added a kick to the kid's ass. The boy was up and running. What a piece of shit.

With this peep hole he thought he could make a few bucks. There was an ad among the pages of ads on the back of a porno mag he stole, someone who wanted candid home shots of family members. He was willing to pay. Rif typed a letter, didn't sign it and enclosed a pic he had taken through the wall of the girls' locker room. The girl had been close and he said it was his sister. He could send plenty more but only after he was paid. He was a natural—15 years old and he already knew the basics; they just came to him. He didn't even have to figure it out, the ways of business were in his blood.

Rif mailed the photo to the post office box written in the ad and within a week he saw a letter in his post office box. He opened it and folded in a letter was a 5-dollar bill. The letter said there was a 5-dollar bill for any candid shots of any female "family" member. The quotes were in the letter and Rif figured that they meant any naked woman would do, even though he rarely went to English class. He immediately mailed a second letter with a pic that he had ready for this occasion. As a means of business expansion he had acquired several more skin mags. He found out that *Playboy* and *Penthouse* didn't have the type of ads he needed but mags with names like *Muff* and *Alley Girl* had plenty. He decided to risk the loss of his remaining capital by sending pics to every ad that solicited candid shots and promised to pay. He sent the same typed letter with a photo with the same post office box. That's when things got interesting. He still received typed letters from either post office boxes or with no return address at all. Some of the letters were weird, especially for a 15-year-old in the early 60's. Someone thanked him profusely then spent 2 pages talking about how he knows he shouldn't do this and that he knows something is wrong with him and he sickens himself, but would he please send more? Rif wouldn't have read further, but this was the only letter with a 20-dollar bill. Another 20 or even more was promised for candid pictures of his "family"—again the quotes. He would defiantly ask for more.

Two letters were definitely scary. One was an unsigned letter from someone who called Rif a sick pervert. The writer said if he ever found out who he was he would kill him and he was going to the police with Rif's letter. He would tell them that the letter had arrived unsolicited. He hoped that the police would track him down and send him to jail where the other inmates would know how to treat him like the pervert he was. Rif was shaken—were the police watching, would they be watching soon? Did they follow him to his house?

Rif could control his mother better than the kids at school; basically all he had to do was stay out of her way, and not interrupt her when she was drinking and got that look. You had to catch the look early and be watchful for it, especially if you didn't know how much she had been drinking when you got home. It would always start out with compliments and expressions of concern; if you didn't find an "out" right away, then it was too late. The expressions of concern would grow more accusatory, more blaming and more outraged. If you left when that started, shit, she could come after you with a ball bat and even if you outran her, where was there to go? If you left the house, when you got back, all your stuff would be smashed to shit. Your room would be torn up and if you got home the next day she would be too hungover to talk about it. If she had a man over, the fuck would take her side, hoping that he was scoring points for a blowjob later in the day. He'd had some of her guys take off after him too, just for those blowjob points, or because they were mean drunks who liked to beat the crap out of someone smaller to make up for their failed lives or at least their perception of a failed life. The meanest one of all of 'em always drove a new Caddie, always had nice clothes, and always brought expensive Scotch. Mom had been seeing him off and on for years but it was always the same after he was drunk—mean son-of-a-bitch that likes to flail on his slut's piece-of-trash son. She didn't care and what was the kid gonna do? Nothing. Well, the kid was getting bigger. Even as a young teenager Rif was almost 6 feet tall and he was quick. Bastards couldn't catch up with him now, and soon he'd have his own little place to store his shit, then if Mom wanted to go breaking things up, let her. She'd always get him a new bed and dresser and clothes, and if his important shit was elsewhere, someplace he could go for the night, he'd be fine—he'd be more than fine. In the meantime, though, it would definitely not be cool at all for the police to come by. He needed just a little more time. Hiding stuff in a garbage can in the alley or in an abandoned building was no longer acceptable. He needed a place to go and a place where he could conduct business.

The scariest letter came back with no mention of the police—it was handwritten and signed. It said:

"You obviously were not aware that the candid photo business is already established and we do not expect any competition. If you want to sell to us we will give you $2.00 per photo. Don't sell to anyone else. We're watching the post office, we know what you look like. We will not send you another letter." Signed Al.

Fuck, that seemed serious. Rif did not want to meet Al or any of his friends. He would have to be very careful. He would not be able to respond to any more ads. He would have to develop a different business strategy. Rif relied on his head for business. Al might know he was a kid but didn't know if he was the one sending photos and he probably didn't know for sure that his letter was read today, but he could probably find out if it was delivered today, probably would only cost him $10. Rif had no idealized notions of how the post office or anything else worked. He knew the world was a shithole and it was every man for himself. Dammit, it was going to be him and not them, not the Cadillac-drivin' son-of-a-bitch and not big Al. He couldn't fight Al but he could play him, he could try, he would just have to be real safe. That would be his new motto. Real safe, let the other people get hurt, he would be safe.

With that attitude it was surprising that he didn't give up his life of crime and become a model citizen—a safe job in a safe neighborhood and a safe wife, 2.5 kids, but those concepts were as foreign to him as studying for a test or self-sacrifice. He had a head for business, he had a start, he liked the excitement, he liked that he was getting over on the little chickies in the gym. He didn't want to stop. So for Rif the idea of safety merely meant that he would have to conduct his business more safely. He took a self-inventory: he could start with what he had.

He had sent out 24 photos and had received 10 letters back so far, 2 threatening letters, 3 with 5-dollar bills, 3 with 10-dollar bills, one containing 2 dollars (possibly from Al) and one with 20. He could potentially receive more threats and more envelopes with money in them requesting more photos. He needed to find out what his return on investment would be. He already had made back the cost of the film and then some and this was definitely more money for less work than he had ever received. He needed to check back in a few days, maybe a week. He needed a plan. Maybe a distraction. If Al's guys saw him they may not think he was behind the business—he was after all just a kid. On the other hand, judging from the ages of the girls in the photo, they might be able to put two and two together. "OK, here's the plan," he said to himself, resigned. If he was going to do this, there would have to be some initial risk, then after that he would live for safety, and cash.

If Al had guys watching him at the post office they probably followed him home. The worst thing that could have happened was that they saw a teenager get some letters from the post office and walk home. They knew where he lived. While they knew where he had gone, they didn't know for sure he lived there, at least not yet. He had little doubt that they could find out but they didn't know for sure if it was *his* business. He could be an errand boy. Already his head for business had formed a plan based on the principles he would continue to follow throughout his life—deception, manipulation and exploitation.

First, just in case he was being watched, he gathered the same number of envelopes that he had gathered from the post office, including the now-empty envelopes he had opened. He went outside and caught a bus across town—he didn't think that anyone was following but they could be professionals. He got off at the last bus stop and walked 2 miles into the good neighborhood to Richard (the Cadillac man) Dawson's house. He was in luck—the big car wasn't there. If it was, this would have been much more risky. He walked up to the front door and put the letters in the mail slot, then walked back to the bus stop, waited, got on the bus and went home. Tomorrow he would find a new mailbox. He had the all important addresses. He didn't go back to the post office again. Instead he started grooming another supplicant.

"Hey Mikey, howzit goin?"

Mikey, an average sized 7th-grader who was an aspiring badass, delighted to hear a friendly overture from the school's main badass. Yet he was wary. "Doing good...whatzup?"

"What's happenin'?"

"Not much."

"Got any cigs?" Rif demanded, thinking it best to get the relationship off to a proper start—Mikey was to give him things.

"Sure," the supplicant answered.

"Lets go." The kids smoked on the corner just outside of school property so Rif didn't have to say where they were going. As the class bell rang they left the building, stood on the corner and smoked.

Over the next few days they shared many cigarettes, lied about girls, and Rif even offered a cigarette on a couple of occasions then asked for small favor. Could Mikey pick up some cigs on his way to school the next day? He was in a little trouble and thought that the law might be watching him and didn't want them to have an excuse to fuck with him being underage and getting cigs. Rif handed him a buck. That was enough to buy them if he knew where to shop. Mikey was delighted. The two buddies hung out for about a week. Then Rif needed another favor. Could Mikey pick-up his parents' mail from the post office? There was a free pack of cigs for him if he'd do the favor. Rif wanted to take care of some business on his way home but he was supposed to go to the post office on his way home and since he was having a little trouble with the law he couldn't skip school right now and the extra time it would take him to do his business and go to the post office would be noticed, so could Mikey skip out, pick up the letters for him and meet him at school and give them to Rif later that day?

"That ain't gonna get you in trouble with your parents or the teachers or anything, would it?" Rif asked, mimicking concern.

"Fuckem if it does."

"Great, tell you what...here's my combination to the padlock on my gym locker. Just put the letters in there by lunchtime, OK?"

"No problem," Mikey was being cool.

"Man, I owe ya," Rif said with apparent gratitude.

By noon the letters were in his gym locker and the new lock he had bought for the occasion was thrown away and the old lock, the original lock, was put in its place. By 1:00 Rif had one more favor to ask. Could Mike leave school again and mail a thick brown envelope? It needed to be in the mail before it was picked up at 3:00 and Rif couldn't risk getting caught skipping school at this time.

"No problem," Mikey said. "Say, Rif, whatzup with the law and you anyway?"

"Man, you don't want to know; in fact, it's best you don't know, that way you're not an accessory if things go bad. I really appreciate your help and wouldn't want you fucked over from helping me, OK?"

Mikey was impressed—this was bigtime shit! "Sure, Rif—thanks."

If Mikey had been followed they would have seen him walk to school with the letters, then emerge from the school a little while later and mail a thick envelope presumably with the letters in it. This hopefully would take the heat off of him as the businessman and make him seem to be just one of several couriers for someone else. He hoped that Mikey wasn't intercepted on his way to the mailbox and the envelope opened, which he doubted would happen, or that the mail was intercepted at the post office, which he also doubted would happen. He was in the clear and if they suspected Cadillac Man and were watching his house, they would see that a thick brown envelope was mailed to that very house in about 3 days.

There were 8 more letters received, all with 10's and 20's. Rif was rich—he could invest in more product and safety.

The second order of business was to find a new means of delivery. This required research. The yellow pages showed several places that not only had mailboxes, but you could request that the mail be forwarded to you for a small fee. There were also places that looked like a street address so that UPS could deliver packages. This was the best of both worlds. He could have his letters delivered then mailed to another box. This would slow down delivery time but it gave him an added layer of security, and if he played his cards right, Al would only have the vaguest hint of an operation—nothing obviously taking a chunk out of his business and not enough to send people out on a mission to track him down. He was sure that they could track him down if they tried hard enough, but now they wouldn't be that concerned that he would be infringing on their profits, and if he didn't infringe on their profits why would they care? Now to enlist the mail service. Ideally he would change services every month. This would be a logistical nightmare taking buses, and using up all of his capital. Screw it—he'd use two companies close to home that didn't have forwarding services for his actual mailboxes, and use one across town that would forward as the p.o.b. he'd give his customers.

His next dilemma was the problem of age. A 15-year-old boy would have difficulty signing any official forms to open his various post office boxes. Rif's original box at the actual Post Office had been initiated by his mom when she was having some difficulty with a boyfriend that she allowed to stay over for a few days that turned into a few months. He wasn't paying rent, was eating all of the food and going through her mail to see if she had anyone on the side. She had asked him to leave, he said he was trying, but when his mom asked he got mean toward her and said he'd get the hell out as damn soon as he could and it wouldn't be soon enough because he was sick of her, sick of her house and sick of her fucking kid. His mom had opened a post office box the next day and had her mail forwarded to it. After two months the son-of-a-bitch finally moved out taking the stereo. Rif had volunteered to go to the post office to cancel the box and to tell them to forward the mail back to their address. Well, when he got to the post office they wouldn't just take his word for it—they needed his mom's signature but they gave him the form to take home. He took the form home and had her sign it, but when he went back, for some reason he didn't turn over the key.

"You still have 2 more months on the box paid for—gonna give it up after that?" the man behind the counter had said.

"Not sure...will my mom have to sign anything if she decides to hang onto it?" Rif had asked.

"As long as it's paid up she won't have to sign a new lease," the man replied.

"OK, I'll go home and ask."

But he didn't ask. He hung onto the key and paid for the box himself, not really knowing why, just knowing that he really liked the idea of having something for himself not under anyone else's control. It had been over a year before the box's true value had shown itself and now he was going to have to give it up.

After calling the mailbox companies he found out that they would really prefer that the person who was getting the box come in to sign up, but since the caller was bedridden it would be OK if they sent someone else down. Yes, it could be a minor, but the signer's identification would have to be presented. Rif then asked the person he spoke with what their hours were, saying that he wanted his son to be able to do business with the person he spoke with on the phone. Each time he was told that anyone in the office could handle the transaction and the working hours of the individual taking the call. Rif made it a point to always present the signed paperwork with his mother's pilfered identification in an hour that conflicted with the schedule that he'd been given on the phone. There was a chance that the person would recognize his voice and think something was amiss; this minimized that chance. All of this planning and deceit came easily to Rif—he was a prodigy, but not the type of prodigy that would be discovered on a standardized test in school.

His means of delivery set up, he next needed to dispose of Mikey. First he would try to finesse his way out of their relationship. Mikey might be useful in the future, so there was no need to burn bridges needlessly. If that didn't work he could always find a pretext to beat the shit out of him so that he would keep his distance. So when he went to school the next day Rif sought Mikey out.

"Hey Mikey," Rif said in a distant offhand way.

"What's going on, Rif? You've been scarce lately." Mikey was concerned and his guard was down. He was daring to ask Rif personal questions but this fit into Rif's plans nicely.

"Mikey, I'm pretty hot with the cops right now. I gotta keep a real low profile for a while. It's best if we're not seen together till things calm down." Rif was talking quietly but seemingly in earnest.

"Fuck the cops—they don't worry me!" Mickey was all bravado. He was a badass.

"Don't do nothing stupid. First, I don't want you in any trouble from just hangin' out with me; if they pick you up for questioning, the less you know about where I am or what I'm doing, the better for you. You've done me some real favors and I don't want you fucked over," Rif said, as though he was trying reason with him.

"I ain't worried about no cops. Hell, I'm 13, they ain't gonna do anything to me anyway." Mikey was too full of himself.

Rif quickly shoved Mikey behind a double row of lockers, his arm at Mikey's windpipe, forcing him up so that he was on tiptoes supported by Rif's arm at his throat. Mikey was struggling to breathe; gasping, eyes bugging out, instantly terrified.

"Look man," Rif said, still being respectful. "They question you, you might give them some information without even knowing that you are giving them information and I'm fucked. I'll be tried as an adult and I go away for a long time, you got that? You've been a good friend but if you get me set up I swear I'll kill you before I go inside. You got that? I will kill you." Suddenly he was nice and concerned again, though Rif still had his arm on Mikey's windpipe. "I don't want to have to hurt you, I don't want you in trouble with the cops so let's just be cool, OK?" Now Rif slowly lowered Mikey to the floor. "I gotta keep a low profile, I'll be here but no one will notice. I will be in class. I will be here every day and we just say hi in the hall if you want, that's it." Mikey got the message. They walked their separate ways and Rif went to the closet behind the girls' locker room to get more product.

Business was conducted with the 18 customers he had established during 2 years. They became accustomed to mailing their requests to different mailboxes periodically. Their supplier never let them down, and he had begun to provide them with requests. After he had accumulated some more money and some years he acquired an new distributor. This distributor didn't require that he have an adult's signature or identification, so a false name and street address corresponding to Mr. Richard Dawson could be used with a little cash. Rif and the distributor had an understanding that if anyone ever asked about the identity of the person at that mailbox, he should follow any standard procedures, then to call a number that Rif provided him, within 24 hours. This provided Rif with a lead of several days, since the letters were forwarded to other mailboxes. A call from his new friend would let him know that Al was actively looking for him.

His customers were offered the opportunity to get reduced rates on pics if they requested 5 or more at a time. If they wanted to have their friend order through them that was OK but he didn't want any new addresses coming to his post office box without an explanation and their old address listed. Several of his customers were entrepreneurs as well and Rif's business boomed.

By the time Rif discovered Alice he had a modest amount of money socked away in a couple of bank accounts and a less modest amount in several safety deposit boxes under different names. He figured he'd need to get his money offshore somehow if he ever made a big score, but his head for business didn't seem to extend to laundering money, just acquiring it through the manipulation and exploitation of drugged women and staying away from the police and other businessmen that he knew would be happy to put him out of business. His clients were getting more demanding. The world of pornography was just starting to open up and the true fetishes of his customers were starting to come out. In addition, even though his original business had been started 14 years ago, the price he commanded for his pictures hadn't gone up appreciably. He was having to turn out more product to stand still economically. Customers who once were happy with a peek of pubic hair now wanted a whole scene including penetration. Still, Rif commanded more money than some, though his pictures didn't show much more than one could see in a skin book from a porno store. His clientele liked having something special that wasn't available to the masses. So his money accumulated slowly, he lived in an apartment and dreamed of something big that his customers would really pay for. But his fear of police and of people like Al kept him cautious all of these years. Now he saw the possibility of paydirt.

Several of his customers had been clambering for special shots—the type of shots he didn't know if he could pull off. Mostly they wanted to see a woman bound and tortured and though he had no qualms about causing another person pain, having a living person to torture either meant a whore who would notice the cameras and may run her mouth off to the wrong people, or keeping one of his conquests drugged which meant no look of fear or agony as she was tortured. The second option was kidnapping someone, torturing her, and either killing her or arranging it in some way that she didn't know it was him or where she was. Both of these options seemed to be far too risky. If the police got involved and he was even a suspect way down on their list their suspicions would be aroused if they ever came to his apartment and saw his equipment and, god forbid, any of his negatives. That type of killing was best left to drifters. Anyway, he still made a decent income, got to have sex with a lot of bitches, and drove a great car. Life was sweet but…but still, there was that gnawing voice that said that the world was changing and this gravy train wasn't going to last forever.

Alice had been exploring a long-known but only recently acknowledged facet of her sexuality. Alice's boyfriend, Mark, had gone along with her initial request to allow her to tie him up because he knew if he did he'd get laid. He knew he would probably get laid anyway, but this was an easy get laid, she wanted to do it and like they said in the movie, *Bull Durham*, "A man will do anything if he thinks it's foreplay." Mark had received more than he bargained for. His girlfriend had ridden him more enthusiastically than he had ever been ridden, and she had cum more forcefully than anyone he had ever had sex with. It was great for his ego to know his woman was in the throes of such pleasure, and since they had started with her games it was all the sex he could handle. In other words, he had more than anything a 22-year-old male could want. There was a drawback, though—Alice didn't want to switch roles. They talked about it and she said that being in the submissive role just wasn't part of her dream. He didn't like the sound of that, that meant that when he was tied she saw him in a submissive role and he wasn't sure if that was something a man should do or something that a man should allow, but there was the sex to consider. If there was something he could do to turn her on that was a sure thing, he guessed he was ahead in the long run. Besides, Alice didn't require expensive meals though they went out sometimes; fucking, carry-out and more fucking was a more usual date. Alice didn't require expensive clothes, and she didn't need him to have a fancy car, which was good since he didn't have one. All she required was that he follow a few rituals that had been established and he would have the best sex of his life. All in all a good trade. They had been seeing each other for 10 months.

They always got together on Friday nights. Lately they had been discussing the possibility of doing something besides fucking all Friday night but by Friday it had been several days since they had seen each other so the biological imperative always took hold. Earlier in their relationship she had left the door unlocked for him but then that creepy guy with the hair and the car started to always seem to be around and she wanted a locked door between him and her. Hairguy was the type that the Barbies went after; he had hair, he had a car, he wore expensive yet casual clothes, but there was no life in his eyes. Alice knew he wasn't a catch but by the way he looked at her, he didn't know she knew. He always had this kind of leer that she guessed some women found sexy, but it made her shudder. When she had first moved in she had attempted to get to know her neighbors, even hair man, but his conversation was empty. She felt like she was talking to a commercial, as though everything he said was orchestrated and rehearsed under the heading "casual conversation." He talked about his car, he talked about places he liked to go to, he talked about his job as a freelance photographer, but his talk seemed empty. Not that the jocks next door had any great intellectual or insightful gifts to impart, but their conversation wasn't staged. At times, one would become desperate in an attempt to get to know her better, but she knew she was talking to guys who could be foolish, and probably oafish, but they seemed whole. That was it. Hairguy had something lacking, like he was missing something. He was like the sleaziest salesman you ever met, only polished. He had the superficial charm thing down, he had a patter of things that would impress someone who was looking to be impressed, but he was missing something important. Alice thought of that missing part as a soul; people in forensic work called it a conscience.

On Friday, as he had done many times before, Mark knocked on the door.

"Close your eyes," he heard Alice say. He knew that the best sex relied on his strict attention to detail. Her details. When they had started playing her games he had been less serious and she had been more unsure of herself in the role of sex director. If he started giggling or if he really didn't close his eyes when she wanted she would get flustered and unsure. On one hand, he liked having that type of power over her. That was the type of power that his friends aspired to have over their women, keeping them off balance and unsure what was acceptable to them. That way the guys had the upper hand and they could parlay their upper hand for sex or having her doll herself up so he could show her off to his friends. Already, through Alice, he was discovering a truth. Keeping your partner off balance may give you a type of control but it can sure get in the way of spontaneous sex, at least from the partner who is kept off balance. How can a person be creative and playful if she is unsure of the rules?

Mark did as he was told. He closed his eyes and opened the door. When the door closed behind him he felt a blindfold being put over his eyes.

"You'll need to let me lead you; the furniture has been rearranged," Alice said as she took both of his hands and slowly walked him from the door to the living room. He walked through what would have been an end table so he know she wasn't lying.

Alice pressed herself against him, holding his arms at his sides. He could feel her tits and hard nipples even through his shirt. She was naked, skin hot, she brushed against one of his hands and he had a brief feel of her pussy, already hot and moist. She was rubbing herself all over him, letting go of one hand as she rubbed his sides, still lightly holding the hand closest to her. She was taking her time, rising to her toes, pressing against him then sensually allowing her body to rub down him. God, it was a turn-on. She moved to his back and rubbed her pubes against his ass. He could feel her, even through his pants. By now he was trembling, hard, ready, desiring, panting, and she hadn't even touched him. She was taking her time at his back, rubbing herself on his ass, pawing his thighs one-handed as she slowly released her slight hold on one hand, caressed the inside of his thigh up to his crotch, then gently reclasped his hand and released the other.

Mark was in heaven; she was in no hurry and he had been with her long enough to know that he didn't need to hurry either. Still he ached for her and started to grind in time with her, pushing himself against her. She maintained her light grasp of his hands, grinding herself against him emitting small sounds of pleasure. He could feel the heat of her—she was trembling too. She lifted his arms behind his back gently and allowed her hands to follow the insides of his arms, his armpits, and down his sides, then gently reclasped his hands. She repeated the process again and again, her breathing heavy and deep. Again she let go, then gently lifted his arms, moved, reclasped his hands, then he felt metal being put around his wrist. Mark was slightly alarmed but any fears were quickly quelled by Alice's continued caresses, her breathing and the sound of her breath as she moved around to his other side, still rubbing her body against him, her tits continually pressed against him, then her body moving in small swirls as she lowered herself. He imagined what a painting would look like if she were covered with paint, her tits making spirals as she lowered herself down the canvas. This was another unique thing about making it with Alice—he imagined color, and form, the shape of her body. On the painting he was imagining now she would definitely be covered in a rich dark yellow and definitely latex, shiny, thick paint so that there were almost brush marks from the swirls her tits made on the canvas. God, he should take art and screw all this business administration. God, he should stop thinking and only see the yellow swirls in his mind's eye as he felt his girlfriend's body making circles against him.

Alice was back in front of him, still slowly rubbing her body against him, thrilled about the power her seduction had over him, feeling his need, his need becoming her need, his excitement transferred to her and changed somehow. She was thinking of yellow. Dark and rich and shiny, the color seemed to fit the mood, and in her mind's eye the yellow color turned into a smoke that filled the room, making small prisms of candles and light bulbs. She unbuttoned his shirt and pulled it down his arms, continually rubbing against him, caressing his chest and nipples before unbuttoning his pants, slowly taking them down, removing his shoes and pants.

Alice began to notice that there was an ebb and flow to the yellow color and it was influenced by the attentions she was bestowing on Mark. The colors grew richer in her mind's eye as she stroked the insides of his thighs. She was almost playing the colors and her lover like music, and she discovered that playing either her lover or the colors added to the excitement and richness of the moment. She wondered what would happen if she put him in her mouth. She circled his cock with her lips. Surprisingly the colors in her mind's eye faded. She was still in her living room, still turned on, but the beautiful daydream had ended.

She still had her lust, her control and her naked boyfriend. Hardly a total loss.

Mark was imagining the canvas, the yellow paint, and the visceral sensations his painting would inspire in anyone. Why hadn't he realized he could visualize like this before? He could see each swirl of the paint, he could see the thin dark ridges and lighter valleys where the paint was thicker and then so thin that the canvas could actually be seen through the paint. Looking at the design the observer couldn't help but experience not the paint, but the canvas, what the canvas felt like with each stroke of the brush, the overall sensuality of the lines and the ridges and valleys of thicker and thinner paint, the paint so thin that you could actually see the canvas through it. Mark was lost and the paint and color actually seemed to start to move ever so slightly. Mark was aware of his shirt being unbuttoned and exposing his naked chest, his shirt pulled back to the handcuffs, then her body, and again he felt the intensity that canvas must feel, the pleasure of being painted, the raw experience when each thick drop of paint slid onto the canvas then covered the surface perfectly so that a visual representation of the pleasure given by the paint was there for anyone with eyes. Anyone who looked would experience this sensuality as the visual receptors of the brain merely acted as conduit for the meaning and experience which could not help but fill them with awe and raw lust. There was more to the painting than raw sensation and naked sensuality. There was almost volition, almost movement, almost…he felt his pants being removed, lowered, shoes and pants removed. Her tongue and lips and hands were on his thighs. He wanted her lips around his cock, he was aching, trembling. He felt her mouth getting close to him. The few seconds it would take her to close her mouth around his cock seemed an eternity, several lifetimes. Then he was in her mouth, the sensation bliss but not whole. He noticed that the painting he was thinking of was no longer in his mind's eye. Try as he could, he could reconstruct only a flat 2-dimensional approximation of what he had experienced, but there were other more pressing matters. Alice gave great head.

Three weeks earlier Rif was not a happy camper. He had been getting some great shots that his customers would love. His neighbor routinely tied her boyfriend to the bed frame like an X. There they would engage in oral sex to regular sex, she would untie him and they would have another round or he would fall asleep. At least that is all the shots he would get. He knew there was more to the story. Rif had taken to noticing his only conscious model when she came and left. He knew her schedule. He knew approximately how long it would be from the time she brought her boyfriend home to the time they would be in the sack. She sure was enthusiastic although her waist was a bit too thick, her boobs a bit too small, and her ass a bit too thin (Rif liked wide hips, bigger than Barbie) and her shoulders were too sturdy, thighs and legs way too muscular. This was the 70's and though Alice liked to work out at the gym, the idea of a woman with defined muscles as beautiful would not become popular for another decade. He was starting to wonder what it would be like to have a woman so alive in the sack. In his fantasies she would be as enthusiastic as Alice, without her physical defects, of course, and she would be quiet, pliable, getting into the positions he liked, but bucking and thrusting with the enthusiasm of his neighbor, quiet but enthusiastic.

Rif knew her schedule, had his fantasies, and knew her body but there were things he didn't know, and he was sure that those things he didn't know had market value. More and more he would see them entering her apartment, the lights going on but his view of the upstairs loft with the bed in center screen was empty. They were playing in other parts of the apartment and he was not getting photos. This presented a problem—the live camera was costly and though it had paid for itself, installing another one would present some problems; the cost of another camera, installing the camera, and most importantly, running more coaxial cable from her apartment to his building. If she ever noticed, she would see that there were two television cables running out of her apartment and if she looked carefully she would notice that one cable ran to a group of cables which ran to a telephone pole where other cables went to other apartments but a separate wire also exited her apartment and went into his building. If she followed the wire she would see that it connected to a place in the roof of the building at the opposite end of Rif's apartment. Rif didn't want to run the risk of yet another cable. That had too much potential for discovery. Rif hadn't been in this business this long by being careless and taking stupid risks. Three cables coming out of an apartment with one television was a stupid risk. But there was a solution.

Stores had surveillance cameras that would take pictures at designated time intervals. The quality of the pictures was usually grainy and indistinct but Rif was informed that the poor quality of the picture made it possible to fit more pictures onto the cassette. Higher quality pictures were possible if he was willing to give up quantity. Rif bought the camera and had a simple plan. He would install it in the downstairs through the air vent. The camera could be turned on and off by connecting power to the camera. This was easy—a much smaller wire was required and this could be connected to an on off-switch that he chose to install at the far end of her building. Nothing else going back to his apartment, nothing else connecting him to her. All he would have to do is go to where the utility people read for the monthly bills and flip a switch.

Rif knew something was going to happen downstairs when he saw his neighbor enter the building and her boyfriend stayed outside. When she entered the downstairs lights came on, but not the upstairs lights. He waited for the young man to enter, then he slipped out of his apartment, went to the utility area, and flipped the switch.

Alice had just finished having her way with Mark. He was naked and flat on his back on the living room floor, hands still cuffed, a stuporous half-smile on his face. Both lovers were naked, sweaty, flushed and panting. Alice rolled Mark over and unlocked his wrists. As he stretched his arms she hugged, entwining legs, kissing him fully. He hugged her, lightly untangled himself from her arms and legs, stood and stretched.

"Hope you have beer," he said, walking toward the fridge.

There was one left; he opened it and drank from the bottle. Mark was pacing and stretching. "Guys," Alice was thinking, "fuck 'em and they either fall asleep or they get up and think you should be grateful."

"Want to go out, meet some people, hear a band?" Mark asked. Like many 22-year-old males, Mark was obtuse in his awareness of his lover's desires. He knew she liked to tie him up and fuck the daylights out of him but it never dawned on him that after they were finished having sex they weren't finished making love. He thought after they were finished having sex they were finished. If they weren't going to have more sex it was time to do something else, like watch TV or go out.

"What are you going to do when I leave you tied up for hours after we're finished?" Alice teased.

"None of that until I get to tie *you* up."

This was becoming an old discussion. Alice supposed that she should go ahead and let him, turnabout being fair play and all, but being tied was not part of her dream world. It was not part of her makeup. As long as she could remember she had always gotten a thrill out of scenes in movies and TV westerns where the young boy or girl was tied up but she never put herself in the role of the ingenue. She just had this feeling somewhere deep inside that this was the other half of the equation she needed to make something. She never knew what that something was but she knew it was something important to make. Something she was supposed to make. Something that was special, that would release something, or do something, or well, just something very special that was part of her, that she was supposed to do in order to be who she was supposed to be. The scene never involved her being tied up. If she was tied up she knew she would not be able to do it, whatever *it* was.

When she was at the age when children frequently satisfy their curiosity about the other sex by playing doctor, she had thought long and hard about the game she wanted to play. Girlfriends in grade school had been talking about playing doctor and she hoped she would get the chance to play too, only her game would be different. She would play war and would tie up her prisoner before satisfying her curiosity. She knew how to tie her shoes but didn't know if that was the right type of knot to use on a boy so she asked her mom.

"Mom, what's the best way to tie up a boy?" Alice asked.

Her mother had that look on her face that said she was thinking that, "there might be something wrong with my daughter," that she better answer this question right, and that she was worried. Alice immediately regretted asking and realized that she had obviously said something very wrong. Her mom was looking at her with eyes that said, "there might be something wrong with you—why are you thinking this way?" Alice was thinking, "Mom won't love me if I ask anymore about this—I'll drop it or Mom will think I'm bad." So Alice didn't ask anymore but her curiosity was strong. She wanted to know, what was the mystery that parents wouldn't tell kids about? If she knew the mystery she thought she would be more like a grownup—she would be more grown. That was the clincher. The thing that children desire the most is age and maturity, the thing they have no respect for is innocence. When she was 7 one of the boys from the street behind her house asked her if she wanted to play doctor. He had come over to play as he sometimes did but this time was different because usually he had a friend or two with him. This time he was alone. He said he had played doctor with some of the other girls on the street and now he wanted to play doctor with her. It was a sunny spring day and they both loved being outside. Where could they go where their parents wouldn't catch them, Alice had wanted to know. He knew a place.

"Are you going to show me your thing?" she had asked.

"If you show me yours," he had replied.

"So that's fair, if you get to see mine I get to see yours?" Alice had wanted to know.

"Yeah, that's fair," he said, feigning worldliness.

"Let me get my purse," she had said. Though she was wearing shorts, sneakers and a T-shirt, the idea of her needing a purse didn't seem strange to him. Alice tore in the back door, ran to her room and got her purse with the rope that she had put there for the day, this day that she knew would come. "I'm going next door," she told her mom on her way out.

"Which next door, sweetie?" her mom had asked.

"Fred's house."

"OK."

Alice left with Fred. They casually walked through her fence into his back yard. She could hear noises coming from the house; it sounded like people listening to a game on TV—every now and then there would be loud cheers in unison. Fred walked confidently into the tool shed.

"In here," he had said. They walked in. "First you show me yours," he said as soon as the door was closed.

"No, first I want to tie you up, then I'll show you mine," Alice said.

"No way," Fred countered, "I'll tie you up."

"Fred, I have to tie you up." Alice was so matter-of-fact, but Fred was having none of it.

"You're bad—I don't want to play with you." Fred left and that was that. From what she had learned from her Mom and a peer with whom she had hoped to obtain knowledge that would help her mature, it was wrong for girls to tie boys up. She learned that lesson too well—she was 20 before she got up the nerve to ask another boy. Now that she finally had a boyfriend who would go along she still didn't know what it was she was supposed to do with him. She had no road map, and was acting on instinct and trial and error alone. Her fantasies were more intense than their play had been, but even at 22 in 1978, Alice was beginning to suspect that the nature of fantasies was that they promised an intensity through certain actions that were not replicated in the real world. Still, where was the boundary?

Things she knew for sure were that her fantasies never had *her* tied, and tonight something had happened—the yellow in her mind's eye, the yellow cloud that she had actually thought she had influenced. That was new and the sensations she felt for that timeless interval could only be defined as...what? As a promise? The color and her supposed influence had actually felt like a promise of bliss, the intensity of which she could not even imagine.

Rif had chosen the time of Mark and Alice's lovemaking to do his laundry. The small apartment complex in which he and Alice lived was composed of two large rectangular buildings each with four loft apartments in the front and back and two on each side. The two rectangles were positioned so that if you looked at them from above they would look like stair steps. On one side of each rectangle was a parking lot. Where the space for the step would be, was a large concrete patio where a pool used to be. At the base of that area fully in front of Alice's building but directly to the side of Rif's building, was the laundry building with two washers and two dryers. Going from Rif's apartment to the laundry required that he walk in front of Alice's building. Each time he walked to check for his laundry he could see if the lights had changed in her apartment, and if he was lucky he would be able to discern movement behind the floor-to-ceiling patio-style windows in each apartment. During one of his trips he could tell they were finished with their fun and games. Even if they did it again it would be more on his terms and not hers. He seemed to need more mobility to get it up after the first time. Rif went towards the laundry building then made a quick left to the utility area to flip the switch before going in to check the laundry. He didn't know it at the time, but a simple business analysis he had conducted several years ago would soon cause a major change in his lifestyle and would create a corner in Alice's mind in which she always looked over her shoulder, always waiting for another shoe to drop.

Alice was entering her standard refrain into the standard argument. "I have no desire to be tied up."

"I do it for you," the standard response.

"I know that you do and I love that you do it, but when I first asked you I said that this was something I wanted to try and you said yes it would be OK to try it. I'm telling you that it's not OK with me to try it the other way. I have never had that type of fantasy and the idea is not a turn-on for me," Alice's standard reply to Mark's standard response.

"Lately I've really been thinking about it." This was a new strategy. His old ploy had always been to argue about fairness and her replies had always centered around the idea that this was a fair arrangement because she had asked him if it would be OK with him, and she checked with him to see if he liked it, which he always said he did. So her argument was that this was fair because they both got something they liked and it was along the lines of something they had discussed.

Now he was appealing to a different type of fairness. "Lately I've been imagining what it would be like to have you as helpless as you make me. Then I could fuck you and have all the control."

"You have a lot of control on round 2 or three when you're usually on top," she offered, but knowing inside that it wasn't the same. Though she enjoyed second or third-fuck orgasms, for her, first-fuck orgasms were always best. Everything else was just icing.

"Alice, this is something I really want to try. Just like me you can stop it at any time. Just say stop. I've just never had the opportunity before and I really want to try." Mark was not only convincing, he sounded sincere.

Alice was beginning to feel like a guy who always wants head, always cums in his date's mouth but never has his mouth near his date's pussy. She wasn't being fair. Mark may be young but she was more than reasonably sure she could trust him. She was quiet for a minute as Mark looked at her hopefully.

"All right," said Alice. "Maybe I've been selfish. When you wanna do it?"

Mark was quiet for a minute. He had been prepared for a protracted discussion in which he probably wouldn't get his way, then he could be mad and complain to his friends about that bitch girlfriend being so selfish. He hadn't actually told them what they did when they were together—that wasn't really guy talk in his circle, but talking about girlfriends doing sexual favors, usually blowjobs or assfucking, did come up in conversation. However, when these subjects came up the sexual references were made sufficiently vague so that either the speaker who didn't have a much of a sex life with his girlfriend could make it sound like he did or, in Mark's case, a speaker who had an incredible amount of sex with his girlfriend could still sound unsatisfied. He had actually been rehearsing his complaints when he heard her capitulate. He had to think fast; his rejoinder about their having a lopsided relationship followed by her accurately observing that he really had nothing to complain about sexually, would no longer be appropriate. If he had had time to think he would have said ,"Tomorrow or later this week." That would have been best. He could have said, "I'll have something special planned for you," said with a sexual leer.

Instead he said, "When we get back from Cues." Cues was a pool hall-beerjoint where they liked to meet their friends.

"K," Alice said. Standing up naked she pressed her body against his and kissed him deeply, then went upstairs. A couple of minutes later the shower was running. Mark was thinking that Alice took less time to get ready than anyone he had ever dated. If they were just going to a hangout she could shower, mess with her hair and be ready to go in about 20 minutes. Of course, she wasn't much for make-up. When they first started going out after extended bouts of lovemaking, they sometimes went out reeking of cum, smiling silly, but in those days they weren't out long—too much lust. That had lasted for about 3 months. On Saturdays, after taking care of business Friday night, they had reacquainted themselves with their friends and in the process made themselves a bit more presentable when they went out.

"Gonna shower?" She was out already, gell and comb in her short hair slicking it back. She was wearing a short jean skirt, T-shirt and old cross-trainers. How could someone so sexual, so into kinky sex, look so ordinary when they went out? His friends' dates always looked foxier, dressed sharper, wore better make-up, and wore heels. Hell, Alice only wore heels for sex or on real special occasions.

"Yeah," Mark went upstairs, turned on the shower and got in.

Alice was on the bed so she could see Mark when he left the bathroom after his shower. He stepped out wearing only his towel, and Alice stepped over and pulled it off of him. "Just like to look at my property," she teased. Mark was strangely quiet, preoccupied. He caressed her ass, then got dressed.

"Since I'm tying you up when we get home, how 'bout if I tell you what to wear this evening?"

"I don't tell you what to wear, " she said.

"You tried, I just wouldn't go along with it."

"There you are."

"I was just going to suggest maybe hose, and a sexier top, maybe some make-up." Then he added "it turns me on."

"I told you it would turn me on if you wore my panties when we went out, especially if I had worn them all day. You wouldn't have any of that."

"Gross," he said.

Alice was more than beginning to suspect that lust and the enjoyment of a few shared friends was all they had in common.

"I like wearing this—it's comfortable, it's a warm night, really humid, and makeup would just feel gross, as would hose and anything but a T-shirt." An impasse had been reached again. Alice liked Mark, though. He was basically a good guy, reasonably honest with her as far as she knew, and she had no reason to think otherwise. He didn't do too much bullshit guy stuff like coming over and making a mess for her to clean up, or expecting her to be so glad to visit him that she cleaned up his place. He had his own mind, which she liked. She liked talking to someone with opinions who could articulate the reasons for his opinions. Mark was even, on occasion, able to listen to her point of view and weigh her opinion against his own. He was muscularly lean and they sure had the sexual compatibility thing going. Plus, he was good to have around in a bar with a bunch of drunk guys. They could be assholes sometimes, and being with a guy could make it easier; he liked knowing that he was indirectly a protector even though they had never had occasion where he really needed to protect. Anyway, her wearing of make-up and heels, and of his wearing her worn panties, was going to be a discussion where they would be at loggerheads, then they'd get over it.

In a couple of decades Alice would be considered to have a lesbian look in some parts of the country. In the 70's, her look was considered more woman's lib or hippie carryover. Mark got dressed and they were off to the Cue, the tension dissipating. On arrival they met some of their crowd—a couple of Mikes, Rob, Dave, Karen, Cath with an ie, who had actually dotted the i with a heart in high school and her freshman year of college, and Beth. The guys were dressed in shorts, jeans and T-shirts. The Cue wasn't air-conditioned but doors and windows were open. It had never been a nice place—more of a hangout for playing pool with cigarettes just as likely being put out on the floor as in an ashtray. When it was closed up it had a stale beer smell; that's why it was best in the summer when everything was opened up, or in the winter when the heat from the furnace dried everything out. Karen and Cathie, who no longer used a little heart on the i, each wore cutoff jeans short shorts, bright halter tops, sandals, perms and makeup. Beth had a jean skirt slit up the side almost to her underwear, a denim shirt tied in a knot showing off her boobs and belly button, and high-heeled open silver shoes. One of the Mikes had had the hots for her for some time. She loved that attention and everyone was thinking that she got off more on being admired and chased by Mike, more than on the idea of actually going out with him. Beth's hair was blond, straight and to the middle of her back, her face all black eyes and pink shiny lipstick. Both Mikes were giving her attention before and directly after the crowd's hello's to Mark and Alice.

"Beers?" Alice said to Mike as she walked toward the bar.

"Sure," he said, meeting her eye then burning a hole in Beth's cleavage as soon as Alice walked away.

Alice walked to the bar, ordered two Buds, and saw Beth being, as usual, the center of attention and loving it. Guys, Alice thought, are morons. Mike had been sent over by Beth to fetch beer. She never paid for her own as far as Alice could tell, always played the helpless female needing a guy to help, move-help, install-help, get beer-help, even grocery shop-help if she could pull it off. Alice had seen Mike and other guys with Beth in the grocery store, no doubt trying to win her favors by helping out where they could. Thing is, she would more times than not go home with some car guy or money guy or in college a sports guy, and still there would be a slew of other guys ready to pitch in just to hang out with her. She defiantly looked like Barbie and played it for all it was worth.

"How long you guys been here?" Alice asked Mike.

"Got here right after work—4 or 5 hours I guess," Mike replied, looking Alice in the eye before looking to the bartender to order drinks, a Bud for him and Heineken for Beth. Alice gave him credit for being polite enough to look at her when he talked to her—though she knew that if she hadn't been there his eyes would have been on Barbie-er-Beth.

"Don't seem too drunk," Alice said, considering how long her friends had been at the bar.

"Just playin' some pool and hangin'—gonna see how the band is." Mike nodded towards a four-foot stage at the end of the room about 15 feet from the last pool table.

"Have you ever actually asked her out?" Alice said. Mike gave her a blank stare.

"Beth, the girl you have the hots for...have you ever actually asked her out?" Alice asked.

"Once, no, twice but the times weren't right. I figure as long as we hang out with some regularity, there's hope," he said like he had it figured out.

"Just curious," Alice said. "If you're going to have unrequited love, the object of your affection should at least know about it."

"She knows," Mike said. "I'm buyin' her drinks."

The group was clustered by a pool table with Dave and Karen, the last two, left in the game.

"Thanks for the beer," Mark said. "You know, you'd look good with an outfit like that." Mark was looking toward Cathie and Karen.

"I know. In fact, I have an outfit exactly like that. I just choose not to wear it because it's too hot out and I want comfortable feet." God, she hoped they weren't going to get into a lengthy discussion. Thankfully they didn't.

The game was over and the group was trying to decide how to make a game that they all could play. They decided on three-member teams and cutthroat. Mike E, who had the unrequited lust for Beth, made sure he was on her team along with Rob; Alice, Mark and Karen; Mike Dave and Cathie. Sometimes the guys got competitive but Alice just saw the game as a chance for everyone to have something to do if the conversation waned—she liked to play, though. Beth was getting ready to break, bending low so that her boobs almost rested on the table.

"She's gonna pork out if she doesn't watch it," Karen said to Alice. "Here we go," thought Alice. "Female competition and cattiness." The observation was correct though; those boobs went with her thighs which were already almost too thick, and her ass, though the object of many guys' attention, was already bordering on too round.

"She's enjoying herself now," Alice observed noncommittally.

"Alice, how's Gloria?" Karen was clearly on a roll and wasn't gonna let anyone off the hook, even Alice. At least she wasn't saying anything behind her back. "Gloria" referred to Gloria Steinem, the person who popularized women's lib. Karen's comment was more directed to Alice's lack of flash and makeup than any political philosophy, however. Of course Karen was sufficiently small-town not to realize that there could be a difference. Friends could be a pain in the ass but it was good to have people one could rely on, even if sometimes they seemed dumb as shit. "See how Mark's ogling Beth," Karen persisted. Mark was talking to Mike S. Mike S. lusted after Beth as well, as did most males, however he didn't have a full blown crush, just the passing fancy in bed on a dateless evening. "Mark's eyes wouldn't wander so much if you dolled up a little, put on some color."

"It's hot. It's summer; you guys will be powdering and redoing and running mascara all evening. I hate it when it gets in my eyes. I'm here to have fun and don't need to advertise at the moment." Alice hoped she sounded assured. "I take good care of Mark—he may complain but I keep him happy." God, why was she being so defensive with Karen, why all these justifications and having to brag about her feminine prowess? She hoped that this conversation too would not last long and the evening would become more laid-back. It did mostly. Beth was too concerned with posing to break well. She failed to hit the ball squarely and the balls hardly broke at all. That was good for a round of laughs and snickers and a pout from Beth who stood back demurely. Mike E walked up to Beth for conversation and rescue. The conversations around the table ebbed and flowed about school and work—asshole professors, asshole bosses, asshole co-workers and classmates, projects and summer plans.

"Hey," Dave said loudly enough to get everyone's attention, "when are we going to the beach? We never did it last year and kept saying we would."

"Next month," Mark said.

"How 'bout the first weekend?" Alice offered.

"Let's DO it this time," Dave affirmed. "How 'bout we set a definite date by next Saturday?" Dave had his teeth in this one. "That way we can all do the schedule thing."

All agreed. Next Saturday, the date would be affirmed.

"I'm gonna need a new swimsuit—last year's is all ratty," Beth announced.

"They have great bikinis at the shop down the street." Mike E. had taken the bait.

Alice knew that Mark had no problems with her swimsuit; she was as practical at the beach as she was going out at on a hot evening. Alice liked her body, liked the sun, and liked to swim, so though her suit was not prone to falling off in the water there wasn't much to it. "Is there a nude beach around? That would be fun," she said.

The males immediately lit up; the women said, "Gross, no way."

The rest of the evening was spent on plans for where to go, where to stay, and much more relaxed conversation. Alice missed a straight-in shot and lost the game for her team and Mark glared at her. "He can be such a competitive asshole," Alice thought. In the next game she buckled down and sank 4 straight. "Good for me," she thought. The band was taking way too long getting ready; it seemed that each instrument, especially the guitars, had to tune loudly, play their warm-up scales loudly, then retune loudly—this had been going on for over 45 minutes. Everyone was getting tired of having their conversations interrupted by the noise. Then came the sound checks, a few "testing testings," then a protracted squeal of feedback that seemed to bewilder everyone on stage.

"This is getting old," Alice finally said to Mark. Mark had been looking at her with a mixture of quiet puzzlement and blank stares, his face showing almost no emotion for the past 20 minutes.

"Yeah," he agreed. "Want to get out of here, go back to your place?"

"Sure," Alice agreed.

Mark was relieved and actually let out a long breath. He had been building this conversation up in his mind for the past half hour, not knowing how to get it started, which was strange since he never had any problems talking to Alice about what was on his mind in the past. But this night was different. This night it was his turn.

"We're getting out of here—this is crap!" Mark yelled at Mike and Beth. The others could see he was talking but couldn't make out what he was saying. When he and Alice walked toward the door they figured it out. Beth looked to Karen and mouthed "lust attack," Karen sagely nodding in agreement.

On their way to the car Mark turned to Alice and picked her up by the waist, and kissed her hard. Alice was a bit off balance—spontaneous acts of lust had been fading the longer they knew each other. She accepted his tongue, sucking on it then mingling hers with his, grinding herself against him. Mark unlocked the door for her, then walked around to the driver's side and got in.

"Cool," Alice thought. "He's in the mood, so much for needing makeup and heels." She reached over and fondled him through his pants as he started the car. The drive was only about 10 minutes but they pawed at each other at each stop light. Alice didn't know if it was imagination, paranoia or what, but she had the impression that this all seemed a little too forced on his part, like he was trying to prove something. "Probably paranoia," she thought. They got out of the car and entered her house. Mark was urging her to the stairs just inside her apartment door. The stairs that went to her bed. Why was he so urgent? He was kissing her, holding her, and they were trying to negotiate the stairs all at the same time; every time they were in a good kiss it seemed that a step would either break contact or cause their teeth to clang together. This was annoying Alice a little but she liked that Mark was in heat and that he was in heat for her, but, she thought, wouldn't this normally be something he would complain about? An uneasy paranoia again entered Alice's consciousness, she was unsure why. They had had a good time earlier today, but Mark had been acting all weird before they left and now this urgent lust attack. "Alice, can't you go with the flow?" she admonished herself. "If you wanted to know the bottom of everything an MBA is inappropriate; that's rules, systems, and hierarchies. You should be in something more academic, and why aren't you getting carried away?"

Mark started caressing her breasts and feeling between her legs. He knew all the right spots; she had shown him where they were and what to do with them, clothes on and clothes off. She was glad she hadn't neglected his education—she responded almost immediately.

Mark was removing her T-shirt and her skirt. She was braless and he cupped her breasts just like she liked and lightly pinched each of her nipples with the sides of his fingers between the knuckle and the first finger joint, just like she liked. Her eyes were starting to roll as they traded tongues.

"Where's the handcuffs?" Mark asked breathlessly.

"Bottom drawer of the closet, one key on the bedpost, one on my key ring," Alice said quietly, heart beating rapidly and breathless as well.

Mark broke off their embrace and walked to the bottom drawer.

"Do you know how to use them? You have to be careful to click the guard on each cuff so that it doesn't keep ratcheting, understand?"

Mark rummaged with increasing frustration even though they were right on top and it took him less than 10 seconds to find them. Alice was saying something about the cuffs. He knew all about them—he had worn them enough.

"Want me to show you?" Alice asked as he walked toward her.

Mark looked at her wearing a short jean skirt, no top, breasts firm and nipples erect. He walked over and snapped her wrists behind her back, forcing her breasts out even further, as though she was offering her nipples to him. Mark took the right one in his mouth and sucked it hard, harder than she usually liked it. He unzipped the back of her skirt and pulled it down along with her panties leaving her wearing only her shoes, which she stepped out of by using one foot to stand on the heel of the opposite shoe. She was completely naked in front of him; he leered, she saw the bulge in the crotch of his pants, dropped to her knees and teased his hardon with her teeth and mouth through his pants. Mark let out a sigh and a small moan as he removed his own shirt, even exciting himself with his own touch as his hands pulled his shirt off. Alice was loosening his belt with her teeth, alternately teasing his cock and working on his pants. Mark picked her up by the shoulders and kissed her, biting her neck lightly; both were feeling each other's heat. He held Alice up and backed her against the wall, holding her up with the force of his body and one arm as he finished unfastening his pants, then he picked her up, one hand in each armpit, and threw her on the bed. Alice landed on her ass and back, her wrists immediately taking away all thoughts of lust, of fucking, of having sex, of making love.

"Mark!" she said, alarmed. "You have to fix the cuffs—they're too tight. I can't lie in them unless they're adjusted."

Mark didn't hear. There wasn't enough blood left for his brain or hearing, it had flowed elsewhere. He was hurriedly taking off his pants, full frontal, looking at her all eyes and hardon.

"Mark!!" she said more loudly but he was already at the bed, already on top, already inside with his weight on her. Alice was trying to protect her wrists but Mark had all his weight on top of her and the cuffs ratcheted tighter. The pain was white hot. Alice was sure something was breaking or being damaged. She screamed, doubled up and used her thighs against his hips to force him off of her. It took all of her strength. If he came back on her, she would not be able to do it again.

Mark was bucked off, Alice screaming, and he finally realized that something was wrong. Years later he realized that he should have said, "What's wrong?" in a concerned voice that matched her urgency, and then attended to the problem. However, it took him several years of marriage to learn that little trick. Instead he said, "What?" in a loud voice that was both angry and hurt.

"The cuffs, you gotta take them off." Alice was almost hysterical.

"What the f.."

"Take them off, please," Alice was crying…this was serious. Mark, still pissy, fumbled for the key on the bedpost and undid her cuffs. Alice's hands were already a nasty shade of red and yellow. She was crying, trying to move her fingers and wincing with each slight movement. "I told you about the switch—you have to set it," she was screaming and crying at the same time. She heard knocks at the front door. The jocks next door were probably concerned.

"You OK in there? Should we call the police? We're gonna call the police if you don't answer!"

"Coming," Mark said as he put on his pants and shirt. The knocking stopped briefly as Mark padded down the stairs barefoot. Mark was at the door. Alice was still upstairs, her hands becoming slightly less foreign to her. She was trying to clench each fist and release. It was improving but wasn't going well. She heard Mark open the door.

"Everything's all right," he said.

"Let's see Alice," one of the jocks said.

Alice was thinking these guys weren't doing so bad at the damsel in distress stuff. "Be right down," she said, pulling herself together. She wasn't going to be able to manage buttons, zipper or even holding something to pull it up, so she slipped on a bathrobe, wiped her face and went downstairs. Mark was guarding the door.

"Mark, please stand back so my neighbors can see everything's OK." Mark stepped back from the door. "This is really sweet of you guys; you're great. I really appreciate your concern." Alice could tell that Mark wanted these guys gone, but dammit they were concerned for her and were doing a good thing so she wasn't going to brush them off.

"You're OK then," the one in front said.

"Yeah, we had a little accident and I bent my wrist—I think everything's OK now."

"Want me to look at it?" The guy in the back was stepping forward. Alice had just become aware that he was carrying a baseball bat. "We get wrist injuries on the football field—I can tell if it's broken."

Alice looked at her wrist and noticed there was a ring which was already bruising which traced the handcuff. She was not in the frame of mind to make up a convincing lie concerning the ring which matched a handcuff around her wrist, nor did she want to give up some on-the-spot medical advice from someone who had seen a lot of wrist injuries. Alice cinched the belt of her bathrobe, walked past an incredulous and slightly seething Mark, and stepped outside. It was night. The light wasn't as good and hopefully he was going to do what he was going to do by feel and touch. She was right.

Her neighbor took her wrist gently and touched underneath and on top, asking what hurt as he moved it slightly. "My guess is a sprain; if it swells up and turns scary colors or especially if it swells and gets hot go to the emergency room. You know how to take care of a sprain?"

"Yeah, I know the basics. Thanks, you guys have been real nice. I owe you a case of beer. What kind do you like?"

"That's not necessary." God, they were being chivalrous, Alice thought.

"I know it's not, but you're good neighbors and did a good thing, and now I would like to do something nice for you; please let me." Alice was speaking levelly and with kindness.

"OK, anything's fine; that would be great," said the jock who held her wrist. Then under his breath, "If you need to get out of there just jump behind me; he isn't getting past us."

Alice was thinking that these guys had watched far to many cop shows on TV but on the other hand, what if....

"Thanks, it's OK really," Alice whispered back.

The neighbors left, Alice went back inside, Mark closed the door and went upstairs, put on his shoes and came back down.

"I'm going home—you OK?"

"Yeah," Alice said, clenching and unclenching her hands. "I'm going to soak in ice water."

Mark opened the door and left.

This did not mark the end of Mark and Alice's relationship but neither one of them ever saw the colors that seemed to move through a combination of will and sex, or thought that it would be a good idea to give up the pursuit of business for the pursuit of art again.

One neighbor knew that Alice was in no danger—at least he knew it after he saw Mark unlock Alice's handcuffs. The monitor which viewed Alice's bedroom as soon as there was enough light for the camera to work, lit up and Rif took notice as soon as they got home and turned the lights on. It had really helped when the bitch's boyfriend had decided that they were going to make it with all the lights on—candles usually made for shitty images. Unfortunately, Rif was not able to capture any of the images. He was lying on his back, his head propped up against the wall where he had been thrown. One eye was swollen shut and looked like a red and black orange, he had a mild concussion, and a laceration on his forehead was dribbling blood down the side of his face in a small but steady stream. Occasionally the blood would get into his eye but even though it stung like hell, Rif's brain wasn't working well enough for him to do anything about it. Blood was also coming from his broken nose, which was splayed to the right like the melted nose on a clay face lying on its side in the rain. Pieces of bloody teeth speckled the front of his shirt, looking like bits of undigested food he had thrown-up on himself.

In agony, Rif watched the flickering monitor. There was no one in the bedroom and the monitor provided his only light. How had they found him? He had been so careful. He would have to get himself to the hospital soon, he knew, but he still wasn't clear-headed enough to coordinate his body. He didn't know that his present predicament was the direct result of his being too cautious and too mean. He didn't know that a decision made 3 years ago that was meant to keep him safe, would in fact cause a chain of events that kept him very unsafe. He didn't know that his decision three years ago would lead him to be a murderer and he didn't know the exhilaration he would discover after having become one.

It had started when Rif decided that his business was doing just a little too nicely. He had done well, avoiding both the law and avoiding Al and the people he knew Al represented. Rif was afraid that his expanding business may have already come to Al's attention once more, only this time if Al put 2 and 2 together he would realize that the kid he thought he had scared off, had actually outsmarted him and prospered over the years. Rif didn't want to think of a confrontation with Al or his soldiers, so he thought he'd do a little double-checking. The linchpin of his operation was the mail service that forwarded his mail to other post office boxes. This was also his weak link. He was vulnerable if someone got to his business associate. He was paying him well just for the assurance that he would have a day or two's lead on whoever might be trying to find him. But what of a double cross? What if he wasn't notified? If he wasn't notified then his post office box could be under surveillance and he would be exposed. Rif didn't like that idea so he decided to put his associate to a test. Several months before the test he opened a post office box over the phone under an assumed name and paid for it with a money order mailed to the service.

He told his connection for 'ludes and psychedelics that he needed a brief favor from someone who would be leaving town. This person would receive 50 dollars for his trouble and all he could drink after the chore was finished. His accomplice for the evening was driven by Rif to his linchpin with a simple message and another 50-dollar bill. He was to present an unopened letter addressed to Rif's post office box, to his business associate and explain that he was concerned because he had received this letter in error and he was afraid that the owner of that box had received a very important letter that should have gone to his mailbox. This letter was almost a week late and it was extremely important that he get in touch with the owner of the POB written on the unopened yet stamped and canceled letter. The associate cited procedures and said all he could do was to put a message in the appropriate mail box and wait for the mail to be picked up.

The accomplice said it was extremely urgent and offered the associate $20 for an address. The associate again cited procedures but his attitude changed noticeably. The accomplice upped the ante to $50. The associate said he'd be right back and left the counter for a few minutes. He returned holding a piece of paper. The associate held out his hand, the $50 was proffered but not relinquished. The paper was put down on the counter face up so that the address could be seen. The $50 was put on the table, transaction over.

"I really appreciate this, man," said the accomplice as he left.

Back to Rif: a ride to the bar, far too many drinks for his new friend. Rif left an extra $20 at the bar for more drinks if needed, then went home. His phone didn't ring the first day, nor the second. He'd been shafted. He waited till his planned lull in business—the 2nd and 3rd week of the month—then paid his former partner a visit. Though Rif was afraid of cops and organized crime he was not cautious when he knew there were no possible consequences for his actions. His associate got off of work at 1AM. Rif met him at the door wearing leather gloves, jeans and a cloth jacket, and escorted him to the alley, where he broke ribs and teeth, at least one wrist, and for good measure, a kick in the nuts hard enough to rupture one testicle. He took the keys, went inside to check his mailbox one last time, went back to the alley and returned the keys. "If I so much as see you again I'll kill you, and unlike today, I'll take my time," was all he said.

After leaving the alley he disposed of his jacket and gloves and went home. He found a new mail service the next day, wrote his customers telling them of his new address and vowed to lay off expanding his business for a while. Maybe his accomplice wasn't the first to get his mailbox—he would be careful.

In reality his accomplice was the first to ask for his address; however, 3 weeks later a check occurred. The pornography business was undergoing a dramatic change. What had looked good for Al's business partners, (the advent of *Playboy* and *Penthouse* increasing the demand for their sleazier wares) had turned out to be the beginning of a decline in revenue. Sex had gone legit, therefore, more businesses were getting into it. Some had sufficient backing to ward off unwanted intrusion, and others actually went to the police if they were harassed. This never would have happened if sex had remained illegal, and almost universally sanctioned as evil.

Freud said that when people think they are losing control of their minds they will frequently try to regain control by exercising it wherever they can. This is why people who wash their hands 50 times a day find such relief in that ritual; it provides control over some part of their lives. Political parties react to a loss of control by appealing to their most rigid adherents, which causes the alienation of the middle ground; industrial managers will respond to losing control over some aspect of their domain by increasing pettiness and intolerance of innovation. This is how Al responded. Goddammit, there were all kinds of little fuckers out there taking and selling pictures to other fuckers who should have been buying Al's product. It didn't matter that all the money that all the little fuckers made combined, would equal only a day or two of income a year for Al. This was money that he should have had, goddammit, and he wasn't going to take it anymore. So, like so many decisions made in fear and rage, Al's solution would cost much more than the problem ever posed and was largely unnecessary because the same social forces that were seriously eroding Al's income were putting the little fuckers out of business as well.

Al decided that he was owed bigtime from anyone who had been profiting from sex pics in his area without his OK, and he didn't mind paying top dollar to assure that the little bastards were tracked down and their assets relinquished. Rif was one of the little bastards. Al knew that there was some type of small-scale operation running out of Baton Rouge but he hadn't done anything about it 'cause well, why bother? Well, now he had his 'why bother.'

When two neatly-dressed men with piercing dead eyes approached Rif's former associate they found him taped, bruised and limping badly. They scared the shit out of him just by walking into the office. Something about them let people know that killing you (or worse) would be nothing special to them. They asked him politely for the address of the owner of Rif's mailbox.

Rif's former associate smiled, wrote it down and said, "Sorry, it's just another mailbox but that's all I have. He pulled out 3 weeks ago."

He was more than happy to give them a description as best he could.

It had taken a few years, but they had time and other little fucks to take care of. They had found Rif's apartment and entered when he was out flipping a switch in the utility area across from the washing machines.

Rif walked in and realized that he wasn't alone even before he closed the door. His captors were professional. He told them everything, how he made his living, where his undeveloped pictures were, even about his lockboxes full of money, anything that might save his life and stop the pain they were causing him. The professionals methodically went through his apartment taking his cameras, pictures and his more expensive developing equipment. They missed the small television that was kept at floor level beside his work table. One of them saw that it was switched on but there was no picture or sound, and turning it on and off again still brought no results from it. Hell, leave the dirtbag a broken TV, they thought. Before giving Rif the blow that would cause him a mild concussion, he was informed that he would be watched, and he would have 3 weeks to deliver $175,000 to an address that was written on a piece of paper and thrown on the table. Before receiving his concussion, Rif was amazed at how they had done all of this so quietly; they had smashed his place, gagged him and wrecked his body and left, yet no neighbor would have thought anything untoward was happening. Then from the chair where he had been tied there was a bright flash and he thought he heard a crackling sound like electricity. He was awakened when the couple across from him came home and turned on the upstairs lights, giving the video camera enough light to transmit a picture. The girl in the other building had tried a different sex role with her boyfriend. It didn't look like it worked out too well, Rif thought as he passed out again.

When Rif came to again he knew he was bad. They hadn't taken the phone or pulled it out of the wall. In fact it was only a few feet away from him. They obviously intended for him to live so he could get them the money he promised. Painfully and slowly he managed to get to the telephone, each move slow and methodical. He managed to call for an ambulance. The last thing he did before passing out again was to turn off the TV. In the hospital he talked to doctors and the police, was held overnight and half of the next day, then released. When he left the hospital a car drove up to him; the back driver-side window opened a crack, then a hand reached out and handed Rif his car keys.

Rif was cleaned out. He had less, not more than he had figured, and had to sell his Vet in order to stay alive. He had never worked a day in his life—the only thing he knew was exploitation and photography, one and the same. After all was said and done he had a total of $1000 and an old slant six with 3 on the column. He got a motel room and rested for a few days and thought. He had never been without money, easy money. He knew only one way to get more but they were onto him, except...those few customers that he always put off, the ones who wanted special pictures, the pictures that he had considered far too risky. As he saw it, there was really no choice. Without his pictures he was a bum, without an education or any previous jobs to put on an employment application. Besides, real work was out of the question; he had to exploit, not be exploited. Over the next two weeks he painstakingly assured himself that he wasn't being followed. Then he bought a camera, black and white film, and developing equipment, and wrote to the addresses he had stored in memory—the ones that offered big bucks for special pictures, asking them how much they would pay. He'd have to rest up; the thought of possible exposure scared him shitless but inside it felt like this was destiny.

Rif needed money and he needed to disappear to a new town. Tayler would be perfect—one of those shit mid-sized towns with dumb cops and dumb bitches who fell for guys driving a Vet. He could stay at the long-term motel for a few months, get himself together, and start his new life selling specialty pictures to a few select customers. He knew his tried and true customers' POBs by heart—he was reasonably sure they didn't rat on him, he had just gotten sloppy. Not again. He rested up for a week in his apartment and finally started feeling like the son-of-a-bitch he always was. That's when he started surveillance on Alice's apartment once more.

Alice didn't like her job. This MBA business and working was bad enough but why was she always working with assholes? Alice was going through her usual Monday; she needed a reason to quit or at least a reason not to go in today, she really wasn't up for it. Nevertheless she showered, dressed in business clothes, headed out the door and began walking the 50 feet or so to the small parking lot the residents used. She hadn't seen hairguy's Vet in a couple of weeks but there was a beat up Dart where he always used to park. She hadn't seen a moving van but maybe he moved. Good. He gave her the creeps. She got into her car, started it, turned on the radio and AC, and started out onto Cedar, then Park, that would take her to the artery into town. "Shit," she thought, "I forgot my lunch and I'm really not in the mood to spend an hour's pay on lunch." So, making a U at Park she drove back down Cedar and entered the parking lot just in time to see someone entering her apartment. At first she was disoriented; had she pulled into the wrong parking lot? She made an assessment of all the cues she used for coming home. A split second later she knew she was in the right place and someone *had* entered her apartment. She thought of confronting the intruder, then thought the better of it. Anyone crazy enough to break into her apartment was crazy enough to do god knows what. Should she call the police? By the time she got to a pay phone and the police arrived, whoever it was would be gone. She could watch, but not from here; whoever entered her apartment would see her in the parking lot as soon as he re-emerged from her building. She had just entered the parking lot and hadn't even pulled into a space yet, so she quietly backed out and parked in the lot for the building across the street. Parking under a tree in the shadow, she was reasonably sure that whoever it was wouldn't notice her car or that someone was in it, unless they were really looking, something she prayed her intruder wouldn't be doing. It only took about 5 minutes and she saw hairguy emerge from her apartment carrying something she did not recognize, about half the size of a shoebox. He entered his apartment with it. Then he made several trips to the old Dart. Hairguy looked wrong. His movements were jerky, like he had aged 40 years, and his posture was bad. She caught a glimpse of his face and again had the disorienting feeling that she was looking at a stranger. His face was misshapen. It too seemed to have aged. What was he doing? After packing the Dart he got in carrying the small box he got from her apartment, started the car and drove off.

Alice had a reason not to go to work today; she had to follow the asshole who just waltzed into her apartment and took something. She had never followed anyone before but that wouldn't stop her. The Dart pulled out of the parking lot. Alice noticed which way he was going on Cedar and pulled out.

Pulling out on Cedar, Alice noticed her first mistake in tailing. Rif's car was a block ahead of her approaching a red light; she would soon be behind him. If he noticed her, the chase would be over before it started. His car was in the right-hand lane. Alice quickly turned onto a side street that paralleled Park, and made the next left. There were two cars ahead of her trying to get on Park; the first made a right, the second turned on his left blinker as the traffic filled the intersection. "Asshole," Alice thought. "Didn't that idiot realize that making a left would be almost impossible this time of day?" She couldn't fathom why people chose to go up this side street to make a left onto a busy street when one block over they could have a light. As she waited she saw the Dart drive by. The traffic let up and still the jerk wouldn't move his car. Alice gave him a short beep. It didn't faze him. Again there was time for him to go, again the idiot just sat there. Finally he moved. Alice was on his tail but of course he moved so slowly that a new batch of cars blocked access. With less space than she should have she pulled in front of a car that was lagging behind the herd. She heard a screech of brakes. "That wasn't necessary," Alice thought; there was a good car length between them. A major intersection, for her, was ahead. Left was where he probably went—that went to town and the interstate, but if he went straight she had lost him. Of course if she went straight and he turned left she lost him too, she thought. Alice was sitting at the light. Well, he's got a car full of stuff so he's going somewhere and if he's going somewhere he'll take the interstate, unless he has some errands to run. Hell, she'd go for the interstate. Turning left onto City Drive she abandoned her usual caution which dictated that she drive the speed limit—hell this was important—and she was consumed by the chase. Fortunately City Drive was 4 lanes; unfortunately the street was always busy and the posted speed limit was 45. Cops just loved to catch people late for work going 55. Alice was going 60, knowing she had one and a half miles until the interstate. If that asshole was going somewhere, she had to know which direction he was headed. Fortunately there were stoplights and Alice gunned through the first just as it was changing; at the next intersection she ran the red. If the cops stopped her she'd tell them that she was chasing a car of someone she saw breaking into her apartment. Of course it didn't look like he took anything except the box, whatever that was. Her mind was on overdrive, giving her confidence, making her reckless. Then she saw it—the Blue Dart, stopped ahead. At the next intersection the street widened to 3 lanes on her side to accommodate people making a left-hand turn. The Dart was in the right lane…he was either going to make a right onto College or he was setting himself up to go east on the interstate one block beyond the intersection. Alice was stuck in the center lane about 5 cars behind him. Dammit, if he made a right she was going to make it happen or get in a wreck trying. The light changed—he went straight through. Alice swerved into the right lane again, cutting off a driver who blasted his horn and gave her the finger. The Dart drove onto the interstate with Alice 3 cars behind.

Once on the interstate she dropped back, allowing 2 more cars between the Dart and her car. This would be dicey if he was only going a couple of exits as she might miss him turning off. There were five more exits before they were clear of town but she didn't dare get any closer. Occasionally as the interstate wound she caught a glimpse of the Dart. It looked like he was leaving town, the bastard. Eventually traffic thinned. Since they were out of town now, tailing the son-of-a-bitch would be easier.

Alice kept a respectful distance then gunned the engine and closed the distance between the cars every time they passed a sign warning of an exit. He was definitely on a mission, going somewhere. What if he was moving hundreds of miles away? Alice hadn't considered that. Hell, what if he was going 1000 miles away? Well, she would follow him for one hour and that was it; she couldn't go on chasing this guy to Maine or Florida if he decided to keep going after hitting the coast.

After an hour he was still going. Alice had to pee, and she was going to have to get gas soon. She didn't know she was going on a road trip when she got up this morning. They passed a rest stop; Alice looked at it longingly. God, she had to pee. She was going to piss herself soon if she didn't take care of this but she needed gas soon also. Could she pass him? Would he notice her? She had to do something—get ahead and get gas or just stop on the road. She thought of her morning coffee. This morning it had been two cups. She always went to the bathroom as soon as she went to work. The bathroom was right down the hall from her cubicle, past the bitch who always looked up and took notice when you went, like she was monitoring how many times you went to the bathroom on company time. But the bathroom at work was close, and always available. From now on, no more coffee before work. From now on, no coffee period. God, she had to pee; she could feel it in her teeth. The gas gauge was in the red; she would be out of business in 20 miles max. She floored it and saw the distance between her and the Dart closing. At least she was wearing sunglasses. He may not notice. Her Fairlane looked like every other Fairlane on the road. She had thought many times what it would be like to have money, just a little money, so she could buy a car that looked nice and was comfortable to drive, but with school and work the idea of extra money was out of the question. Now she *loved* that Fairlane. You couldn't tell one from the other, and with luck the driver of the Dart wouldn't give her a passing glance, a glance that would reveal the driver to be his neighbor, suspiciously on the same road just after he broke into her apartment.

Alice passed him, looking straight ahead, keeping it floored, so that her figure would soon fade from his vision. In 10 miles there was a turn-off with the promise of gas. She pulled off, went to full service, said, "Fill it up," ran to the bathroom, paid for her gas, got in and was back on the interstate. She knew she had only put a few miles between them before she pulled off so the question again was how far ahead he was. Again flooring it she was on the road, hoping there were no police. Again she wondered how long she was going to continue doing this—her stated hour was up. Again she wondered about the wisdom of this chase. A second decision was made—she would do it until she decided to stop and she wasn't ready to stop just yet. Fifteen minutes later Alice again caught sight of the Blue Dart, or *a* Blue Dart anyway; she was going to take this on faith. If he saw the Fairlane again he might become suspicious if he wasn't already. He continued driving just at the speed limit, like a man who wants no hassles.

They had been on the road for over 2 hours when Alice decided she was definitely going to call off this chase if it lasted one more hour. "Screw it, he's going to Maine," she thought. He wasn't. Twenty minutes later he took the first exit, of three according to the highway sign, for Tayler. Alice took it too. The Dart turned left toward town. They were on a 4-lane highway populated with a few gas stations and a Tilly's Kitchen restaurant. As they got closer to town they passed car dealerships, then a series of motels. The Dart crossed the street and pulled into a one-story aging U-shaped motel with a brick circular island in the mouth of the U containing living and dead flora. The Scenic Highway Motel advertised short and long-term stays at reasonable rates. The Howard Johnson's across the street from the Scenic Highway Motel was angled toward the oncoming traffic to entice travelers by reminding them what the front of a Howard Johnson's looks like. Alice pulled into the restaurant's parking lot and parked on the side of the building facing the street where she had a direct view of the Dart. She turned off her car and watched. Hairguy, who didn't look so good, got out of the Dart and went into the office, returned to his car, parked it in front of number 4, just down from the manager's office, and began to unload. Alice realized that her car was directly in his line of sight if he looked up, but he seemed to be preoccupied with unpacking. When he turned toward his room and entered with an armful of clothes Alice started her car and continued towards town, thereby avoiding having to pass directly in front of the motel. Rif heard a car start so he looked up when he went out for another load. He noticed a Ford Fairlane pulling out of the Howard Johnson's parking lot heading towards town.

Alice drove 2 miles into town, turned left onto Franklin Street, a street which looked like it might be another main artery, and took that street until she found a gas station. She called work, explained that her car had broken down and the police had notified a tow but she had had to stay by her car until the truck came. She then went into the station and asked for directions to the interstate. The attendant tried to direct her back the way she had come but Alice said that she had never been to Tayler before and wanted the opportunity to see more of the town. Her new directions snaked her through a town that looked like it had never really been prosperous but had definitely seen better times. The downtown was almost deserted, trash and grit blowing between empty 4 and 5-story office buildings; only the banks were open. The people looked dirty and poor. No, this town had definitely seen better days; the buildup of motels, including a nice-looking Ramada and Sheraton, had not prepared her for this. The town reeked of early rust belt, a malady that would befall many towns throughout the 70s as business moved for cheaper goods from overseas, goods made with nonunion workers and automated factories. While she drove she saw that this town, which couldn't have more than 50,000 people, mirrored many larger cities. The houses got better, not grand, just better, as she drove away from the center of the city. As she left downtown the streets were better swept, yards better tended, and people looked cleaner and in better health. Next Alice saw the reason for the town's center city neglect, a new mall by the interstate. Like most malls it hadn't created jobs or opportunity for the local businesses; it merely shifted consumerism from the center of town to the outskirts of town and transformed store owners into managers of chain stores owned by holding companies. Alice again thought about her future MBA and that she, in a way, would be contributing to the decay of the private business ownership that was part of local communities, and in return she would help to bring the organization/business paradigm of Wall Street, where business owners made decisions on the bottom line, eliminating that messy human factor.

"What'cha gonna do girl," Alice thought as she pulled onto the interstate heading back towards home. "Change the world?" If nothing else Alice was practical. Though she thought the rhetoric of many of her friends who were planning to be activists or counselors to the needy was seductive, she really believed that it didn't make a difference in the scheme of things and besides, if someone was gonna get fucked chances were it was gonna be someone towards the bottom and those who were nearby helping them. "Get out of middle-management as quickly as possible," her classmates had said. "Shit flows down from management brass and backs up from nonprofits. Alice believed them; her course had been set, not by a consuming drive but from the simple perception of self-preservation and safety. Besides, she didn't have to turn into an asshole, she could be comfortable without being part of the problems; she was merely a participant in the changing economy. At least that's what one of her professors had said.

Alice had more than a three-hour drive home, and during the trip she wondered why she had followed the son-of-a-bitch, and what was she going to do about it? What had he stolen? What could she prove? Nothing. Yeha! At least she knew where Tayler was and what it looked like.

Alice drove home, still curious about what she had expected that she would do when she found out where hairguy was going. The deed was done to no end that she could see, however she had discovered something new about herself: when she was good and pissed off, she was definitely a person of action, though not necessarily well-thought-out action.

When she pulled into her parking lot she couldn't take her eyes off of her corner apartment. It was as though she was seeing it for the first time. It looked like the day she first moved in, foreign, full of other people's vibes, not knowing if it would eventually be a place of familiarity and comfort. She looked at her front door. It was strange, betraying no sign that it had let in an uninvited guest. She examined the lock and the door—no tell-tale scrapes or signs of entry. Did the asshole have a key? She would have the locks changed today. She opened the door and crossed the threshold. All of her belongings, her furniture, books, records, clothes that needed to be put away, appeared untouched, giving no hint that her space had been violated. She felt vulnerable, ill at ease. Suddenly she wasn't up to this and only hours ago she had been involved in a car chase, caution to the wind. And now, now she was afraid of her own apartment. Maybe she should see if any of the guys next door were home. They had come to her rescue the other night; maybe she could go over for coffee just to chat, make contact with a friendly face till she calmed down. She went next door and knocked; no answer. "Well, it's just me and you I guess," she said to her apartment, once again crossing the threshold, this time closing the door. She examined everything with a critical eye. What had he stolen? Where had he gone in the apartment? He had been in there only 5 minutes or so. He had known what he was coming for. She looked in drawers, on her bookcase, upstairs in the bedroom…nothing. She examined the floor looking for footprints. If she was a neater housekeeper her floor would be regularly vacuumed, the carpet fluffy, and telltale footprints noticeable. She could hear her mother's voice in her head saying, "I told you so. I told you that you should always keep a clean house; you never know when you will have unexpected company." Did Mom vacuum twice a week to detect burglars? The thought of her mother, daily examining her vacuumed carpets for burglars made her laugh out loud. "I'm getting punchy," she thought. She looked at the walls and windows—no clues. Back to the floor…wait, there was something, not a footprint but…two indentations from the chair to her dining room table. Her loft apartment had a living room and kitchen downstairs with stairs going up to the bedroom and bathroom to the left of the door. Underneath the stairs she had put her television, and a stereo speaker. The far end of the downstairs had two doors, one for a nice closet and another housing her water heater and an intake vent for the combination air-conditioning and furnace; the vent for the outflow was above the door in the wall. The kitchen table was under the stairs with three chairs against it, though only the one with the back to the galley kitchen could be sat in comfortably, the chair close to the stairs having limited head room and the other chair too close to the doors to be moved out. She and Mark usually ate off of the coffee table in front of the television or in bed. She thought of her fantasies about Mark eating his food while on all fours, but he would have none of it. Aside from allowing her to tie him up he didn't seem interested in exploring alternate roles further. "Too bad," she thought. "Too bad he doesn't want to play," she thought, looking around. The chair nearest the two doors had been moved. She wouldn't have noticed it if she wasn't looking, but that chair was hardly ever moved and the carpet under the table hadn't been flattened by her trips to and from the kitchen. Those two dents in the carpet meant that the chair had been moved, and on closer inspection she found the other dents where the back legs had been as well. Why had the chair been moved? She opened the closet and it looked exactly the same, boxes, stuff she didn't use but wouldn't throw away, a fine layer of dust on the shelf above the coat rack. She picked up the chair that had been moved and put it in the kitchen so she could open the door to the utility closet. She noticed a small fleck of sawdust fall when the door was opened, looked up and saw nothing. Examining the closet she found even more flecks of sawdust and loose wood shavings, but nothing to indicate that anything had been moved. Then she noticed the top vent. It was wrong somehow. One of the louvers was hanging down while all of the others were parallel. Alice moved the chair and touched the vent trying to right it. It moved too easily to her touch. When she lifted it, it went up too far, almost completely under the louver above it. She gave it a slight jiggle and discovered that the entire vent was a little loose, still secure to the wall but not tight. She checked the vent in the door; moving it moved the door. It was solid. The vent in the wall was going to have to come off.

Alice's father had given her some basic tools when she first notified her parents that she was getting an apartment in college. "I know that young men will be happy to help you," he had teased, "but I want you to be able to rely on yourself to fix the basics. I want you to have someone fix things because you want him to, not because you need him to." With that said he presented her with a small toolkit —screwdrivers, hammer, pliers and a socket set. She got a suitable screwdriver from the toolkit and started to remove the vent. The screws turned easily, as if they had been screwed and unscrewed into the wall several times making the hole a little too large. She removed the vent and then she saw it— two small holes in the side of the vent and a hole with what looked like a thin cut wire at the end. She could see the insulation and the shiny copper center, and around the two holes the duct-work was slightly dimpled. Something had been screwed tightly into the vent. She guessed that it was probably about half the size of a shoe box.

Mark and Alice's relationship was definitely beginning to cool. She was thinking that Mark was a decent honest guy, liked sex as much as Alice, was attractive and, as far as she knew, had never been unfaithful to her after they had become an item. Mark was a guy and guys like sex, but then there were men who liked the process of sex. "That's what I mean about liking sex," Alice thought. To Mark it wasn't just about making sure she had an orgasm, though she knew he did his best and was usually successful. He sure wasn't a guy who just wanted to stick it in, get off, then go talk to his buds treating their women like some fuck-doll. No, he appreciated the build-up, excitement and anticipation, and when they had regular sex he always took his time like he was savoring her. Alice liked that. Lately though, he seemed so preoccupied with other people's opinions. He didn't like how she dressed because his friends all want to date Beth girls. "Not that there's anything wrong with Beth," Alice admonished herself. "I mean she does dress for the guys and loves to flirt but I will give her this...she has never walked up to me and said anything derogatory about anyone in the group. The other girls had and it was mainly about Beth but not always. Anyway, back to the problem with Mark. It was so easy to let your mind wander when it was working on something difficult or unpleasant, Alice thought. "I wonder why that is...you would think I would want to get this business over with, but instead"...she stopped herself and before letting her mind wander in an entirely new direction she resumed the unpleasantness. Mark seemed increasingly unhappy with her the way she was, and she was becoming increasingly distant from him because of this. Was this a rough patch? At 22 Alice had experienced boyfriends but the older she got the more she knew herself and the more of herself she invested in a relationship. This made letting go harder. Hell, it's like money on a car; after you spend your time and energy with a car, get it broken in and comfortable, then when things start to go wrong, you never know if it's time for another or if you just have to get past this present inconvenience. Mark is someone who is basically comfortable, safe and really knows me, she thought. How much was too much? What is not enough? Anyway Alice was beginning to notice that dates were taking more and more energy and there seemed to be more and more topics to avoid. She had an old undergrad friend, Kate, whom she kept in touch with, that is, they dutifully called each other several times a year unless one of them was in crisis, then the calls were more frequent. She also had an old boyfriend Phil, also from undergrad, who had remained a good friend once the passion had cooled and they had gone to seek other relationships. Both had the same advice; may as well try to talk it out, she had nothing to lose. That had been useful information but what she and Mark were going to talk about, she wasn't sure.

Before going to the beach they had a talk. Things were definitely cooling. Mark was a typical male, unable to discuss his feelings and being noncommittal, Alice just wanting to know if they had anything to work with. Neither wanted to hurt the other. They still liked each other but something had changed and they both knew it. Now what to do about the beach...if they didn't go together that was a big deal and if they went together that didn't seem practical, at least right now. Screw it, they both decided. Alice was getting shit from work anyway about taking a long weekend and Mark really wanted to go. Why didn't he just go, and come what may? "Damn, we can be a good team," Alice thought. "We even decide how to cool it without a fight. Maybe Mark could be friend material like Philip the undergrad."

A week later Alice had done her best to forget about her vent. She had started her life moving by cooling things off with Mark, buying albums by John Prine and a new band everyone hated, the Sex Pistols. Alice figured if everyone hated them so much they had to be worth listening to. Thoughts about the car chase, son-of-a-bitch next door and a small box started seeming to be in the distant past.

The biological imperative was making itself known but she really didn't want to call Mark over for a fuck. That would make things real messy. Of course he would come over but then what? Well, they'd fuck. But would he still let her tie him up or would it be regular sex? If it was going to be regular, what did she think about it? This was all too complicated. She'd just read some of her favorite *Penthouse* forums and take care of herself. This brought up another notion. Porno. She should have some real porno. Guys always have it, why shouldn't she? There was a porno store, a storefront in a run-down section of town with front windows that were painted yellow three quarters of the way up. It had the classy name of MAGAZINES printed in yellow but this time outlined in black above the three-quarters-high yellow paint. Hell, she'd go during the day; the real scumbags liked to hide in the dark. Alice was excited thinking that in the porno store she would find magazines that would detail all of the fantasies she lived with. She would be able to watch them performed, see various subtle variations, and hopefully find a clue to the question that had been forming since adolescence when the hormones kicked in with a vengeance and she quickly realized that she was different from her friends. Even then her thoughts weren't of Prince Charming, the football captain who would make her a complete person, make her someone in everyone's eyes. By listening to the conversations of others she kept her secret, remaining silent, hoping that one day someone would understand and have similar interests. But there was something else, too. Something that said this was only the beginning, a first step in a journey that would show her why she was different and, more importantly, a journey that would show her that even though she was different she was OK, she was special. Even in puberty she knew that there was something within sex for her that wasn't there for anyone else she talked to. That thought was scary; it kept her alone and apart from the friends that are so necessary for teenagers. She was only apart that one way though, in the way that she was looking for a special quality that she quickly found was not one of the qualities that any of her dates possessed. In other ways, she enjoyed the company of her friends, sharing gossip and secrets (except one that was very important), and having friends she competed with and felt accepted by at the same time. But there had always been that question. Why am I different, why do I want something no one else seems to, and why does it seem like this is what I am supposed to do? What am I supposed to do? Why do I only seem to be able to know what I'm *not* supposed to do when I'm doing it and I'm unhappy but there seems to be no clear path to knowing what I *am* supposed to do. There was another question underneath all of this, the one which, when asked, never promised an answer for any human being unless they are filled with faith. Why?

Thinking that some of the mystery of her journey might be explained by a trip to the porno store increased Alice's excitement; she imagined some of the things she had always wanted Mark to do—being displayed for her. She was imagining an epiphany of body and mind, sensory and cerebral. She also had a nice orgasm.

The Saturday that everyone went to the beach, Alice went to the porno store at 2:00 in the afternoon. She figured there wouldn't be too many scary people out at that hour. "They don't like sunlight," she laughed to herself. Her heart was thumping and she noticed that she was more nervous than she thought she would be at the prospect of going in. Taking a deep breath she entered. The front part looked like a dusty magazine store—*Popular Mechanics, Playboy, Penthouse* and *Hustler, Guns and Ammo.* What was conspicuous was a large, high cashier's booth against the left wall. Customers had to actually lift their purchases up to almost head height to put them on the counter. The entire place was wood—the floors, the bookcases, the cashier's booth, all lighted by fluorescent lamps outlined in yellowing plastic. Magazines were held in place with a wire strip that threaded through a hole in the wood frames of the bookcases. The man at the booth looked to be in his 30's, at least 6 feet tall with the distinct look of "not-too-bright," beergut, dirty T-shirt, with stubble from at least three days' growth. A cigarette burned in his mouth as he operated the cash register, every movement of flabby arms displaying pit stains. Beside the cashier's booth was a swinging door with a hand-painted sign that read ADULTS ONLY.

"Well, I've come this far," Alice thought. "May as well go all the way. Anyway, I'll look stupid backing out now," she thought even though this environment gave her the willies. She took a breath that she hoped wasn't noticeable and walked toward the door.

"Wait a minute," the fat cashier said. "Need to see some ID." His voice wasn't gruff like she expected, just matter of fact, almost gentle, as if he realized that she was ill at ease.

"Sure," Alice said as she retrieved her wallet from her hip pocket—she only carried a purse to the office. She flipped the wallet to her driver's license hoping that she wouldn't fumble in the process. The cashier gave it a cursory glance and said OK, nodding his head toward the door. Alice entered.

Inside was much like the outside, only about 4 times larger. There were three long magazine racks in the center of the room. The walls too were lined with glossy magazines. At first it was overwhelming with the glossy pictures reflecting badly from the overhead lights, but as she walked the aisles she noticed that the store was broken down into topics that people wanted. Alice concluded that the customers were mostly men as most of the mags had pictures of naked women, either being fucked on their backs, fucked doggie style, fucked in the ass, fucked in their mouth, and pictures of women's body parts with the accompanying fluids. There were three other customers in the store, nondescript males who made no eye-contact with each other or her as they perused the stacks. There was a section of naked men. At first, Alice thought, "Ah, something for the ladies," but then she realized that in this section there were usually two men in the picture. The men were also getting fucked in the ass and mouth and showing body parts with the fluids from having been fucked. She noticed that some of the men had shaved pubes. "I like that," she thought. Then there was a section with women tied to beds, walls, and high wooden stands. Most of these women had a look of distress on their faces, as if something terrible was about to happen. By the time Alice had circumvented most of the store she had seen fat women, Asian women, black women; then, in the back corner there were men tied to beds, thick wooden stands and walls. These pictures usually showed another man about to whip or paddle the bound man. The difference was, in most of these pictures the bound man did not have the look of panic that was so popular with the tied women. Alice liked that. Next to this section on the wall were two columns of magazines depicting females wearing leather outfits; some of these mags had tied males looking up either fearfully or expectantly. Somehow none of these magazines seemed to offer the magic she was hoping for, but she thought she would try them anyway. She selected two—*In Charge* and *His Keeper*—they were sealed so that all she had to go on was the cover and the titles of the picture segments with names like Savage Mistress, and Her Bound Husband. At least these had pictures of expectant-looking males, not males who looked like they were fearing for their lives. $10 for a mag was steep—$18 for two seemed exorbitant but she wasn't going to leave empty-handed and the promise of what she would find inside excited her. The cashier took her magazines and didn't leer at her; she was thankful for that. He bagged the magazines, took her $20, gave her $2 and said, "Thanks for stopping by," as she left.

Alice drove home anxious to look inside the plain brown paper bag. She had intended to go shopping first but her curiosity was getting the better of her and she was yearning to know if the magazines would answer some of the questions she had about herself, questions about why she was different. Were there others like her, people with desires that were forbidden? How many times had she sat around with Karen, Cathie and Beth while they talked about sex—what they liked, what they didn't like, what their boyfriends liked that they would or would not indulge. Through all of these conversations she had been pleasant, appropriately enthusiastic when a friend mentioned an act or technique they loved or hoped to get their boyfriend to do with them, but she never shared her own. She had a fear that her desires were too different and in being different, shameful. She was at the age where she realized that being ashamed about what she secretly longed for, was not healthy and she had sometimes caught herself feeling that she was defective. She also knew that this was not the case. A battle that used to rage inside her now took the form of a dialogue, with self-acceptance of her uniqueness winning most of the time.

At the same time she knew, or took on faith, that disclosure of her turn-ons might alienate her from her friends. She reasoned that friends who accepted you, even though you were different in many other respects, were a prize worth protecting, even if the cost of that protection was the withholding of information that was dear to her. The cost was also not knowing, not knowing if she would be accepted if her secret was known. Because if it was known her friendships would be even closer and she wouldn't have such a large part of herself that she felt she had to hide, but at this time the risk seemed too great even though she was paying a price much higher than she imagined.

Alice hoped the magazines would show her that others shared her special interests. First, Alice did some figuring to see where she stood; there were two adult book stores in town. In the one she saw, magazines representing her interests made up only a small percentage of the total compared with the other topics that were represented. Most important, however, was the fact that there had *been* some. Other women who bought the magazines, would share her interests and the men who bought the magazines, if she could meet one...there were so many possibilities. Alice didn't realize the truth, that most of the magazine buyers had chosen different lives for themselves, and their yearnings were met only through fantasy while their wives or girlfriends were either not aware or were not interested in the activities described or shown in their purchases. These buyers had decided that their desires were less important than other wants such as social standing and business, or chose their partners based on a desire for the approval of others and not based on a compatibility of a deeply personal desire. The more bold of this group sought out professionals with whom they could pretend that they had a relationship which possessed qualities lacking in their spouses.

Alice parked in the lot purposefully taking the space where asshole used to park his Corvette. She entered her apartment and locked the door.

She was already aroused by what she hoped she would find. She opened *In Charge*. The front cover had a picture of a man tied on the floor with a leather-clad woman standing behind him. Inside there was a black and white picture that took up about half of one page—the rest was stories. Alice started reading the first story; in it, a teenage boy was sent to boarding school and was at the mercy of women who humiliated him in front of his female classmates. His role was largely that of confusion, victimhood and humiliation; however, at the end of the story he decided that he wanted to stay at the school because he had learned his proper place.

Another told of a man who went to fix the phone who was kidnapped, tortured and forced to please his captors sexually. He too decided to stay when after 3 days he was given the option to leave. These stories excited Alice though she saw them as incomplete. The actions between the sexes seemed correct but in each case, in every story, the males were forced against their will, as if they did not have the knowing inside of them like Alice had, but through the use of force and torture their true selves could come to flower. The thought of having a man in such a vulnerable submissive position excited her. As she read the text and stared at the pictures she had casually loosened her clothing and slid out of her pants so that only her shirt remained. She masturbated three times while reading, though her masturbatory fantasies changed the tenor of the stories to become one of romance, where a man offered and pleaded for the opportunity to serve in the submissive role. Alice didn't like being forced to do things and didn't want to have to kidnap someone in order to find the mate she had dreamed about. Another thing disappointed her in *In Charge* was the pictures—they had absolutely nothing to do with the stories. Apparently the stories were just filler for the pictures or vice versa. Following the stories were match-ads, most of which appeared to be advertisements for women who charged a fee for torturing men.

His Keeper was a black and white picture series showing a naked man asleep and chained in what looked like a cramped prison cell. His leather-clad jailer came and awoke him with a caress of her gloved hand and lead him to a room full of heavy wooden fixtures on which he could be fastened. Picture by picture his legs and arms were fastened to a wooden horse and he was paddled. There was a full-page color picture showing him bent over, his ass red, and showing considerable distress on his face. Picture by picture he was released, then she saw it—a picture that drew her in to the point that she was almost living the scene. She felt her breath becoming shallow, her face hot, her hands moving immediately to her crotch, where their dance seemed to release a bolt of energy that had burst inside her. The picture showed the captive and jailer looking at each other, but not from a position of submissive and dominant, but of lovers. Their eyes were locked in what could only be called mutual adoration, as if they had achieved something for which they had no words. Alice played with herself and imagined herself in such a relationship...she imagined a partner who wanted to share these things with her, imagined their lovemaking, and saw it all through a filter of yellow light. In the magazine the man left the room in which he had been paddled and, still naked, began to cook breakfast.

Alice wanted to do more than she knew Mark would be comfortable with, and at this point she knew that their relationship was on the wane anyway. "Damn, now I know what I want in a relationship even more and I don't have anyone to be in a relationship with," she thought. Alice imagined the intimacy in sharing her brand of sexuality in terms of relationships; the idea of nameless partners didn't appeal to her. When she first became sexually active in college she had had a series of one-night stands but soon found the process pointless. Why go to bed with a guy who you don't want to talk with in the morning? Besides, there were diseases and jerks out there. She came to find that a nice dildo was much better, to her, than sex with a man she didn't know or care for.

Alice wasn't too surprised when Mark called after the beach weekend saying they needed to talk. He said he had given it a lot of thought and had decided they should cool their relationship for a while. He also mentioned that he thought he was getting that vibe from her as well. Alice agreed and said that she thought that his weekend alone at the beach would be a good way for him to decide what he wanted to do. She said that she half-expected that he would become enamored with one of the available females in the group. Mark admitted that Beth's string bikini caught his eye whenever he had the opportunity to ogle her and that he and Cathie had had a good time together, but they hadn't fooled around because things weren't clear about what was going on between him and Alice.

Alice appreciated his honesty and, if it was to be believed, his chivalry. Though she regretted that they would not be together as they had been, she thought he could definitely be friend material—after a while. She told him that she appreciated his honesty, she wished him well, and hoped they could still hang out in the same group. Alice suspected, however, that if his and Cathie's relationship was consummated no one would be seeing much of either of them for a month or two as the lust of a new relationship would probably take up all of their time.

And that was that. Alice was now single, she knew what kind of relationship she wanted and had absolutely no idea how to make it happen. For the next couple of weeks she went to school, went to work, stayed to herself, periodically reading her magazine and dreaming. Surprisingly, to her, it was Beth who called to say hi and wondered if she could come over.

Beth entered her apartment typically dolled-up like she was going out on a date in Hollywood, sparkly sandals, short shorts, full make-up, hair perfect. Alice was dressed in a T-shirt, cutoffs and K-Mart strap-over-the-big-toe sandals.

"Haven't seen you around for a while and wondered how you were doing?" Beth said as soon as she entered.

Alice had her sit, got some iced tea and said, "Pretty good. Mark and I have cooled it. I'm just hanging out getting my bearings."

"So how are you doing?" Beth was clearly concerned, not wanting to say the wrong thing.

"Really, I'm fine. I expect Mark is going out with Cathie, and that's really OK with me. Mark's a great guy but it was time to split."

"I've seen them together; that's when I realized you probably weren't dating anymore. He doesn't seem like the two-timing type, but you didn't have to be a hermit! I started worrying about you, wondering if you were moping around. You have friends, you know?"

Alice was genuinely surprised that she had been touched by someone she didn't think had this much substance. Beth had not come with gossip, or to play the blame game, or to tattle—she was just concerned. "This is really nice of you, Beth. I really am OK."

"Then let's go out now, it's a summer day, it's Saturday."

"Where?" Alice responded quickly.

"Don't know. Let's cruise to the country, find a bar, get a beer and drive home."

"K," Alice said, getting her wallet.

The road trip was nice, and the fact that Beth was the only one of her friends who had checked up on her, though she really didn't need checking up on, did not go unnoticed. They stopped at a redneck bar, bought Buds, had Buds bought for them, then drove home.

"I thought you were OK, everyone was whispering but I thought you were just hanging, just wanted to check you know? You seem more together than most of us, except for me of course," Beth said laughing.

"I always saw you as so girlie, then you go and do something so nice, not gossiping, not blaming. I think there's a side of you I don't know," Alice said, seeing if the gap between good acquaintance and friend would be breached.

"I had brothers," Beth said simply "We all have sides others don't really know about."

Beth dropped Alice off at her apartment, saying that Alice should meet the gang tonight. Alice said she'd think about it but would probably take it easy, Beth wasn't to worry, she would go out with the gang next week if not tonight. On the way back home Alice had been thinking that the side of Alice that Beth didn't know about was more substantial than having brothers and being less of a girlie-girl than appearances would lead one to suspect. She also thought that it was time to add to her magazine collection. Her last trip to the dirty book store was relatively painless, as it was still light. She would go over, pick up a mag or two, then decide if she wanted to go out later.

Alice entered her apartment for long enough to pee, then got into her car and drove across town to the same seedy building, same fluorescent lights with formerly-white-now-yellowed fixtures, same guy behind the counter. This time, thankfully, he had on a clean shirt and his stubble wasn't any worse than the last time she saw him, so at least he had to have shaved at least once since a month ago. She presented her ID and it was given the most cursory of glances; making eye-contact, the man nodded and Alice crossed the threshold to the stacks.

There were more men in the store this time; some took notice of her but no one returned her glance. Knowing where she wanted to go, Alice went to the corner with the two columns of magazines which held her interest and, starting from the top, glanced down trying to find a cover picture that would pique her interests. Again, most of the covers depicted leather-clad women and cringing, mostly unattractive men, some looking adoring and some looking silly. Still she had already selected two and held them in her hands. "I'm getting more selective," she said to herself with an inward smile. About halfway down the second rack at eye-level—the first magazine anyone would look at if they just happened to walk down this aisle—she saw it and remained motionless for what, to her, seemed like 5 or 10 minutes but was actually less than 3 seconds. Her eyes wide, heart pounding in her ears, she stared entranced, her grip on her selected magazines involuntarily loosening, magazines falling to the floor. She did not notice that they had fallen or that the noise made by their dropping had turned all eyes toward her. Without color and dazed, she walked toward the entrance, her stride increasing as the pounding in her head and narrowing of vision increased. She didn't notice the man behind the counter looking at her strangely as she flung the front door open at a brisk walk, body tense, stone-faced. The door slammed behind her and she further quickened her pace until she got to her car and drove off.

The man behind the counter was puzzled. He remembered her, because not that many cute girls came into the store. "What bee got up her butt anyway?" he wondered. Well, he'd better pick up the magazines before they got all walked on, wrinkled and useless. As he was re-slotting the magazines he noticed a magazine at about eye-level in the second column: unlike the other magazine covers, this one had a black and white picture of a woman dressed in a garter belt and nothing else; she had a man tied spread-eagled to a bed and was sitting on his face, burying her crotch in his mouth. The man had a full erection which she held in her left hand teasing the head with her thumb, her right hand tweaking her own nipple; she looked straight at the camera, her eyes unfocused. The woman looked exactly like the young lady who had just left his store.

Alice drove home in a daze, driving carefully and more slowly than the drivers behind her would have preferred. When she got home she opened the door, crossed the threshold and did not feel safe. She did not feel alone. She did not feel up to dealing with it.

She went to her sofa, curled up in the fetal position, hugged herself and rocked for what seemed like hours.

Rif the photographer was about to turn from a sexual predator, to a predator even more dangerous and hunted. The idea still scared him to the core. Once taking this road, he knew he would have to increase his precautions. It was one thing if a stranger in town happened to have sex with one of the local girls who just happened to get too drunk and end up in a strange bed—it was another if the appearance of a stranger in town resulted in the disappearance or death of one of the local girls. He would have to be able to arrive unnoticed and leave the same way. No more Vettes or flashy clothes—he had to be invisible. His plan was to take a 3 1/2 hour drive to Livingston. Hopefully an idea would come to him, hopefully opportunity would present itself.

He had set up a crude darkroom in the bathroom of his motel room/apartment. Pans of developer and rinse solutions were placed on top of furniture in the room when he used the shower. Hopefully he would be able to move into more satisfactory quarters after the money started flowing in. He had a nest egg already. The pictures from the girl's apartment had been sold to his few customers. He might have been able to market them to regular skin magazines but he felt that the risk of incurring Al's wrath was too strong, especially if he inadvertently tried to market the pictures to one of the magazines controlled by Al's organization. He had received promises of a big payoff for special pictures and the photographer wanted a big payoff. He would send his pictures only one or two at a time to see if his customers made good on their promises. If they did he would send a couple more until he was able to amass the maximum return for the investment of what was left of his soul. He started preparing for his trip. Three 35mm cameras, tripods, remote shutter release so that all cameras would shoot and flash simultaneously, heavy-duty battery for the flash, handcuffs, rope, pocketknife with a 6-inch razor-sharp blade, and pliers.

He packed everything in the trunk of his car, ate supper at the Howard Johnson's across the street and hit the road at 8:00. He should arrive in Livingston around 11:30 on Friday night. Prey would be partying, and would have been drinking for probably two hours—enough time for lapses in judgment. He had driven through Livingston several times previously, he knew where the bars were, and he also realized that people who disappeared from seedier bars were less likely to be quickly missed than people from bars that were more upscale. The photographer was surprised how quickly opportunity presented itself—why hadn't he thought of it before? He had never considered using prostitutes because he was accustomed to getting his rocks off on a regular basis as part of his business. While Rif stopped at a light, a young, plumpish girl in hot pants, heels and a sheer blouse, walked up to his car and asked him if he knew where a party was. He reached into his hip pocket and showed her a 20-dollar bill folded in his palm. The same palm he used to motion her to the passenger door. Looking around quickly he assured himself that no one was nearby or watching. He reached over and unlatched the door. She opened the door and slid in.

"Where should we go?" the photographer asked.

"Just up the street to the alley's fine," she said as she closed the door.

Closing the door was his cue and had been the whole reason for his asking where they were going. As soon as the door closed he hit her in the jaw with a clenched fist and she crumpled. "Bitches can't take a punch," he thought as he drove out of town with the first model for his new enterprise.

The project left him literally shaking. His knees and arms were shaking so violently that he had to put all of his concentration on driving without looking drunk. She had become really noisy after he slapped her awake, moreso when he ripped off her clothes and started fucking her; he had had to stuff her blouse in her mouth just so he could hear himself think, and still she was shrill when he really got down to business for the money shots. He could still hear the high-pitched scream turning guttural and mechanical, as the photo shoot progressed. And the mess! He was sticky with it. He had put a blanket over his car seat cover and still it might soak through. God, if he was pulled over now it would be all over. He had to drive carefully, concentrating on breathing deeply throughout the process, and still now he found himself breathing in rapid, shallow breaths until he became lightheaded. "Fuckin' whore," he thought. "Shit, if she gets me busted from all her shit all over me, she fuckin' deserved it. No one's gonna miss a fucking whore anyway. But still the cops. Those assholes wouldn't care if it was just a whore—they'd just see a chance to put another arrest on their record, no sense of proportion. Hell, no one will even notice or miss a fuckin' whore. Oh, god I've got to get home and cleaned up. I can't even check into a motel room—I reek and my clothes are sopping.

The photographer's assumption that no one would notice the whore's passing was almost correct. She had escaped from her abusive family by marrying poorly. After the police were called to their apartment 3 times in one week her husband had left her with a baby, no job skills and no education. Welfare had helped a lot but she had developed a drug and drinking problem and frequently missed appointments with her caseworkers. Her checks had stopped and she never seemed able to show up on time even after she had marshaled her energies to make an appointment. Some people had theories about learned helplessness brought on by a life history of powerlessness and abuse. People who do not believe they are capable of achieving anything because they never have, tend to live up to their own expectations. The overworked caseworkers saw her as merely an irresponsible case who took up their time for appointments that were never kept or plans that she never followed through. Though she did drink to excess and occasionally used street drugs, she had always fed her baby. Crack cocaine had not yet made significant inroads; if it had, she probably would have lost that one remaining achievement. On the evening of her death there was no food in their apartment. She had given the child, now 5, the last of the Count Chocula cereal, dry, and had told him to be good, that she was going out to get some money for food. Prostitution hadn't bothered her much. The men were usually assholes but all the men she had ever known had been assholes—they used her and left her. For her, being a whore was just more of the same. The baby didn't sleep that night; his mother hadn't returned home and even if she had, without food the boy was too hungry to sleep. The next day he was found on the street and taken to the police and child protective services. Thinking that he had been abandoned by a woman who had a long history of irresponsibility, he was fed and put into a foster home. The body wasn't found for several months.

The photographer had gained control over his breathing; he was almost calm and had started to reflect on his accomplishment. That is what it had been—an accomplishment. He had faced his fear and had conquered. He realized something else too—if he got away with this, he was truly special. He had done something that few others would dare, and as he looked back on the act, the procedure, he noticed that he was aroused, his hardon straining in his drying, tacky pants. As he thought about it more he realized that his driving had deteriorated and he had almost cum. He had been driving like some guy getting a blowjob. He found an exit off the freeway and drove down a two-lane highway until he could pull off in relative safety and privacy. There he remembered and savored, going over each sweet detail. He came without even touching himself, without even releasing his hardon from his pants. At that moment he moved from murderer-predator to serial killer. He was really going to like his new job and the pay was going to be great.

After about an hour Alice decided that she should do something, but she wasn't sure what. What kept nagging her was how much of her private life had been published? How much did other people know about her? What was in the magazine? "This couldn't be legal," she thought, for she hadn't signed a release and surely there were laws. But mostly she wanted to know how much of her life was now public domain. But she couldn't go back to the store—she just couldn't. To buy the magazine with her on the cover, with that sweaty, hairy fat guy looking at her, would be too much. She needed help. She had risked with Beth and had found acceptance—she would try again.

Alice went to the phone. "Beth, could you come over, it's important."

"Sure, when?"

"Now," she said, then added "if you can."

"Anything you need to talk about now?"

"If you could, please just come over here now. I'll explain then, OK?" Alice answered.

"See you in 10."

Beth was over in 15, full makeup, different hot pants, every hair in place, Barbie with chunky thighs. "Alice, you look like shit—what's going on?" she said with concern and urgency.

"Beth, I need a friend, a real friend. You were the only person I could think of to call." Alice's voice was strained; she was trying to hold back her desperation.

"Thank you for calling me, Alice, I'm glad you think of me that way," Beth answered with sympathy and concern. "What's up?"

"I need you to keep a secret, maybe more than one," Alice said.

"OK, as long as you're not robbing a bank or anything." Beth was trying to calm things down, the strange urgency in Alice's voice scaring her.

"Nothing like that, but it's something about me." Alice was breathing deeply, composing herself.

"OK," Beth said simply.

"First, I like to play with rope during sex," Alice said, trying to hold back the fear in her eyes, fear that that she would be rejected outright.

"OK, I've done that with a few guys—they get off on having a girl tied up. In fact one guy…Brad, really got off on it. He liked to tie me up and we'd fuck our brains out," Beth offered with a smile.

"Why did you leave him? Was it because that is what he liked to do?"

"First, I'm in no mood to be tied down," Beth said, then smiled and added quickly, "in a relationship. Second, he wasn't that much fun to take out; get him with a group of people and he'd either clam up or just talk to the guys, and third, no foreplay, he wanted to tie me up then fuck if I was ready or not. We didn't go out that long."

"Well, I like to tie men up," Alice offered again, looking for a sign of disapproval.

"Hmm, don't know if I'd like that," Beth said, slightly puzzled. Alice felt a sinking feeling. "But whatever turns you on, you know, whatever floats your boat."

The floodgates opened. "Well, I've always wanted to, and finally got up my nerve to ask Mark and he agreed. It's all I really want...for me, sex, regular sex is almost nothing compared to the feeling I get when I have him helpless. He got plenty of foreplay, in fact sometimes more than he wanted, but he can't stick it in till I get in position. It's almost like I leave, like my consciousness changes; I feel almost magical, and so sexy, so charged. Anyway, I know that Mark loved the sex and he got a lot of it. More than he could handle sometimes, but that was nothing to complain about, but I knew he really wasn't that into it. He wanted more control, more of the masculine seducing role and I couldn't give that to him. Not and be honest with myself, anyway. Mark's a great guy, was always honest with me, didn't fool around, wasn't too critical. I mean, I know that he wanted a girlfriend that he could show off, one who was more traditional, but he's a real good guy. I wanted more control and he gave up all he was comfortable with." Talking about their relationship was helping Alice put the pieces together, helping her to understand herself and her relationship. She hadn't really thought the relationship out this completely until she could tell her story with someone she trusted. "But here's the thing..." Alice's voice dropped noticeably; she was struggling for words and composure. "I found out that someone had a camera in my apartment over there," Alice said, motioning toward the airvent above the door. Beth's eyes widened. "I think it was the creep that used to live over there," again motioning, this time towards the front in the corner of the next building. "I saw him leaving my apartment with something and followed him, then I figured out what it was."

Alice told of her trips to the adult book store and of seeing her picture on the cover of the magazine. Beth was understanding, accepting and outraged.

"Son-of-a-bitchin' pornographers! If it was *Playboy* or *Penthouse* you could have a good lawsuit on your hands, but those guys, that's still mainly a mob operation. They probably figure that if you started something legal they'd splash your pictures everywhere...you'd have no other career opportunities except porn queen. Besides, they'd just go out of business so you wouldn't have anyone to sue. It's the distribution, not the company for them. If the company says they used models the distributor is not liable. If a company has to fold, a new one can be started for about $500 a lot cheaper than legal fees.

Alice was impressed with Beth's legal knowledge. Beth explained that one of her brothers was a lawyer, a budding DA.

"Beth, I need to know what's in the magazine...will you go buy it for me?" Alice said softly and evenly but her eyes were pleading.

Beth said she would buy the magazine but Alice had to wait in the car with the car running. Beth was a little fearful of going to that part of town at this time of night so she wanted someone who would be nearby in case she got into trouble. Alice said they could even take her car, she'd drive and wait right in front with the car running, and if Beth took longer than five minutes she would start honking the horn and flashing the lights. Beth said she doubted that there would be that type of problem—she just wanted company and was just a little nervous. She had brothers who had porno mags, she had just never bought one herself.

As they were neared the store called "Magazines," Alice pulled into the yellow line directly in front of the store. A sign said, "Delivery Only." It was dark and a light rain had started. Alice said, "Left hand wall just before the corner, eye-level. There's hardly anyone in there anyway, and you'll need your ID."

"I know. That's the third time you told me, Alice. Don't worry, get a grip." This was said nicely, without impatience, just mock exasperation that served to quell Alice's nerves.

The fat man behind the counter noticed Beth first. Not too many women used his store, even fewer clean-cut types, and this was the second today. Besides, Beth was an eyeful dressed more for a bar across town where the kids hang out than here. He ogled the young woman who seemed not to notice or at least not to care.

Beth walked up to the man, wallet in hand and flipped it open to her driver's license. The clerk gave it a cursory glance and motioned her in. At least one of Alice's stated facts about the store was incorrect. The store was full of men, about half of whom looked up and took great interest in her arrival. Beth treated them like she treated men at a bar when her date was at the far end, politely nodding to those closest while keeping her eye on her destination. She walked past several men perusing the racks till she got to the back left corner and noticed two columns of magazines with leather-clad women stepping on or whipping naked or bikini-clad men.

The clerk lost direct sight of Beth and did his usual survey of the store. On weekend nights he was too busy to watch the small black and white television he had just under the counter next to his .38 and Louisville Slugger. Looking outside he noticed a Ford Fairlane parked in the loading zone with the motor running; the driver looked like the girl who had dropped the magazines a few hours ago, the one that was on the cover of one of the leather magazines in the back. He had an idea.

Beth saw the magazine in question, about where Alice said it would be, about 5 feet up, second column. It was Alice all right, in a magazine called *Bound for Mistress*. Alice looked like she was really enjoying herself. Beth got the magazine and made her way around men, having to back out of one narrow aisle between magazine racks because a man wouldn't move out of her way. He took a step towards her, locking his eyes on hers when there was a loud thump from the counter, as if a box had been dropped. The man quickly dropped his eyes and bent over to examine the magazines, his ass taking up the rest of the aisle. Beth resumed her journey to the counter with a ten-dollar bill already in her hand.

"She wants to be able to get out quickly," the counter man thought, "probably had the ten in her hand the whole time." He rang up the $9.00 purchase. As he was about to give Beth her change he said, "You know you could advertise in the *Match* and probably get a lot of customers." He was holding a thin newsprint magazine-sized newspaper.

"I'm not looking for customers," Beth said, just wanting her change and to get the hell out of there.

"Boyfriends then," the man offered. "People with the same interests. Tell you what—take the rag, I'll keep the change and make up the difference." He put the paper in her brown paper bag. Beth accepted her purchase and left.

The cashier was hoping that one of the women would be looking for a date in the *Match*; neither one of them looked jaded or tired, and if he was real lucky, maybe one of them would answer his ad.

Alice was tense behind the wheel. She had locked the passenger door and was a little too slow in reaching over to get the lock so that Beth's first pull on the door handle was met with a locked door. Alice tried to unlock it by pulling on the handle just as Beth tried a second time, resulting in the door still being locked. Finally, Alice held up her hand in a stop-motion for Beth, unlocked the door and Beth entered.

"That was graceful," Beth said as she got into the car.

"I didn't like the way the men were looking at me as they walked down the street," Alice said.

"They think we're hookers," Beth said. "Let's go."

Alice looked blank for a second.

"Let's go," Beth said more firmly.

Alice put the car into drive and entered the traffic.

"I just felt like all those men had seen me and they knew," Alice said softly.

"Alice, you're shook; I'm sorry, but get it together! Most of the guys in that store just see the body parts, and on top of that most of those guys aren't looking at the leather-women-tied-men magazines, and if they were they would have to look directly from the magazine to your face to make any connection." Beth was being firm and was also becoming increasingly concerned about her friend. They rode in silence.

"You're right," Alice said almost 5 minutes later. "It's hard not to let my imagination run away with me. I imagine these guys obsessing on my picture and looking for me, but you're right—that is a real long shot. I just need perspective."

Beth told of the *Match* mag "He thinks we could find boyfriends in there," she said laughing

"That's rich," Alice joined in.

Conversation on the rest of the way home was easier, each woman recounting her experience buying the magazine and each laughing at their own fears about making a simple purchase. When they arrived at Alice's apartment Beth asked if Alice wanted to be alone in looking through the *Bound for Mistress*. Alice said,

"Well, you've seen the cover—the rest is more of the same. I'm appreciating your company. If it doesn't gross you out and if you're not busy, I'd like you to stay."

"Cool," Beth said. "None of my brothers ever had any domination magazines." She regretted saying it as soon as it was out of her mouth but Alice was laughing.

Pictures of Alice and Mark took up three quarters of the magazine, but by the time they were on the second page Beth realized that there was more to this story than perhaps even Alice knew.

The photographer arrived at his motel just before dawn. The exhilaration and fear of the night's kill had worn off shortly after his orgasm. He was tired and his skin was chafing from the chunks of congealed dried blood on his arms and stomach, which made every movement of his arms and adjustment in his seat smart as his chafed skin was rubbed by the rough surface. He had to slap himself to stay awake and rolled his windows down even though he drove into a light rain. He almost drove off the road after only allowing himself one long blink of his eyes. He frequently was unsure if the road ahead went straight or turned, his vision so close to dreams, but he could not fall asleep, could not even pull over, no one could see him at this time. He dared not get coffee and was thankful he had had the presence of mind to fill up his gas tank and bring spare gasoline before the hunt. "Next time," he thought, "I'll bring a thermos of coffee and a change of clothes. That would make all the difference."

After arriving at his motel following his nightmare of dream-wakefullness and chafing clothes, he stripped, showered and put on sweat pants, leaving his bloody clothes on the floor. "Shit," he thought. Even through his tiredness he wanted to see the results of his work. He wanted to see his new product, the one with which he could start a new life, even better than before. More money, a new car for show and an old one for the hunt. He started the process of setting his darkroom in order. Two hours later he had pictures hanging over the bathtub. When all of his pictures were no longer vulnerable to light he opened the door and hung some from the walls of his bedroom. Some of them were precious, almost too good to sell, the look in his model's eyes as she realized what was going to happen, the expressions on her face almost taking his breath away in their...beauty. He felt himself getting aroused again and stroked himself to climax in a matter of seconds. Now he needed sleep. He walked unsteadily over to his bed and fell, instantly asleep, soundly and deeply.

    Alice was looking through the magazine, enraged, embarrassed, humiliated and fearful that her new friend would think of her as some kind of freak pervert and that would be the last she would see of Beth. She was afraid she would start to see curious glances in her direction from former friends, then a quick glance away as conversations started at her expense. "Son-of-a-bitch had a camera right next to my kitchen!" Alice said, hoping for a similar type of response from Beth. She didn't get it.
    Instead, Beth said with a broad smile and a look of approval and maybe even envy, "Well, you sure look into it. I can see why Mark stayed on even though he wasn't comfortable with the role you put him in," she said, giggling. "You're hot, Alice, are you always that into sex?" This time there was admiration in her voice, something totally unexpected for Alice.
    Caught off guard, Alice said, "Yeah, mostly."
    "And you guys were together how long?" Beth asked.

"Almost a year." Alice responded to Beth's questions a little puzzled. Instead of getting rejection she was getting curiosity; was the rejection going to follow as soon as Beth's curiosity was abated? Nothing in Beth's face betrayed any kind of disapproval, only curiosity and approval.

"Let me tell you something," Beth said. "That degree of lust lasts a month or two for me, and even then I can't say I ever get as zoned as you do." Beth was holding open the magazine where there was a full picture on each side instead of the quarter picture shots that comprised most of the magazine. On the first picture Alice had moved herself down from Mark's face and was inserting his erection into her. Her eyes were feral, forehead creased, jaw clenched, hand gripping his erection. As she lowered herself she looked like a starving person who had to climb a fence in order to get a steak dinner, her complete focus and entire body devoted to the task. In the second picture she was on him, eyes closed, face completely relaxed—a look that was almost angelic. Whoever printed this mag had an eye for a good picture. After a brief pause, Beth said, "Alice, you are so lucky to enjoy sex that much; I hope you know that."

Alice knew she was different, knew that her difference was important to her and that she didn't want to change it, but she had never considered herself lucky. "I always figured if I talked about it, it would freak people out," she said.

"Probably would freak a lot of people out, sex does. Can't imagine Cathie approving but on the other hand Mark's likely to get more blowjobs while he's driving nowadays," Beth said.

"Don't bet on that," Alice smiled, "but I always made him wait till we got home before he could cum."

Both laughed, and appreciated each other's company, sharing the joke. It felt good to discuss her sexuality with someone else. Alice was fulfilling a need she hadn't known existed until now.

Beth looked thoughtful then lowered her bombshell. "Alice, these are pictures of your bedroom. You showed me where you thought the camera was taking pictures of you—that was downstairs."

There was silence for 2 seconds then, "BASTARD," Alice shouted as she tore up the stairs, the old feelings of exposure, rejection, and embarrassment taking over again. Then she realized, she wasn't alone, that there was someone who didn't think she was a freak, and if one person didn't think she was a freak, there were surely others who felt the same way. Slowly, amid the anger and making circles in her bedroom to try to locate the lens, a new realization took hold. She had been violated, but not shamed; fuck the guy that did this, fuck the magazine, fuck the goddam sleazy asshole son-of-abitchen-motherfuck'n-cant-get-it-up-so-they-have-to-fuckin-peep-into-someone-elses-fuckin-life-bastard-motherfuckers anyway. She got on her bed and knelt where Mark's crotch would have been...and looked directly into the airvent.

Beth was still downstairs. Alice said, "Mother-fucker's consistent, used the airvent again I betcha." Before Beth could walk up the stairs Alice was running downstairs to get her toolkit. Alice was a ball of motion, adrenaline rage and focus combining into rapid movement and chattering. "Dad always said, learn to use tools. You can have a man fix things because you want him to but don't have him fix things because you need him to. He was so right. I don't want to need any motherfucker to do any fucking thing for me, I'll do the motherfucker myself."

Laughing out loud, Beth followed her friend upstairs. When she arrived at the top Alice was already standing on her desk unscrewing the vent. Beth said, "Alice, could you do me a favor?"

"What's that?" Alice said, working on the second screw.

"Could you try to use the work fuck a few more times in a sentence? I think you missed a few opportunities to say fuck a minute ago."

The modifications to the inside of this vent were different. Instead of a slight dent where it looked like something had been bracketed, there was a single screw hole in the top of the vent, and instead of a thin brown wire that had been cut off there was a thick piece of wire, black insulation, a copper wrap, plastic insulation and a thick single strand of wire. "What the hell?" Alice said as she stepped down and motioned Beth to look.

"Don't you mean what the fuck?" Beth said, climbing onto the desk after Alice had vacated.

"A lady doesn't use that language."

Beth looked at the wire. "Looks like a wire for cable TV," she said.

"That's what I thought. Let's check something."

Alice was walking now, the picture of calm. She opened the front door and started looking at the exterior of her apartment. She noticed the electric wires going into the building from a nearby telephone pole, the phone wires going onto the side of the building from a nearby telephone pole, her cable wire going into her apartment from the nearby telephone pole and something else. She noticed a cable wire running into or out of her apartment along the side, then connecting to the building across the walkway. The wire ran to the exact opposite end of the building from where her former neighbor lived.

They examined the wires, agreed on what they meant, and were re-entering the apartment when Alice, her voice matter-of-fact and rising only slightly, said, "Motherfucker thinks I don't know it went into his apartment. What was he doing sitting there jacking off can't get a date can't fuck a real woman has to watch me and jerk off safely in his own apartment? Alligator-boot-tight-jean-corvett-drivin-bastard-fuck-bastard."

They decided it was time to eat; a temporary change was called for. There was an Italian restaurant just down the street next to the SaveMore food store. Amid red wine and the comfort of starchy pasta Alice was thinking out loud. "I wonder if he's sold those other pictures yet? The ones from downstairs." Then, trying to look demure and embarrassed, she said, "We did it downstairs too." Beth put on a shocked expression. Alice continued. "I don't like being spied on and I especially don't like people making money off of spying on me."

"Can't blame you for that."

"I know where he lives, or at least where he lived a few weeks ago," Alice mentioned.

"And?" Beth said, sure of what was coming.

"Wanna take a road trip?" Alice finished.

The photographer arose in the early afternoon. Shit, it was bright outside. Even through the curtains it was bright. He squinted as he reached over to make sure the curtains were pulled. Slowly at first, the memories came back. He smiled, then in a rush he started a mental checklist. If he had made any mistakes he was in danger, the most danger he had ever been in. Were there any telltale signs on the car? Were there any telltale signs on him? Did anyone see him get in late last night? God, was he leaving fucking bloody footprints? He scanned the floor fully awake; if there were bloody footprints on the floor there would be bloody footprints on the sidewalk leading to his door. Oh, god, and he had slept through the entire morning. No, there were no bloody footprints on the floor. He would have to check the sidewalk just in case. Yes there were bloody clothes on the floor and Jesus H Christ they had probably stained the rug. Why didn't he undress in the tub? The clothes were against the wall next to the head of the bed in plain view. Anyone walking into the room who looked left would see the dresser with TV on top and a pile of bloody clothes on the floor next to the wall, shit. The blood had dried. There was even a raw spot on his arm where the dried blood had rubbed and rubbed. He went over to the clothes and picked up the stiff handfuls of material and felt a tug as he lifted. Yep, there it was. A reddish brown stain with fibers of his shirt stuck to it, just as fibers from the worn rug were sticking to the midsection of his shirt. Shit, now what? He dodged the dresser with the television on top as if he was going towards the front door, then turned left in the narrow walkway at the end of the mattress and went into the bathroom. He soaped a washcloth and scrubbed. A lot of good that did. The stain spread, getting a little lighter around the edges but that was it; now there was a damp, soapy, reddish-brown stain on the floor that he knew he had to get out as quickly as possible. If someone saw him and the police came to question him that stain would be all it would take. Forgetting his pictures for the time being he went out to his car, got an old rag from the trunk, wet it with gasoline from his emergency 5-gallon can, and returned to the motel. On the way back he slowed his pace, just to see if anyone was looking. No one was. The Howard Johnson's across the street looked just like it always did. No one was in the motel parking lot except for a Charger, though there was the usual assortment of drawn and undrawn shades. No one was looking at him. No one even noticed him. He started breathing easier. Back in his room the gasoline-soaked rag did a much better job of cleaning the stain. It wasn't removed exactly but it was much lighter and with a little shoe dirt would be indistinguishable from the rest of the worn and dirty carpet. With the incriminating spot much less distinguishable from the rest of the carpet he decided he needed to take a little more care of his pics; they were hanging all over the bathroom but he wanted a shower—he already smelled of sweat brought on by panic and gasoline. He also wanted to check the news to see if there were any reports of a murder last night. He switched channels until he found a news program, then went to work on the pictures. He placed them carefully on the bed, the dresser, on top of the television and the small desk. There were no news reports about a murder, in fact nothing except local news about a new initiative to curb marijuana use among local teenagers, then a report on local and national sports. A town only three hours away, may as well have been in Europe, he thought, feeling safer. He went into the shower. As he cleaned off he felt refreshed. No one was looking at him. He was safe as long as he wasn't stupid, and he had only been stupid once. The problem was, he didn't know when he had been stupid, he only knew that Al's men had found him. God, he was hungry. This was the first time he had thought of food since early last evening and now he realized he was starved. He made a list. "Here's what I'm gonna do," he thought, "eat, clean the car inside and out, get plastic bags to carry last night's clothes, take them out and burn them, get envelopes and mail just a few of my pics just to see if the return is going to be what I know it will be. The rest of the pics will be money in the bank." The photographer felt his confidence returning, and walked to Howard Johnson's for breakfast. He was going to get away with it. He was going to have lots of money and he was going to have fun, the most fun he had ever had. He was going to have the most fun ever.

Beth wasn't sure. "What are we gonna do when we get there? What do you have in mind?"

"I don't know. What I do know is I don't want that son-of-a-bitch making another dime off of me."

"Do you intend to ask for the pictures back?" Beth was trying to show how absurd such a venture sounded.

"No, but I'll take them if I have a chance, maybe wait around for him to leave and sneak in and take his precious pictures," Alice said, sounding haughty. "He broke into my place, I can break into his."

"So you plan to go to his place, then, when he's not home, break in, search his place, find the pictures and the negatives, steal them and leave. Is that all?" Beth was attempting to insert reason or at least some sort of plan into her friend's actions. "Do you know how to break into a house?"

"It's a motel room," Alice offered, "not a house; it's an old, run-down motel with monthly rates."

"OK, I'll look out," Beth said. "When do you want to leave?"

"Now," Alice said fiercely.

"No, tomorrow, we need sleep and we don't know what we're gonna step into tomorrow—we need to have some rest. You have been running on adrenaline for over an hour and you're going to crash."

"What?" Alice was confused. "What makes you an expert?"

"Having a brother who went to Nam, always said he tried to sleep as best he could when he knew shit was going down the next day, no matter how pumped he was," Beth said. "And we don't know what shit is going to go down tomorrow."

"Will you stay over?" Alice acquiesced.

"Sure."

Alice brought out bedding for the sofa and could feel herself becoming more tired by the second. Some sleep was a good idea, the thought of driving for 3 hours then facing who knows what seemed like a needless risk. Besides, if he was there at night all they could do was wait for him to get up the next day anyway. Alice didn't think she'd sleep a wink but she was wrong.

They should have set an alarm but didn't, so after getting up mid-morning Alice and Beth managed to get themselves fed, dressed, packed and into the Fairlane in less than an hour. The trip to Tayler was uneventful and mostly silent. This wasn't for fun, the trip was serious. Both made several halfhearted attempts at small talk, the seriousness and danger of their impending act outweighing any other topics of conversation. The trip took longer than expected with a stop for gas and an unprecedented 3 additional pit stops for a three-hour drive. Beth made the observation that perhaps nerves shrink bladders after Stop 3.

They arrived in Tayler. Alice parked at the Howard Johnson's, the front of her car facing the restaurant. Looking over her shoulder Alice took an inventory of the parking lot. There was one car on the far side of the office which probably belonged to whoever was working the desk, and a rusted-out red Charger in front of the last available unit, the shades still drawn. Alice noticed that the curtains were also drawn on the room where she had once seen her former neighbor unpack his belongings from a Blue Dodge Dart.

"I don't see the Blue Dart; that means he either moved, got a new car or isn't in his room," Alice said, her speech slightly pressured.

"What's your plan?"

"First leave the car here, walk over to the motel. You knock on the door, he doesn't know you."

"Hope not," Beth interjected quickly.

"Lets go with that, he doesn't know you, you knock on his door looking for a friend, fifth door from the office, OOPS wrong motel sorry and go—then we watch and wait for him to leave."

"Think he'll make a grab?"

"Hell, it's broad daylight, you scream someone's gonna see," Alice said. "Besides I'll be just around the corner."

"What if there's no answer?"

"I'll get in somehow, go around back and break a window if I have to," Alice said, holding a small crowbar she had taken from her toolkit and sliding it up the sleeve of her baggy shirt.

Beth and Alice exited the car, walked across the parking lot and stopped at the four-lane highway with grass median. Gaining confidence from each other with a mutual glance they worked their way across the two lanes, median, and other two lanes. The motel was shaped like a U with a small D-shaped island that created the entrance and exit from the parking lot. In its better days the island probably had flowers and a tree as evidenced by a dying evergreen in the center, now it was just weeds gone to seed. Alice walked to the side of the building and Beth walked up to the door, took a breath, exhaled slowly, put on a cheery smile and knocked. Nothing. Again a knock, louder this time, still nothing.

"Hey Linda, ya in there?" Beth said loudly as she knocked harder. As loud as she was yelling, and the with racket she was making, she doubted that a scream would be any more effective in getting attention than her knocks if he did open the door, and decide to grab. She looked over at Alice, stating the obvious with her eyes. They waited two more minutes, then Alice walked toward the rear of the building. Behind the building was a narrow cement walkway littered with pieces of broken cement, a retaining wall for Thistle's Furniture Specializing in Early American and Quality Designs. The wall was cracked, grass growing out in places. Alice wondered how many more years it could go without having to be replaced. The Motel was lower than the newer Thistle's Furniture so that you would have to be on the side of the store where there was not even a walkway and looking down to see her. The road was completely obscured by weeds. Counting 4 rooms from the manager's office, Alice tried to look into the bathroom window but the shade was drawn. She put her left ear to the window sticking a finger in her other ear to block out the road noise and listened for any sign of life. Nothing. She tried the window. It jiggled. She tried it again. The window would open just a fraction of an inch, then stop. She could see the lock—not a standard window lock, more like a door lock, closing the window automatically making the mechanism lock. Alice slid the crowbar from her sleeve, put it under the window and hoped the window wouldn't break loudly when she pushed. She pushed and the lock shifted in the soft wood allowing the window to rise past the locking mechanism. Alice's eyes took on a gaze fired by adrenaline, fear and the lust for revenge. She let go of the window intending to just look in for a second before crossing the threshold. As soon as she let go, the window shut, automatically locking. Panting and almost trembling she forced the window open again, this time propping the window with the crowbar. She took a breath and crawled through the window.

Beth remained out front. She didn't know who she was looking for, just that he was about 6'5", lean, drove a blue Dart and was a major asshole. She was confident that if she saw the car she could yell for her friend and take off. She was glad she was wearing a pair of Alice's athletic shoes; though they were a little tight, the traction and ability to move made it worth it. She should have gone home and got her own; Beth was an avid runner, but Alice had been so upset. She'd be OK, she thought, they would be out of here soon, the sooner the better.

The photographer was on his way home. His car had been cleaned outside twice, inside three times. He was thinking of mailing pics, burning his shirt and airing out the room. In two hours I can relax, he thought. As he stopped for a red light it caught his eye, nothing particular, just a white Ford Fairlane in the Howard Johnson's parking lot off to the side so you wouldn't see looking out of the windows of the restaurant even though there were plenty of closer parking spaces available. The image of a white Ford Fairlane made him nervous but he wasn't sure why—there were a million of them and this one looked like all the others. Still his guard was up. Better play it safe; instead of staying in the right lane to turn into the motel he eased into the left lane so that he wasn't at the front of the line of cars and wouldn't be as noticeable. Driving by, he saw what looked to be a clean-cut college bitch in the parking lot. He had never seen one of them there before, and why was she standing so close to his room looking all around?

The first thing Alice noticed was the smell, chemicals and gasoline mixed with something rotten. Her eyes teared up immediately, blurring her vision. Wiping her eyes, the first thing she saw in the bathroom were two flat rectangular pans on top of the john; they were both filled halfway with fluid. From the hooks on the walls and the clothesline on the floor it looked as though in addition to being used as a shower the bathroom was also used to hang dry items with the rope. Alice approached the bedroom which was illuminated by light shining through the curtains and the flickering of the television. She noticed that the bed, bureau, nightstand and chair all had small sheets of paper on them, neatly spaced about an inch apart. She took a step closer to the bed and was confronted by horror. A woman about her age was bleeding from deep punctures in her stomach and chest, her eyes were wild with fear and the photographer was holding a knife-point less than an inch from the woman's terrorized left eye while his hard-on was in her mouth. Looking from picture to picture she could see pieces of the story unfolding in front of her, each picture focusing on the damage done to the young woman's body and the terror in her eyes. Alice felt the bile rising in her stomach and willed it down with all of her strength.

"Shit," she said loudly. "OH shit, oh god."

Beth was knocking on the door now. "Alice, are you OK, Alice?!!!"

Shaken, Alice lunged for the door.

The photographer parked at Thistle's Furniture store and walked around to the front of the motel, staying close to the wall. "Why is that bitch standing so close to my door and where have I seen her?" he thought. Peeking around the corner he could see that the bitch was pounding on his door hollering for Alice. That was the whore next door's name! The whore who had recently made him some money but had previously made money for Al's boys. Before he had pictures of her he had never had any problems, then shortly after using her pictures his luck had changed, his looks had changed, he had lost everything, his car, his money and his apartment. He had also gained something, knowledge of a level of excitement that he had never imagined, had it not been for the whore's pictures and their great price. Was she now offering him even more? Were she and her bitch friend now offering themselves as models for his new endeavor? It was perfect. The object that had served as his downfall was offering herself to launch his new career. He was almost sorry that he had consummated his career change last evening. This time there were two of them. They looked healthier, so he knew he would be able to have a lot more fun with them—they would last much more than two hours. Could he make it last for days? He felt himself becoming erect just as his door opened and the bitch in front was looking at the whore. The whore was white as a sheet.

Alice was wild-eyed, all color drained from her face. "He killed her and took pictures, he killed her."

"Who?" Beth asked even as she had started to know. Even though she had not yet entered the room, all she had to do was look on any flat surface—they were covered by the photos.

The photographer knew instinctively this was the time, his prey was off guard, distracted. He ran toward the door covering the distance in seconds, less time than it would take the bitch to register, her eyes mesmerized by his product. He was surprised how quickly his brain worked and how right his plan felt. Though he had never used the word aloud he could only think that this was destiny. He would knock out the bitch with a forearm to push her to the side; granted she would be outside but it wouldn't be for long and he needed quick access to his place. He didn't want to stumble over an unconscious bitch—that would give the whore too much time to prepare. The lone tree in the island protected him from being seen by most traffic and the restaurant unless cars were parked on the side. Like the whore's Fairlane. Chances are a few seconds of a bitch knocked down wouldn't be noticed, and he'd have them in his trunk and be out of there in 15 minutes tops, 10 if he hustled. "Fucking bitches can't take a punch," he thought smugly as ran toward Beth, his forearm raised to her eye-level just before contact.

    Beth looked Alice in the eye. "Alice we've got to call the pol...." That was all she got out before her body fell violently like a doll thrown down in a tantrum.

    Alice was aware of two things—the motionless feet and ankles of her friend and the photographer coming towards her. Alice did something the photographer did not expect. She was standing in the narrow walkway between the base of the bed and the bathroom. In front of her was an indentation in the wall—this was the room's closet; it went in about 18 inches and had a single rod with coat hangers. The photographer expected the whore to cower in front of him like that whore last night had done. He was on top of her, starting to wrap his arms around her, expecting her to cower as he threw her to the floor. Last night's whore hadn't had any fight; she had never attacked. Alice wasn't the whore last night. She put her left leg against the wall and used that to spring against him, knocking him back, off balance, slightly winded. He began to see red. Alice was slightly off balance as well. The photographer attacked again, this time grabbing for her neck, intending to lift her by her neck to squeeze and shake till she was unconscious or dead, now he didn't care. Both hands outstretched, he lunged for Alice's throat. This may have been an attack of rage but it was not an attack which held good balance. Alice was able to actually bat his arms away and in so doing made him lose confidence in his attack. He saw what was coming next, however, and prepared. Alice had righted herself and pulled her right leg back to kick him in the crotch. That is what gave her away, pulling her leg back for the kick. Seeing it coming, the photographer batted her leg aside and used the split second it took Alice to regain her balance to encircle both hands securely around her throat, lift her into the air, her head now above his as he smashed her head against the wall, not letting go. Alice saw stars, became disoriented and started ineffectually flailing punches and kicks that lacked both force and direction. Her closed windpipe increased both her panic and her inability to launch any further attack. Alice felt her strength and consciousness slipping.

Unlike a woman, 75% of a man's strength is in his upper body. The photographer used this strength to continue to hold the struggling and conspicuously weakening body of Alice. Unlike a man, 75% of a woman's strength is in her lower body. When that strength is used by a woman who in later years would be inclined to big thighs but now had them controlled by constant exercise, the force is considerable. When Beth kicked the crotch of the photographer from behind he was literally lifted off his feet. Immediately dropping Alice, his whole body felt the shock. He knew he was going to go down and he had to connect now. If his attacker was down too they would be on even ground. Putting all his force into his forearm he was surprised by three things. His arm was expertly deflected, he was face to face with the bitch who should be out for the count, and she clocked him hard on the side of the face so that as he fell to his knees he reeled around facing the whore who was only now starting to stand up. Incredulous that he could possibly be beaten by bitches, he quickly staggered to his feet and made a quick punch toward Alice's face. She ducked and shoved. The photographer fell against the dresser, upending the television. It fell to the floor with a loud bang as the picture tube exploded. The photographer was on top of the mess, glass imbedded in his side and his face jerking as he was shocked by electricity, flames from the gasoline erupting over the upper half of his body. An agonized scream loud enough to be heard across the street emitted from the room.

"Lets get out of here now," Beth said.

"Out the back," Alice yelled as they ran toward the bathroom.

In the few steps to the bathroom Beth and Alice were already coughing from the smoke. Alice dived through the window followed by Beth. As Beth was exiting Alice regained her footing, grabbed the crowbar and shoved it up her sleeve, then lowered a hand to Beth who was already in the process of standing. Walking behind the motel Alice noticed a break in the ivy-grown link fence behind the motel and what looked like an alley behind. She squeezed through the opening, Beth behind her. "Walk or run?" she wondered, her mind racing. "Walk, it's far less conspicuous," she thought. Looking around on the other side it didn't appear that anyone was in the alley. On the other side of the alley was a row of older homes—many had junk in the yards and gray porches in need of painting. Hopefully no one was looking out of their window at the moment that they had entered the alley.

"Let's stroll," Alice said.

Nervously they walked toward the end of the alley breathing raggedly, trying not to cough. Though it was only a block it seemed to take ages, time being compressed from adrenaline, fear and lack of motion. Before reaching the end of the alley, sirens could be heard in the distance, coming up fast. At the end of the alley, each one silent, they turned left then stopped at the corner. Simultaneously they allowed themselves a glance toward the motel. A plume of dark gray smoke was already high in the air broadcasting the fire. This was the first time they noticed that the photographer's high-pitched screams had stopped. "God, don't let anyone notice us," Alice prayed, wondering immediately if she had the right to make such a prayer. "Please don't let anyone notice us," she said to herself again and again trying to will it to happen. She glanced at Beth—her friend was stone-faced, looking straight ahead at the light, waiting for it to change. Traffic was heavy; cars were stopping on either side of the road, now creating a traffic jam. People were getting out to look at the fire. The fire engines with lights flashing and sirens screaming were visible to the left three lights down—less than a mile. The light changed. Alice and Beth ran across the highway, dodging cars now stuck in slowed traffic. Gaining composure they continued walking toward the car; people were out, but all eyes were on the billowing smoke and flames coming from the open door 4 doors down from the manager's office of the Scenic Highway Motel. Starting the car Alice began backing out as the first firetruck pulled into the motel's parking lot. A fireman got out and began motioning cars to move out of the way. A State Police car had stopped at the intersection Alice and Beth had just walked across. Lights still flashing, the trooper too was directing traffic, trying to move the traffic to clear the way for more emergency equipment. Alice made her way to the parking lot entrance. A policeman looking directly into her eyes held up his hand. Alice froze and returned his gaze, keenly aware of the crowbar on the seat between her and Beth. If the trooper saw that, he might start asking questions that would lead to disaster. The hand moved, he was motioning her to merge with traffic. She pulled out slowly and joined the parade of cars towards town, away from the interstate.

"I know where to go from here," Alice said a few minutes later. "I've been here before." Beth nodded, eyes straight ahead.

These were the only words spoken until they had finally threaded their way through town and were on the freeway headed home.

"Beth, he hit you so hard, I thought you were out cold," Alice said after they had 20 miles between themselves and Tayler.

Beth took a deep breath and shook herself, color and animation returning immediately. "I had brothers," she said simply, smiling too broadly as if the memory was being savored and seen in an entirely new light.

"You always say that—what do you mean you have brothers?" Alice said, impatience brought on by their ordeal.

"I mean," Beth began, "that I had two older brothers and one younger brother. We were stair-step kids. My oldest brother is only three years older than me. We lived way outside of a very small town, with a big yard and woods. If I wanted someone to play with, my brothers were it mostly. My brothers were active and rough, always competing with each other, and if I wanted to play I had to learn to take it. In grade school my Dad got real protective, not wanting his thug boys to beat his little angel but I realized that I could be protected and left out or join in and get knocked around sometimes."

Alice made a pitying face. "They weren't mean brothers—I have a great family, but they were active and competitive. If I wanted to play football with them I could but it was a real game. When we fought I learned to hold my own. I was a real tomboy all through grade school and highs school. My brothers respected me 'cause I wouldn't take any shit from them and if they chose to fight me I might lose, but they knew they would be hurting, even Terry, the oldest, and he was a linebacker," Beth said proudly. "I didn't date much in high school; was too much of a tomboy and the whole school knew that if any boy treated me wrong not only would they answer to me but there were three very protective brothers to answer to." Beth was on a roll, her nervousness from the motel fueling her monologue. "This guy Chuck was mouthing at me in the parking lot after a football game saying I was too much of a tomboy and he was gonna make a woman out of me and I would like it. I told him to leave me alone, and he grabbed my arm and pulled me toward his car. I hauled off and broke his nose and kicked him in the nuts and ran. That Monday at school he came up to me all apologetic, saying he was way out of line, promising that it would never happen again, and saying "I'm sorry" about 100 times. Though I hadn't said anything, word had gotten around school and to my brothers who had had a talk with him. I'm sure it was just a talk cause he just had the black eyes and broken nose from me, nothing else, but they must have put the fear of god in him." Beth was smiling, obviously proud of her family and herself.

"I never would have guessed," Alice said. "You're always so made-up, such a flirt, dressed sexy."

"I decided to try a new image in college and it was fun, still is and besides," Beth paused, "I once rode my sled through a barb-wire fence, so I have these little scar lines but you can't see them through makeup," she laughed.

"So that's Rif's and I guess Beth's story," Alice said. She and Lar had been trading off in the story-telling.

"That's quite the story." Yo was staring at the floor. "What happened to him—did he die in the fire?"

"Don't know," Alice said evenly.

"Did the police find out who he was?"

"Don't know. I should have taken a photograph but didn't think of it at the time."

"What do you know?....Sorry, I hope that didn't sound condescending, but what do you know about what happened to him?"

"Not much. We checked the news when we got back, but news of a motel fire in a town almost 200 miles away doesn't make the local news and doesn't make national news so I never learned the outcome on TV or in the newspaper and I was spooked. I was responsible for the motel fire and maybe someone's death, a trooper looked right at me, other people saw me and my car, so I was afraid to go back to town and ask around. I was freaked and wouldn't go near the town for fear that my car or my face would trigger some recollection in someone that would lead to the police getting involved. Probably unfounded but there you are"

"It was self-defense," Yo offered.

"Yeah, I know that now, but it didn't feel like it then. Besides, I had broken into his room in the first place."

"He was a murderer, he killed someone."

"I know, I didn't say I felt all that guilty. I knew what he was. He would probably have used Beth and me in his next photoshoot if he could, but something didn't feel right about leaving him, even though I knew I had to, that if we helped him he would be just as likely, or even more likely, to hunt us down and kill us. We knew he killed someone. It didn't feel good. You know in the movies when the bad guy gets killed it feels good? This didn't feel good. It felt wrong. You're the lawyer—what do you think, legally?"

"I guess if the DA was a real jerk and the photos were burned you could be in big trouble."

Alice's face had gone from animated and showing her emotions to expressionless in less than a minute. Now her eyes were staring as though she was not in the room and she was seeing something that made her incredibly sad and afraid. She took a deep breath, looked both Lar and Yo in the eye and said, "But I felt it would be dangerous to go back to the town, so Beth and I set out to see if we could find out who he killed. We took road trips on weekends to towns a day's drive from Tayler and checked old newspapers; that's where we got some of the information about the woman who was murdered."

Yo had a questioning expression but Alice interrupted. "Tell you what, Lar can fill you in with any other questions. I really don't like to go over this. In fact, I didn't remember how much I don't like to go over this until Lar got us starting the story again."

"Sounds like issues," Yo said.

"Issues I'll deal with sometime in my own time," Alice answered. "Let's talk about you guys' relationship for the next month." Alice was changing the subject and was finishing up the business she had started when she invited her friend over in the first place. "Yo, you've never had a sub and you're going to have a very well-trained one. Remember safety, and what he can be used for. A rule of thumb for you is, if the relationship is based on fear, it's no good, that's abuse."

Yo was starting to speak but Alice interrupted. "I don't mean that there won't periods of time where he won't be fearful; just that the overall relationship needs to be based on trust, mutual understanding, and mutual enjoyment. Is that something you want to try out?"

"Sure," Yo said. In the back of her mind she figured that if Alice hadn't found her own time to deal with the Rif issue in over 20 years the issue is probably not going to be dealt with, but this definitely wasn't the time to bring it up. With that thought tucked away, she was free to allow her other ideas to return, ideas of lust and exploring a new way of pleasure.

"Lar, this is what I want for now. I've always told you and never asked. We are so attuned, I read you, I know you will like this too."

Lar smiled, excited but with a knot in his stomach, the same one Alice felt.

"I thought so. I want a report of your scenes once a week and I want the door open for conjugal visits. You are not to call here unless directed to do so by me or Yo. Do you understand?"

"Yes, Mistress," Lar mumbled.

"Very good—why don't you guys get ready to leave? I have a project I have to work on," Alice said.

The atmosphere was hard to define. Yo was having a lust attack, Lar was packing, eager for the prospect of serving a new Mistress, learning how to give her pleasure; seeing, hearing, and tasting her response. His relationship with Alice was in many ways predictable, though unparalleled; why did he have to keep telling himself that this was her idea, it was only for a month, and he hoped she was OK? Was this going to be a stepping stone to the demise of their relationship? He felt a moment of panic. Alice had been his first and until now his only Mistress; he had always thrilled in serving her, providing her with pleasure and the travels that they took together, travels that began with his body tested, but then they went through the door, and when they went through they went together. He couldn't lose that level of pure sensuality and sharing. He needed assurance that he could continue to be with Alice. She had said there would be conjugal visits, and he would be able to see her, but he was uncertain. He was in the bedroom putting some clothing and toiletries in his backpack when Yo entered.

"Continue," she said as he put things in the backpack. Yo walked over to him and, pressing her body against his back, began massaging his chest gently, rubbing his nipple. Lar began to get aroused.

"Good boy," Yo said. "We'll have to find more ways to keep you like that."

Lar had almost finished packing. He was finding it difficult to concentrate as Yo continued to play with him. "Mistress Yo, should we bring toys?"

"I have money. Anything we use I'm going to want to hang onto. Are you ready?"

Lar nodded.

"Good, get dressed," she said as she turned to go into the living room.

As they were leaving Lar wanted to have just a couple of words with Alice but she was in the bathroom with the door closed.

"Have a good time, Yo—be good, Lar, show off your training," Alice said from the other side of the door.

After the door closed, Alice finished in the bathroom, entered the bedroom and began to disassemble the instruments used in their latest journey.

After getting her bedroom in order Alice began an activity that is usually not associated with a dominatrix. She went into her closet, retrieved her briefcase, put papers from her briefcase on her desk, turned on her MAC, slotted a disk, and began to look over budget projections. She studied the figures until 11PM, realizing that some hard choices were going to be necessary and that she was the one who was responsible for those decisions.

Alice's MBA had provided her with what it had promised—well-paying jobs, availability to switch jobs and employers when things got either too boring or too bloodthirsty, a decent IRA and portfolio. It also provided her with frequent long hours, interrupted vacations, and the knowledge that loyalties and friendships at work are always suspect. She had been pleased with her promotion to managing Human Resources, but she soon found out that her department had been given the responsibility for budgeting payroll and benefits, and that a large part of her job was cost savings. Therefore, a large part of her job was being able to lower the cost of labor.

She remembered when she first got the promotion. She and Lar had been able to move to this apartment. It was larger than their last place and closer to Alice's job. Though Lar was degreed she liked having him at her disposal, knowing he was waiting for her, so Lar worked part-time two days a week just so he could contribute some money to the household and save the rest. Primarily he worked because Alice knew how bad periods of unemployment looked to people in Human Resource departments. Lar was no object, no toy to be discarded if she got bored with him—he was a person, too, and if either he or she decided that their relationship was to end he would have to work. She didn't want their time together to result in ultimate harm to his life, though she sure liked knowing that he would be there when she got home, meal waiting, and wanting her. Well, all of life was a balancing act, wasn't it? Balancing her lust and desires with the needs of her partner, balancing proximity to work with size of living space and traffic congestion, balancing the need to remain physically fit, pursue her hobbies, travel, her friends, her help with the literacy program downtown; balancing time with Lar, their lifestyle and her job; the realities of her job, the effects of her decisions and her view of herself as a person. "Why didn't I just become a professional domme?" Alice asked herself, already knowing the answer. A professional domme doesn't always have the luxury of choosing her subs—her subs choose her, and that means certain expectations of costume, demeanor, availability, but the main thing was the subs. As a pro she needed to be able to read a sub and know what his greatest turn-on was. Alice could do that but she didn't like it. It was so much better for her to find a sub whose greatest turn-on conformed with her own, and with so precious few, a sub who understood the journey and who was as fascinated, awed and desirous of more such journeys, as she, a sub who was a partner and shared her interests in music and politics.

Alice realized what she was doing. Revelry was good for self-examination—it was also a good way to avoid a task. Alice went back to work and realized that with the mandate she had been given at work, a new type of balance was needed to make personnel benefits conform to the budget figures that had been targeted at the last meeting. She had been through this balancing act before. Last year she had initiated a transfer from private insurance to a preferred provider that had used a capitation formula that far exceeded their competitors'. Employees were given a 30-day notice of the benefit change, with the option of continuing with their old benefits as long as they paid the difference between what the company was paying the managed care corporation, and the private payer insurance. This generally translated into about $400 a month for a family policy. There had been a major squawk from the employees, and a number had left, but not too many. They were replaced with workers who were generally younger, cheaper, and healthier, so that they were less likely to need the services of their managed care provider, anytime soon, anyway. Those who stayed tended to be older workers with salaries that were higher, due more to their longevity than their present value to the company. The fact that the CEO of the corporation received a year-end bonus for profits resultant from cost savings which exceeded the savings the corporation realized by the benefits change, was not unnoticed by Alice. She rationalized that one had to balance the desire to do the right thing with the realities of the workplace. At 1AM, Alice had the beginnings of a plan and its structure. It was time for sleep. She made sure she had work clothes ready for tomorrow and went to bed.

To say Yo was excited would be understatement. Her mind was in overdrive just imagining all of the delicious things she could do with a male, let alone a male slave. This was going to border on too much fun and she couldn't wait to get started. One of the things that separated Yo from Alice was that Yo came from money. Unlike Alice, she had it and, unlike many of her cohorts she was bright enough to realize that there were many circumstances aside from laziness and fear of risk that determined people's fate. So when YoLynn wanted friends she didn't look first at their portfolio and when she was psyched she didn't mind spending cash. Yo was psyched.

"Slave"—she liked the sound of that,—"where can we buy some toys?"

"We get a lot of..." Lar began.

"Stop!" Yo interrupted, liking this more and more. Though she wanted to put on a stern face a very wide smile broke through mid-sentence when she said, "You need to call me Mistress if I address you as slave."

"Yes, Mistress, sorry, Mistress," Lar began.

Yo pulled the car into an illegal parking area at the corner. They hadn't even gone two blocks. "How do you address Mistress Alice?"

"During any scene or whenever she addresses me as slave I call her Mistress; if we are out in public or relaxing and she calls me by any other name I call her Alice or hon," Lar continued. The tonal quality of his voice had taken on a higher-pitched, almost adolescent quality.

"Slave, are you from Balmer?" Yo was using the dialect Baltimore natives employed when referring to their hometown.

"Nearby, Mistress, why do you ask, Mistress?" Lar answered quickly.

"The hon, in Baltimore everyone's hon, you can't get a cup of coffee without being called hon." Yo was giving a lecture and also still trying to get into a severe domme role—not too successfully. Maybe she should try a different approach. Lar was her slave for at least the next 30 days; during that time, did she really have to conform to her stereotype of a dominatrix, stern and cold? That isn't how Alice was, ever, well unless she was real pissed but then who isn't when they're pissed? Maybe a different strategy would work a little better for her. If it didn't work for him...well, she'd deal with that if she had to.

"Slave," Yo began conversationally. "I know we're going to have a good time, or I know I am going to have a good time and I don't want you to forget your place. I think I need to set a tone but I don't want to go around acting pissed all the time—that isn't fun. So I have a question for you: is it appropriate for a slave to be punished if he behaves incorrectly?"

"Yes, Mistress," Lar stated, his voice also becoming conversational.

"How much punishment?" Yo asked.

Lar thought for a minute. Was this a trap? His standard answer to Alice would be, "As much as Mistress thinks best," but he realized something. Alice knew the limits, Alice knew the effect of everything she did. She knew it because she seemed to have a gift for combining their two psyches during a scene. But she knew it mostly, Lar thought, because they had been together for almost half a decade and Alice had plenty of time to practice and learn his reactions. Lar wasn't exactly sure why Alice had sent him with Yo, though he wasn't knocking it, you understand, but he sensed that one purpose of his temporary servitude was to show (he didn't want to use the word "train" even to himself) YoLynn how to top effectively. After all, he did have far more experience as a sub than she did as a domme. Instead of giving short responses he would elaborate and see if the additional information was appreciated or not. Lar was sure that he would find out soon enough if the information was not being solicited or appreciated.

"As much punishment as Mistress thinks is appropriate based on her desires, sounds from her slave, or prearranged safewords," Lar offered.

"What do you mean?" Yo asked.

"Well, after a Mistress gets to know her slave she can tell how much effect she is having on him by the volume of his cries, facial expressions, or safewords," Lar began.

"I've heard of safewords—we need to give you one, until I get to know you better." Yo was appreciative of the suggestion.

"We can do this a couple of ways, Mistress," Lar continued. "A safeword can mean stop, but you also may wish to attach consequences to a safeword. For example, use of one safeword can mean stop and my consequence can be going without orgasm for a certain period of time....like maybe 2 or 3 days," Lar was hopeful.

"I would think that a week would be better." Yo was catching on much too quickly; that is exactly how Alice started.

"Or, we can have a series of safewords with varying degrees of consequences," Lar began again.

"Tell you what, slave: let's just keep it simple for now; if we need to add additional words and rules we'll do it later. Do you have a safeword?" Yo asked, then before he could respond, "No I'll give you one—it's widdle fwafey, like a 3-year-old saying little fluffy. Can you say your safeword? Let me hear it."

"Widdle fwafey," Lar said quietly.

"I'm not sure I heard you," Yo said with exaggerated patience as if she was addressing a kindergartner.

"Widdle fwafey, Mistress," Lar said at normal volume.

"Very good, and if I hear that, I will stop what I'm doing with you and you will not be allowed to orgasm for 7 days, even if I choose to tease you every night. Is that understood?"

"Yes, Mistress," Lar answered, eyes downcast.

"Very good, slave. Now you need to be punished for not calling me Mistress earlier, don't you?" Yo remained pleasant and conversational.

"Yes, Mistress," Lar answered.

"Very well. Unzip and pull it out." Yo was quickly learning how to integrate her new role into her normal personality. This was easiest for her; it made her interactions seem more real, thereby allowing her to use her natural creativity without having to go through an additional step of filtering her creativity through a persona.

Lar did as he was told, aware that they were on a street corner and that a pedestrian could pass at any time or maybe a car coming close, even a cop—they were in a no-parking zone before a corner. Their car would make it difficult for other cars to negotiate the turn—they might look in, or the police or....All consciousness was immediately focused on his cock, his face an expression of surprise and pain.

"1,2,3,4,5," Yo said matter of factly behind a whack whack whack sound of an open hand slapping skin. "That will do for now, zip up." Meekly, Lar did as he was told, stuffing his semi-erection into his pants. "Now, where can we buy toys? I'm thinking Pleasure Toys—it's on the way home."

"Pleasure Toys is OK," Lar offered. "I'm not sure what you want to buy."

"I have money," Yo began, "and all I have at home is two vibrators."

"Pleasure Toys is OK," Lar said again. "You probably have more fashion stuff there—you might want to try Leathers in Woodside for more DS toys," Lar answered, returning the conversational mode that Yo was using.

"Thank you for the suggestion. We may go there. I'm going to stop off at Pleasure Toys tonight; however, Woodside is farther than I wish to drive, and one more thing…" Yo said, continuing in her conversational tone but finishing her sentence before Lar could respond. "Pull it out again—you didn't say Mistress,"

This time she counted to ten, smacking Lar all the harder after he became fully erect at 7.

When he and Alice went to Pleasure Toys, part of the trip usually involved circling around looking for parking, part of the shopping downtown experience. Yo pulled into the self-park underground parking lot on the same block—$8.00 first half-hour, $4.00 per half-hour thereafter. "Stay here for a second," she said as she touched a switch opening her trunk. She then got out of her car, went to the trunk and started rummaging. A few minutes later she opened the door to the back seat and started dumping: a briefcase, overcoat, gymbag, sweater, windshield cover, plastic briefcase-shaped container, box filled with oily rags and jumper cables. She closed the trunk then reached to the back seat and unlatched a side of the back-rest, exposing the dark interior.

"I would have had *you* do this but I wanted a surprise for you. Chances are there is a camera somewhere, so, slave I want you to stay in the car—put your seat back like you're going to take a snooze, then crawl into the trunk, remove all of your clothes and hand them out to me. Do it now," she said as she sat in the driver's seat, again turned on the radio and pulled out a map as though she was looking for directions.

Lar's look of surprise and anxiety did not disappoint. Lar did as instructed, first lowering his seat so that he probably would not be noticed as a car passenger, then he slithered into the trunk and in the cramped quarters removed all of his clothes, noticing how tender he had become as he removed his jeans and the heavy cloth brushed him. He handed his clothes out piece by piece until he was naked in the trunk of Yo's car.

"I'm going to crack the windows and this back-rest. I'm reasonably sure that the trunk's not airtight but there's no point in taking that risk. This seat back is marked—I'll know if you've moved it and if you do, you better have a damn good reason. Anyway, if you enter the back seat or even move too much, you'll set off the car alarm and you wouldn't want that," Yo said, just before he heard a car door open and close, then receding footsteps echoing from the concrete floor. Yo's voice was becoming more forceful and commanding, but without the pissed-off quality. She was getting more and more into it, a natural, Lar thought. Of course Alice would have seen that before Yo had been invited to come over this evening in the first place. After thinking that comforting thought, Lar was left with other thoughts, namely that it was dark, cool—not cold—mostly that he could feel the air, the metal trunk lid and the rough trunk carpeting on his bare skin. What if someone tried to steal the car, he thought. What if someone nudged the car, setting off its car alarm? Shit, he'd be stuck in here with the damn thing blaring for who knows how long! He heard footsteps; was she coming back? No, it was more than one—he heard voices too—they were getting closer to the car. "Oh shit," he thought, "here they are, they're going to try to steal the car! The alarm is going to go off, then they'll either run and I'll be stuck with the alarm or they'll disable the alarm and steal the car with me in it." The footsteps got closer till they sounded like they were directly in front of the car, then began to recede in the other direction. Just people going to their car after an evening in town. No biggie. People used garages because not only were they more convenient but they were safer than the street; garages had cameras and only one entrance, the street had more than one entrance and no cameras, much better odds for a thief. Lar decided he should stop or at least cool down some of all this worrying. He had a new Mistress and very quickly she had him in a very vulnerable and potentially exposed state…wonderful. When the next group of footsteps and voices approached the car Lar's imagination and fear were much more under control, and with subsequent groups his emotions began to turn from anxiety to appreciation. Appreciation for the scene he was in, the control his new Mistress had over him so quickly, appreciation that each approaching footstep reminded him of his nakedness, vulnerability and position as a slave. He loved being able to step outside of himself to assume this role where everyday worries and stresses were no longer relevant to his life and for the time being, he was relaxed and free.

Lar didn't know that Yo had returned until he heard the beep beep of the car alarm being disabled; he had fallen asleep. He heard the back door open and a large, thick piece of cloth was thrust in his direction. "It's a cape—I think if you exit the trunk head first you can tie it around your neck then make your way to the front seat with the cape wrapped around you. This vampire stuff has so many uses."

Lar struggled to get his head pointed towards the folded seatback. As his head popped out of the opening he looked towards Yo and stared, unblinking. She was every inch a classic picture of a dominatrix. High black boots with stiletto heels, black stockings held by black leather garters visible at the bottom of her black leather miniskirt, long-sleeved leather skin-tight shirt that zipped up the front, black gloves and a black cape like Lar's. She was wearing dark lipstick and severe makeup. Yo was looking stern but the corners of her mouth were twitching trying to force down a smile.

"You look like a 7th-grader seeing his first real tit," she said, bursting out laughing. Lar continued to stare. After composing herself she looked at Lar still staring and went through a round of guffaws. Trying to compose herself she said, not looking at Lar, "Into the front seat wearing only the cape."

Shimmying out of the trunk, fastening the cape around his neck then into the seat, Lar wrapped the cape around himself then stretched broadly and wiggled his back to overcome the slight cramping that had occurred in the trunk. He noticed that Yo seemed to have bought out the store—there were more bags in the back seat and still outside of the car than he thought she would be able to carry, especially with her heels.

"You can have a good stretch in less than an hour. For now I want the seat up and you sitting still in front seat, eyes front." Yo's voice was almost pitying, noting how difficult it seemed to be for Lar to take his eyes off of her.

Lar complied and said, without moving his eyes toward Yo, "Mistress, did you carry all of that yourself?"

"I didn't carry any of it," Yo started. "Don't think I could have if I'd wanted to in these boots anyway, but you can get lots of help if a clerk knows you're going to drop a bundle. Didn't you hear a more than one set of footsteps come up to the car? I thought these heels made a quite distinctive sound in the concrete."

"No, Mistress, I fell asleep," Lar admitted.

"Terrorized by fear, I see," Yo said sarcastically. "Anyway, first to you, then to the car; I'd have you pack but I don't want you to know what's coming. I think I'm pretty well-equipped and will be moreso after the carpenters arrive tomorrow. I'm calling in sick tomorrow so that I can tend to the carpenters who are to arrive at 8AM, otherwise no bonus; and an STD check so that you can tend to me more than you will tonight. I've gotten so wet just planning. Wait one sec—arms back behind the seat."

Lar tried to comply but there was no room in the car to get his arm between the door and the back seat. Was this going to ruin her scene, Lar worried. How would she handle learning that fantasy and reality frequently don't match up? Would her fantasies crumble when things didn't go according to her expectations? Would it cause her to doubt the validity of her dreams and her ability to make at least part of her dreams reality? Is this where she says screw-it, why can't we just fuck?

"Oh well, plan B," Yo began. "We'll use these instead of handcuffs."

One thing that could be said for YoLynn was that she was organized—there she was with bags and boxes and she knew exactly which bag to go into and without much rummaging produced two thick wrist cuffs. He could remember himself and Alice rummaging forever through a single bag in a comedy of DS, looking for a particular toy, the search becoming more and more important while thoughts of sex and play were set on a shelf to gather dust from disuse as the search consumed playtime.

Lar put on the cuffs, then put his hands behind his back where Yo padlocked them into place and to each other.

"Now sit up," Yo instructed as she pulled on his cape, Lar writching to help her free the fabric that was folded behind him. Yo was buttoning some top buttons with her gloves on and doing a good job, and Lar glanced towards her with every opportunity.

Finally she was satisfied with her work and she cinched the seat belt on Lar. From outside the car, Lar would look like he was wearing a cape like the woman he was with; if anyone cared to look in further, they could see that he didn't have shoes on. Well, who would do that anyway and if they did, who cares?

"Next step," Yo explained. "I originally planned this because I wanted you to feel more isolated, helpless, and dependent on me. Now I'll have the added benefit of not having your eyes popping out of your head."

Yo produced two thick pieces of flesh-colored cloth that looked like the moleskin people use to prevent blisters on their feet, each piece slightly larger than a quarter. "Eyes closed," she said. Lar complied immediately. He felt the material being fitted over his eyes; the side touching his skin had a tacky quality holding it in place. Lar then felt what he assumed to be sunglasses fitted on his face. To the casual observer he was sitting in a car wearing a cape and probably very dark sunglasses, being driven by a woman wearing an entire cow's worth of leather. With his vision gone there was an almost claustrophobic feeling, even more closed-in than when he was in the trunk. He couldn't move or see, he was totally dependent on his new Mistress. Without sight his other senses strained to provide him with orienting information. Sitting still, eyes forward, Lar heard things being put in the trunk and back seat. Then he heard the trunk and back door, the car shifting as if someone was sitting in the driver's seat.

"One last detail," Yo spoke softly, as if she knew Lar's remaining senses were straining to make up for his lost sight so that even the softest spoken words would take on an increased level of significance. Lar could tell that she was sitting next to him. She was almost whispering when she said, "As I mentioned, planning for the enjoyment you are going to give me has made me very wet and my wet panties are chafing and uncomfortable." Yo stopped talking but he could hear her movements in the car.

"What's the matter, can't speak? No 'yes Mistress?' Is this too much to ask?" Yo's voice was louder with an edge of indignation. Lar felt Yo reach under his cape and grab his cock. "10 more I think," Yo said as if she was proposing the answer to a puzzle. "Aren't these gloves great? No seams at all, fit like a second skin. See how you like them." Then she began to count.

"Yes, Mistress," Lar said through clenched teeth several times until the ten count was finished.

"That's good, slave," she said at normal voice. Lar was sitting straight in the seat, tumescent penis exposed. Yo tucked it under the cape then said in a whisper, "You are going to keep this in your mouth." At first Lar could only smell the thickness of her fragrance—he realized she must have removed her panties and was now holding them under his nose.

Yo dabbed them on Lar's nose and whispered, "This is what I smell like, the smell of your new Mistress. Can you tell the difference between my smell and Mistress Alice's smell?"

"Yes, Mistress," Lar replied.

"Good. We may blindfold you sometime and have you pick us out—there may even be other women there—you'd like that, wouldn't you?"

Lar was starting to get hard. "Yes, Mistress."

"I thought so," then at normal volume, "Men are dogs."

"Yes, Mistress," Lar responded.

"Now, I've promised no unprotected fluid contact until I'm tested, so open wide," Yo said with just a hint of resignation in her voice. As Lar opened she squeezed vaginal lubricant with Nonoxynol-9 into Lar's mouth, and onto her panties. She said, "This isn't the safest safe sex, but its pretty darn safe—it has been 6 months, I've had a physical and I haven't had a lot of partners or one-night stands since my 20's, and I'm getting checked again tomorrow." With that she thumbed her panties into his mouth and placed the palm of her hand under his chin indicating that he was to close his mouth. "Now you don't have to worry about not 'Yes, Mistressing' me," Yo said as she started the car.

    Alice was up late and up early. Work today was going to be a bitch. Budget meetings meant assholes from other departments vying for any piece of any other department they could get their hands on. Salary meant responsibility for dollars and the demonstrated ability to do more with less. Anything that looked like a dropped ball in a meeting, or even the hint that a ball may be dropped, would let the vultures swoop down attempting to take whatever project, or responsibility, away from the hapless presenter. Who cares if the department vying for the project had any real expertise in the area that was being fought for? What mattered was *apparent* responsibility for results in the area being vied for. Short-termers could always just lay a few people off, then present the reduced cost projections to their higher-ups, meanwhile asking for either a transfer to another department, preferably in another town, where they would be, "more challenged and able to put their demonstrated skills to use." The fact that the negative impact of these floaters' decisions was never dealt with by, or attributed to, the floaters was something else about this business that was not unnoticed by Alice. She frequently wondered if she was the only one who noticed. So many well-paid managers at this meeting had never seen a project through from beginning to end in their entire careers, and though Alice was starting to close in on six figures, many of the floaters who played the game of production instead of actually producing, made considerably more.

Like always Alice took the elevator to the lobby, walked to the corner for the bus to the train that would let her out a block from work. Every day she gave herself a pep talk; she was good at her job, better than anyone else at the company, her immediate supervisor was a decent person unlike most of the other assholes in the company, she was being rewarded for good work, had a good salary, good retirement, good benefits, though the medical benefits were not what they had been thanks largely to her, and she definitely was challenged by her job. Still, she had the feeling that something wasn't quite right. How had this started?

Well, it had started shortly after she graduated with her MBA, a year after the creep had fallen on a broken TV and burst into flames. She had gotten a job right away with an electronics development company, overseeing contract fulfillment, that had lasted only a year since most of the government contracts were drying up in the late 70's, but she had been able to springboard to a company that was working with computer applications. With the 80's and Reagan, government contracts for defense or anything that could even be inferred to be defense-related were rolling in and she was able to go back to her first company. Each move along the line had been by the book. More money, more responsibility. The fact that she wasn't married hurt her at first but as she moved through her 30's promotions and responsibility seemed to be easier to come by. Alice always thought that it was because management had become less concerned that she would want to get married and start having babies, thereby not having sufficient time for that all-important job of making the company money.

Three years ago she had settled here at DemLab, a company that had absolutely nothing to do with laboratories, or any type of development. The name had been devised by a consultant who determined, or theorized depending on your point of view, that DemLab was a name that would appeal to government contractors, giving them a slight edge on contracts, and would impress the management of both Demonstrated Physics Inc., a huge electronics firm, and Demographic Software Corp., a subsidiary of the even larger software company with an obscene market share in both business and personal computers. The hope was that either Demonstrated Physics or Demographic Software would want to acquire DemLab for its name, thereby causing DemLab's stock to go up, the CEO to get a handsome bonus, and whatever employees were left to gain increased salaries in the new company. Rumors were always rampant that now was the time to buy DemLab stock; it was the announcement that a merger was nigh and the stock was going to soar. Alice had a nice little stash of DemLab in her IRA and was quietly buying more.

So Alice had taken and steered her career with her eyes open and things were going just as one would expect them to go, but god, she was tired of the assholes, male and female. She had gotten to the point where she needed to make a plan about how she was going to structure her career and her future, and the intense nature of work lately had left her drained and distracted at home. Lar was there except when he worked 2 days a week and he was helpful, but the stress at work and her belief that a plan was needed, was starting to interfere with her emotional availability to anyone. Now she needed a clear head and having Lar around hadn't been helping. They had been together for so long that he always knew when she was upset, always commented on it and always tried to make it better. The problem was that the mere act of being together broke her concentration. Alice wasn't actually sure what it was that she needed to concentrate on, but she did know when her concentration was broken and Lar broke her concentration every time she saw him. Best to get a break—something he will enjoy, something not too permanent. This had lead to the teaming of Yo and Lar. Lar hadn't been there in the morning, which was somewhat disquieting but reassuring, she told herself. Now she would be able to think about what had been vexing her, whatever that was.

Alice was at work an hour early but still the atmosphere was charged, electric.

"It's gonna happen this time," Sam the security guard said as she entered the door. Sam was in his late fifties, with an ample middle-aged spread, and a ready smile in the mornings that faded into a blank mask in the afternoon. "Both Demographics and Demonstrated just bought a big chunk of stock." The man was excited as if the news would be a major life event for him instead of for the CEO and senior managers who had huge amounts of stock.

Alice, known for her detachment, remained detached. "I've heard it all before, you know," she answered. "Besides, how much stock do you have?"

"Oh, I have a bit" the security guard said, smiling with the sides of his mouth turned down, the expression he used when he wanted to look sage.

"Well, good, hope it happens for you then; thanks for the news," Alice said pleasantly but without conviction, moving toward the elevators.

At her office Alice checked her voicemail. Vicki, VP in charge of research, human resources, and generally keeping things stirred up so that no one can get their jobs done, still insisted on being called Vicki so as to differentiate herself from her male counterparts, who always used their surname when talking to their subordinates. But since Vicki was female she said that she was demonstrating a more feminist, egalitarian management style. While some people adopt philosophies because it resonates in their lives and provides them with a meaningful understanding of themselves and others, other people use the trappings of a philosophy as a means to network and bully others. Vicki was the latter, President of the Association for Woman in Business, VP of the League of Women Managers, and on the board of the Coalition for Feminism in American Business Today. Vicki had called Alice's office phone, apparently from her home, at 10:30 last night, leaving a message that there was to be an emergency meeting of management at 7AM. "Good thing I got in early," Alice thought. "I have an entire minute to get to the meeting on the 10th floor—won't be too late. Damn bitch," Alice was thinking as she ran down the hall. "She couldn't call me at home—that way I would be able to get to the meeting on time. She's not the only woman VP for nothing; anything she can do to sabotage another woman so that she can keep her status as the only woman VP for DemLab, she has already thought of and implemented without a second thought."

Alice entered the conference room at 7:03. Vicki was talking and made a pointed frosty glance in Alice's direction, as if she should know to be on time but didn't have the self-discipline or will to do it. The look was not unnoticed by the other managers who sensed there might be blood in the water. The upshot of the 120-minute meeting confirmed what Sam had said. Large, but not huge, chunks of stock were bought by Demographics and Demonstrated, and both had approached the CEO with feelers regarding a friendly takeover. Obviously both parties did not want to get into a bidding war because it would decrease their bottom line, so there was nothing definite, however this was the first time there had actually been something. Since the meeting lasted an hour into Alice's normal working day and she hadn't been able to play catch-up this morning, she began her day two hours behind. "I'll just stay—Lar's not at home so there's no one to call with my schedule, quite liberating," Alice said to herself.

That evening she finished up at 9PM, went home and prepared for work the next day.

 Yo took to her new role with the enthusiasm of a disciple. Their first night, in the interest of safer sex, Yo tied Lar spread-eagled to the bed and gagged him with a latex gag that covered the lower half of his face but had a dildo sticking out where his tongue would be. Lar's safeword had been replaced with a hand gesture. The gesture would mean he would be untied, no more slapping and no orgasm for at least a week. Her periodic pauses to tease him and bring him to the brink kept him focused on what a great sacrifice it would be to be denied orgasm for a week. This would also have a consequence for her—no more slave play for the evening and the realization in her mind that she hadn't read him or played him properly. After securing Lar, Yo stripped and rode for hours, sometimes pausing to tease her naked slave or to slap the area which was becoming increasingly sensitive and was beginning to show signs of bruising. How he winced, even when she just flicked him with her finger and her timing was right. Not once did Lar use the safe sign, though his muffled cries and the look on his face plainly showed his distress.

 It wasn't till the next morning that Lar was acquainted with his surroundings. Yo lived in a 1950's-style rancher on about a half-acre of land. Judging from the length of the drive to her home, he figured they were either still in town or just outside of town, not in the distant 'burbs where such houses would be more common. In the city these homes would be pricey, far more than he would ever be able to afford. The street was lined with similar homes and rolling topography. The next day, promptly at 8AM, a man and a woman arrived in work clothes. After taking measurements downstairs in a room off of Yo's "family room," they emptied the room of boxes and furniture, then assembled a wooden structure that would do any dungeon proud. The structure was rectangle-shaped with an X on one of the sides, a table that could be snapped in or out with 4 bolts, 6x6 beams, and supports of dark-stained sealed wood with holes at 2-inch intervals. Yo, wearing only a short silk robe, beamed as the apparatus was installed, asking frequent questions and delighting in her new knowledge. The workers agreed to take the former contents of the room to Yo's storage area and before they left she paid them each a $100 tip. Lar was seeing how the other half lived; it sure seemed more convenient.

Keeping his promise to Alice, Lar wrote copious reports detailing his adventures with YoLynn. After a week there was a message from Alice on Yo's machine stating that she appreciated the reports but that things were just getting too busy at work right now for her to read such frequent detailed reports, and she would appreciate it if Lar would just send a shorter weekly report that she might find entertaining.

Over the next week Alice's job and life became more and more consumed over the possible merger/takeover/buyout of DemLab. She wasn't eating regularly, didn't have time for exercise, and sleep was caught in the time between arriving home and leaving for work, be that 2AM, 6AM or 8PM. Vicki wanted new year-end projections, and 5-year projections with and without various contingencies built in. For example, what will be the five-year cost of labor given the present economy's growth, with increased growth, with a recession, with decreased benefits, with a tiered benefit system (where new employees were given less than old employees) and with the inclusion of human resources from all of

Demographics Corp. Figuring these projections was incredibly time-consuming, and the end result was meaningless because if the company was purchased all of the factors used in her computations would be null anyway. Alice's mood declined, painting her outlook with a distinctly negative patina.

Waking for work Alice realized that not only was the apartment too small and messy, and inconveniently laid out, but that she didn't like her hair and nothing she had to wear looked right. Following her morning routine of showering, eating and dressing she went outside to wait for the bus to take her to the Metro. She could take her car but that wouldn't save her much time and the potential for much-increased aggravation was ever-present.

Across the street was another depressing sight—that homeless guy with the hood of his sweatshirt pulled up so Alice couldn't see his face. He had been across the street now for how long? God knows, but at least a week. Probably living under the stairs of that building, Alice thought as she remembered the problem over in Cleveland Park, a neighborhood only a few blocks away. In Cleveland Park a homeless man had taken up residence in a small local park, and his panhandling had become increasingly aggressive and violent because of his crack habit. The police continually hauled him away where it was rumored that he was detoxed, medicated and put out on the street where he would find his way back home to Cleveland Park. Car windows were smashed, people moved out, others were continually harassed. "How did that story end?" Alice wondered. "He's probably still there," she said to herself, "probably still hassling the residents while the police do nothing and the rest of the city calls the neighborhood NIMBYs. "Oh, you're from Cleveland Park," Alice started a conversation in her head, "the 'not in my backyard' neighborhood tsk tsk. People not living with a problem sure like to look down on people who have one," she thought. Alice's negative patina had taken over her daily ruminations as well.

The bus arrived, Alice got on. The bus drove to the end of the block and turned left. The homeless man in the hooded sweatshirt arose and shuffled down the block.

Alice was on time for the now customary 7AM meeting. The company was going to make a move that would further enrich someone's coffers, Alice just wasn't sure whose. Most of the stock that was owned by employees had been purchased through a discount program where the employee paid 10% under market value for the stock, up to 1/3 of their salary per year. The 1/3 figure had been implemented in order to prevent employees from just buying discounted stock and selling it all day. Employees were provided with a hedge when stock went down and could generally make a tidy profit when the stock was sold.

"What we're doing," Vicki began—she always used the term 'we' to imply that this was a team decision and she was part of the team—"is exercising the company's option to buy back all of the stock that was purchased through the discounted employee program. This will increase the company's net worth as DemLab's stocks are continuing to rise and can be expected to top out with a 43% growth over the present value when the buyout is announced."

Alice had a notion to access her account and sell, switch all of her DemLab stock now just to spite them.

"This option will be exercised in 20 minutes, at 9AM today. Staff who are expected to be absorbed into the acquiring corporation are being encouraged to keep their stock, as they will not be affected by the buyback." Vicki was handing out personalized letters to everyone at the meeting.

Alice spoke. "When will those who are having their stocks bought back going to receive compensation?"

Vicki made an exasperated and tired expression. "Alice, I am sure you are aware that everyone in this company is stretched very thin right now, we have all been working very hard."

"Great," Alice thought, "I'm being painted as the person who doesn't think anyone here is working."

Vicki continued. "As you should know, our contract says the company has up to 30 days to compensate employees in the event of a buyback."

"I was thinking of people who are getting laid off," Alice started. "If the stock's getting ready to take off and their money's tied up for 30 days they won't be able to take advantage of the merger."

"There's nothing preventing any of our employees from investing their savings or even borrowing to participate in our windfall," Vicki said evenly with a hint of anger.

"Like Sam has a lot of spare money to invest while he waits for his money from DemLab," Alice thought.

Vicki continued with the meeting's agenda. "Each of you has a personalized letter indicating whether it is anticipated that you will be absorbed into the new entity"

"This is sounding like the Outer Limits," Alice thought.

"Regardless of your letter's contents, I look forward to working with you during this next phase of our corporation's growth. It promises to be an exciting time," Vicki concluded and walked out of the room indicating that the meeting was over.

Alice opened the manila envelope with her name on it, the paper inside indicating how much company stock she had acquired, its worth when purchased, and its present worth.

Underneath that, next to the word "Consideration" were the words, "Not Absorbed" and a handwritten note from Vicki which said, "See Me."

Report to Mistress Alice

"I am in charge of all your movements," she said. "Now and for as long as you are here."

I couldn't dispute that now I was bound head to toe and couldn't move a muscle. Mistress had been leisurely as she first tied my ankles together, taking her time to make sure my ankles were snug, wrapping the nylon braided rope around and around, tying it off and then wrapping another piece of rope between my ankles. Circling the rope, she assured that my legs couldn't move but the circulation wouldn't be endangered, for a while anyway. As she moved on to other parts of my body Mistress checked back making sure my feet weren't getting cold, assuring that the circulation was maintained. Next, she wrapped the rope below my knees, again tying it snug, again wrapping another piece of rope around it. My wrists were over my head; they were cuffed and the cuff was fastened to the wall. Mistress had wrapped rope around my arms above the elbows under my head. While she wrapped a rope or inspected her job Mistress would periodically smack my cock making me flinch and letting her know just how much movement I was capable of. After my arms were made snug by the rope behind my head, I feared I would cramp soon. Next my stomach—she wrapped a belt around me and pulled, fastening it off. Then she wrapped another piece of rope around my waist, doubled it and wrapped it around again. Repeating this, Mistress tied it off. I could only breathe by moving my chest with my stomach drawn tight by the belt and rope. Occasionally I thought she would stop, but of course I couldn't say anything, rope having been wrapped around my open mouth, so I couldn't close my mouth to swallow, a trail of drool sliding down my cheek. She would survey her work, perhaps smack my cock, even leave the room briefly, but always she came back with a new inspiration. Mistress wrapped a belt around my chest below the nipples. "Exhale," she said. I complied as she pulled the belt tight. Making a band around my chest again, she used rope this time above my nipples. My breathing was now only in shallow gasps. She watched me, amused by my helplessness, a slap to my cock eliciting only the slightest movement, my breathing shallow. I was sweating and straining. I hoped I didn't cramp. I wanted her pleasure.

"Now for the fun part," she said, and began to wrap rope around my balls.

Alice put down the paper. She was surprisingly unmoved. The reading had been enjoyable but she had felt no particular arousal and more surprisingly, no strong emotions regarding the fact that her slave and lover for the past four years seemed to be having the time of his life with a good female friend of hers. When it came right down to it, Alice really didn't feel much about anything except that she was perpetually tired and perpetually annoyed. "Well," she had said to herself, "this is the first acquisition I have ever gone through, and to think some people thrive on this stuff!"

After the meeting Alice had gone to her office and transferred what she could out of her mutual funds into DemLab through her online broker. Those shares were not touchable by the company. Then she invested her savings in DemLab stocks with a wire transfer, and finally she maxed out her credit cards on DemLab—she would sure be up shit's creek without a paddle if the stock tanked. She had just broken two of her rules: one, don't put all of your stock in one company; two, don't borrow money, particularly on a credit card, to buy stocks. She rationalized that in 30 days she would be able to pay back her credit cards and this was the closest thing to an insider tip she would ever have. The fact that she might be unemployed in 30 days was disquieting; severance would pay just a couple of months' rent.

Alice's business with her stocks took more than an hour. When she was finished she walked to Vicki's office and caught her as she was leaving. "I had hoped that you would come to the office following the meeting," Vicki said, stonefaced and somewhat disappointed.

"I had some business that couldn't wait," Alice said. You're screwing me, remember, she thought.

"Well, I don't have time now—see my secretary, I'm swamped," Vicki had said as she left.

Now a full three days later, Alice was preparing to go to work and face the morning meeting, then an 8:30 with Vicki. "Come to think of it," Alice mused, "the report from Lar was a nice diversion."

Waiting at the bus stop, she again noticed the homeless man in the hooded sweatshirt. Well, he hasn't caused any trouble yet, she thought; maybe this won't end like Cleveland Park. With that thought in her mind Alice boarded the bus and her mood improved, but not substantially.

What she didn't hear was a soft click emanating from the form of the homeless man. As before, after the bus rounded the corner he stood up and shuffled down the street. At the corner where the bus made a left he turned right, quickening his pace for two blocks till he reached his destination.

"Like you say," the man began, "it's an old picture 'n people change in 20 years, but it could be her. I gotcha a picture." He handed the all-in-one camera over and retrieved three $20s. "You want I should look out for her tonight too?"

"That's OK, let me take this picture to my people," his benefactor replied. "Meet me here in a week then I'll let you know if they want anything else. Best you not be around here till then, I don't know what they're gonna do and personally I'm not keeping my ass in this town to find out until I hear from them again."

"You the boss," the sweatshirted man said as he walked away. As he walked he thought, "Hell, this has been easy money." Working for a private detective was great, he could panhandle, smoke, even drink on the job as long as he stayed put and watched for whatever he was supposed to watch for, and being a detective paid good too. Hell, that man was giving him 40-60 dollars a day to just sit on his ass in the morning and watch some lady leave her apartment. "I wonder what the detective's making if he can pay me that," the man thought. And flashy, shit, no Beamer or Lexus for that guy—he got hisself a brand new Vet, a red one. Yes, the bum would definitely be back next week, not knowing he had already received his severance.

Vicki got right to the point. "Presently you are considered in the 'nonabsorbed' category; however, I think if we can increase your performance level...."

"God, I hate how she makes everything 'we' when she means 'me'. It's like she's avoiding the responsibility of telling me what to do by pretending this is a team effort," Alice thought. Alice's dislike for Vicki and Vicki's management style was making it difficult for her to focus on what was being offered and what she was being told to do.

"What do you mean by increase my performance level?" Alice said, fearing the response.

"Our labor costs are higher than both Demographics and Demonstrated. As a member of the senior management team I know that we have been able to adapt some operations to conform with the paradigms of both entities and we will make whatever adjustments are necessary to tie up any loose ends, thereby assuring an easy absorption. I am more than reasonably sure that if you were able to conform your operation to their method of operations you would be absorbed as well. In fact I will get you that in writing by the end of the day."

This sounded like good news. Perhaps Alice wouldn't be out on the street after all.

"If you are to be absorbed, your stocks, of course, will not be subject to buy-back by the company. Confidentially, we expect a large spike in stock value in 10 days to two weeks." Vicki smiled.

To Alice this was sounding even better. "So my job is to bring our labor costs in line with the labor costs of the two entities?"

"Correct," Vicki said.

"By labor cost, you mean you want the cost of a permanent employee here to be equal to the cost of a permanent worker there?" Alice asked.

"Alice," Vicki sounded disappointed as if she feared the confidence she had shared with her new friend was going to be breached. "Labor cost means average cost per worker."

"Vicki," Alice began, "two more questions. One, if we are only going to exist for the next couple of weeks, what does it matter? Any changes in salary or benefits will be moot after the company's absorbed anyway. Two, both Demographics and Demonstrated produce products on a cyclical basis—that means they have a regular influx of large numbers of temporary workers without benefits, something not relevant to our company."

Vicki responded, all business. "That was one question and a statement. The purpose of bringing our costs into line with theirs is to show them we CAN, to show them that we are team material. I expect you to be creative." With that Vicki stood up, indicating that Alice's audience with her was over. Alice stood and walked to the door. Just as her hand was on the doorknob Vicki said, "You will have a written guarantee of your absorption signed and on your desk by the end of the day. Things are moving quickly so there won't be time for committees and the normal wrangling that usually comes with policy changes, so here it is: you present a proposal to bring our labor costs in line, one that's legal, and you will retain your stock and receive a 30% raise with your new employer. That's a good deal of cash and could substantially improve your standard of living." With that, Vicki sat down and began looking at papers on her desk, indicating that this time it was really Alice's time to leave.

Over that past two weeks, a combination of fatigue, loss of familiar grounding with Lar, and her depressed disposition impaired Alice's decision-making abilities. Perhaps that is why it was so easy for her to make a pact with the devil. Before closing the door she said, "You'll have it in one week or less."

Lar was sitting on a high stool at the breakfast counter working on his weekly report to Alice. As usual he was naked as he had not been instructed otherwise. YoLynn was pouring herself a cup of coffee.

"The only thing we have heard from Alice was that I should send a brief weekly report and that was a phone message—I'm getting a little worried about her" he said.

"Me too," Yo responded. "I haven't said anything but we used to talk on the phone a few times a week and have lunch now and then, but now, nothing."

"She did mention being real busy from work," Lar offered.

YoLynn was pensive, holding her coffee cup, eyes focused at the wall. "You've known her longer than I have. Has she done this before?"

"If you mean ignore her friends and fail to return their calls, no. If you mean loan out her slave, double no," he smiled.

"We should call again," Yo said.

"Maybe stop by with take-out if all we get's the machine," Lar added.

"Slave, I have to work late tonight. The good news is that I'll go in late today to make up for it. Last night on the X we had a problem because your hands kept going to sleep and this required that I lower your arms and restore circulation every 20 minutes. I think I have a solution to our little problem—your arms were above your shoulders and I bet that's why you were having circulation difficulties, so now we'll use the cross." Yo was into giving little declarative lectures lately. Lar enjoyed her enthusiasm.

"Slave," Yo said, pointing Lar toward the dungeon and the wooden T. "After you're secured I'm going to use some rubber bands to give you a nice set of blue balls.

Yo had to leave at 10:30. To her delight she had been correct about Lar's arms; keeping them level with his shoulders meant she didn't have to worry so much about nerve damage and she could relax and enjoy the show her slave put on for her. His nuts were another matter, his face registered increasing discomfort as his testicles darkened, so she frequently checked on them, gauging their temperature and color, allowing the circulation to return after they darkened and cooled. How he squirmed and whimpered when the rubber bands were removed. After getting dressed for work Yo got her car keys and left, leaving Lar secured to the cross. Returning just a minute later, she said, "Just messing with you," as she unhooked one hand. He could do the rest.

After his release Lar stretched and went back to his report. He thought this would be a good time to try to catch Alice, so he called her office and got no further than the secretary who would under no circumstances put his call through, though she would take a message. This was unusual because Lar knew Mrs. Anderson and had spoken with her repeatedly ever since Alice went to work in Human Resources. Mrs. Anderson was widowed with 3 grandchildren and looking to retire when she was 65 which, judging from her looks, was 5 or 10 years ago. She had always been pleasant with him, and was competent in her job. "The only messages she has answered this week are from upstairs—everyone else has to wait. People have been asking about their benefits and retirement for days and she hasn't got back to them, so I wouldn't expect a call from her anytime soon," the secretary declared, then added, "If you had married her when you had the chance I'm sure you would be on the A list for returned calls. Wives do that for their husbands."

"Thank you, Mrs. Anderson," Lar said as he hung up. Poor Mrs. Anderson! If she only knew the realities of their relationship she would be at least confused, most likely shocked. "If she only knew," Lar said aloud as he picked up the phone and again dialed Alice's apartment to leave a message.

"This is Alice, leave a message after the beep," her answering machine said.

"Alice, what's going on, how are you doing?" Lar began. "Hey, let's get together this week. We don't have to play or anything. I'm worried because I haven't seen you and Yo's worried too. We don't have to play or anything…just wanted to say hi and all, well, hope to hear from you soon, bye. "Well," Lar thought, "that was certainly an incoherent and inarticulate message."

The bitch wasn't keeping regular hours. That meant that he would have to do more surveillance than he had intended. He'd planned for his subcontractor to do all of the surveillance that was necessary but her sudden change in work habits had nullified a good part of the intelligence he had been able to gather. The motherfucker was going to be back in a week and the driver of the Vet had no intention of being within 500 miles of this city in a week. Hopefully the motherfucker wouldn't decide to be a go-getter showing up a few days earlier just to show his enthusiasm for the easy money he had been making. He would have to make his move soon. At least he knew that she lived alone and that she took a right turn outside of her apartment to go to the bus stop when she exited her building. This meant he could park down the block to the left and chances were he would not be seen. He could stay in his car with its tinted windows and not be a conspicuous spy or mistaken for a vagrant living in an expensive car, but there was still the necessity for a bathroom and food that put holes in his surveillance. Ideally he wanted to catch her outside the building at night, use his stun gun and carry her to his car, but her irregular hours had made that plan impractical. There was only a small window of opportunity from the bus stop to her door, and he would be conspicuous covering the distance from his car to the steps of her building. For the past two days he had missed her arrival home. The time for action was imminent, even if it required increased risk.

Alice had gone over all employee costs and contracts. Though many personnel actions appear arbitrary to employees of a large corporation, there are many laws that hinder management's desire to take certain personnel actions. Though Demlab's employees work "at will," meaning that employees are employed at the will of the employer and no justification is legally necessary for firing someone, employers are sanctioned if the firing can be construed to be discriminatory or if it appears that people are being let go when they are within 2 years of retiring. The main difficulties, though, are contractual. In order to obtain skilled people, companies must make certain promises regarding their benefits, including vacations, medical insurance and retirement, and what procedures will be followed if they are to be let go before their contract expires. This is what makes quick personnel actions difficult. Though employees may try to use a governmental agency to show that a labor law has been violated, the procedures take years and the outcome is capricious, depending on how "pro-business" the current political climate is. Meanwhile, the individual taking action is unemployed and is on record as making a complaint against the former employer, generally meaning no references and an uneasy feeling in any prospective employer's mind, that this person may be a troublemaker. The other route employees may take is legal. If the procedures laid out in their contract are not followed they can sue the company for breach of contract. Many lawyers will take such suits on a contingency basis, meaning that there is little risk to the employee because the lawyer gets a percentage of the settlement. This is can be quicker and the longer it drags out, the more in lost wages and lost earning potential a lawyer can sue for. Making sure that risk of future lawsuits resulting from any employee cost reductions was minimized, was Alice's present concern and the reason for her upcoming meeting with the Legal department. "If this project was so damn important, why did they make me wait two days to see Legal?" Alice thought. For the past day and a half Alice had read, underlined and reread the contracts and employment categories where she could target the most savings. She was reasonably sure she had a handle on it and writing the explanation was both detailed and time-consuming. The questions for Legal were meant to confirm her conclusions. However, the implementation of her conclusions was what had kept her up nights and at work early. Without the proper formulas in place for the proper employees, the plan would crumble into a plethora of lawsuits.

Alice was compiling her documents for her long-awaited meeting with Legal when Vicki walked in.

"Jim is glad you're coming aboard," Vicki began. "Jim" meant James R. Hollings, the CEO, Mr. Hollings to all managers and employees, even Vicki when she actually spoke with him, Alice suspected. "Things are moving much more rapidly than expected. It's like an avalanche—the stock's already taking off and we fear that if they take off too much it could jeopardize the offering, so we need to know if we can rely on you or not. I need your proposal this afternoon."

"Vicki!" Alice started abruptly. "I can't do anything until I speak with Legal, and it's taken me two days to get an audience with them. I don't know how long they are going to let my proposal sit around till they actually get around to getting back to me after I make my case to them. Then, if they have no changes, it will take at least a day to finalize the proposal. I told you I could have it in a week—I can still get it to you a day early, it would have been 3 days early if I didn't have to wait two days for an appointment with Legal."

"You should have a proposal ready for the eventuality that it is accepted as is," Vicki retorted.

Actually Alice did have the draft ready, however she was exercising some gamesmanship of her own. If the proposal was accepted she could have a final draft in less than an hour. It never hurt to show your boss you could do the impossible. "I can get you the proposal within 24 hours of Legal's approval," Alice said agreeably.

Vicki went to the phone and dialed. "We have 24 -36 hours," Vicki muttered before saying, "Sherrie, get me Tom, I don't care where he is, get him." Sherrie was Ms. Danforth, second in command in Legal, a high-powered corporate attorney who Alice suspected was not accustomed to being spoken to like an indolent secretary.

"Sherrie, this comes directly from Jim," Vicki began, again using Mr. Hollings' first name to give herself more clout. "I'm sending Alice over and I want Legal's full cooperation. We need answers fast and we're only interested in major liability, understand? Don't hold this thing up for nickels and dimes." There was a pause. "The net worth of our future corporation will be measured in the neighborhood of 115 billion dollars, so consider *that* when you consider what I mean by nickels and dimes. And remember, even if everyone COULD get money doesn't mean everyone WILL get money—you people always seem to forget that. Alice will be over there in..." Vicki looked at Alice.

"My appointment's in 10 minutes," Alice said.

"In ten minutes," Vicki finished forcefully, and hung up the phone.

It wasn't lost on Alice that Vicki had said that she was sending Alice over in ten minutes even though Alice herself had made the appointment two days ago. It wasn't lost on Ms. Danforth that she was being treated like shit. "I'm out of here and away from that bitch," she thought, "after I cash in my stock when this buyout's over."

Alice's meeting with Ms. Danforth was straightforward and courteous. She wanted to make sure of Corporate responsibility in regard to obligations concerning bonuses and the implications of corporate restructuring on departmental seniority. Sensing that her profits on stock sales were on the line, Ms. Danforth insisted that two other staff lawyers assist her in reviewing the contracts and relevant laws to be certain. Legal was encouraging and said she should have her answers by the end of the day.

Back in her office Alice, encouraged by her reception at Legal, inserted a disk in her computer and began printing out her proposal.

Mrs. Anderson knocked and opened her door. Alice knew she meant well but her proposal was not the type of thing she should be seeing at this time—it could be all over the building in an hour. Alice was visibly perturbed. "I just wanted to say," Mrs. Anderson began, "Lar called for you today. I know you're busy but I thought you should know." Even though Alice was visibly put-out, Mrs. Anderson still managed a motherly gleam in her eye.

"Thank you," Alice said, softening immediately. "I'll get back to him as soon as I can," then, feeling like she owed some explanation added, "Things are crazy right now."

Mrs. Anderson looked at Alice, not as if she had been a subordinate insulted or dismissed in a businesslike manner by her boss, but instead glanced at Alice with wide somber eyes that seemed to be conveying pity as she left the room.

Alice would not have been able to come up with this plan if the company had not made such huge profits for two years running, three years ago. After the first year's profits there was clambering up and down the food-chain for more money and benefits. The company could not make excuses of competition or paying down debt anymore. Unemployment of competent workers was low and DemLab's salaries were just barely competitive with other corporations in the area. So DemLab had to be mindful that it could lose many of its best employees quickly if a plan was not devised. Employees had been strung along with promises of a payback if only the company could make it through its present difficulties. Two banner years negated that argument as far as DemLab's employees were concerned. Just as Alice joined the company, senior management had found a way to reward the workers of DemLab. Bonuses were instituted as a form of profit sharing, but the bonuses were not only monetary—everyone had a huge increase in retirement contributions, medical benefits, training assistance, even daycare. The employees were happy to see that not only did they get what amounted to an extra paycheck, but suddenly DemLab seemed like a much nicer place to be, more than competitive with other local corporations. The institution of the new perks had necessitated that this be legitimized through Legal, therefore everyone had to sign new contracts agreeing to the new arrangement. As long as the company stayed profitable everyone prospered. Alice had reviewed the contracts and was able to come up with a very creative definition of the words "bonus" and "profit."

The phone rang—it was Mrs. Anderson, "Your notes are piling up! Things are going to get out of control unless you at least speak to some people."

"I'll do a briefing soon...within 48 hours," Alice said, dimly realizing what she was asking Mrs. Anderson to put up with for the next 2 days. By then it would be a done deal anyway.

Alice just wanted some time to breathe, to think. If she could hold it together for two more days it would be OK. She'd have what, to her mind, was big bucks, and a good job. Then maybe things could get back to normal.

She called Mrs. Anderson again. "You can tell everyone that nothing is settled yet with personnel. I just don't know what severance package will be available for those leaving or how our buyer will absorb personnel. You can tell that to anyone who asks and can return calls to anyone who left a message if that's what they want to know."

"Me, I'm taking the early out if I'm laid off," Mrs. Anderson began. "The retirement would be a bit less but the lump sum severance and my stocks should tide me over till Social Security. Have you heard anything about your secretary?" she asked quietly, even though they were on the phone.

"Mrs. Anderson, I don't even know if I have a job," Alice said, which was partially true. What she omitted was that she did know that only the senior staff and certain key employees were going to be absorbed—this wasn't a merger, it was a takeover. Their buyer would own DemLab and its personnel and if they went by the book they'd replace non-essential personnel as soon as possible. This would remove a large portion of corporate memory and minimize the chance that there would be friction between the new owners' method of operation and a group of employees who wanted to do things the old way. If they were lucky and wanted to do so, former DemLab employees would probably be hired in small groups so that they could become accustomed to the new employer without having too many allies to breed discontent.

Vicki called. "How did it go?"

"They're going to get back to me by the end of the day. If it's a go, I'll pull an all-nighter and get it to you by noon tomorrow at the latest," Alice said with the proposal almost half-printed in front of her.

The phone rang; it was Legal. Though they didn't have the details of the contracts that would be necessary to draw up the proposal—Alice had kept that information to herself, otherwise she was expendable and she knew it—but the definitions they had discussed and Alice's creative interpretation of the term "bonus" appeared to be mostly legal with a minimal chance of liability.

Alice buzzed Mrs. Anderson to tell her she was going home early to finish working, because there was too much chaos here, but there was no answer. Mrs. Anderson had left. Legal must have been able to call her directly because the rest of the employees had also left. "Oh well," Alice thought, "I'm leaving earlier than I have all week."

"Mistress, is it all right if we stop by before we do our errands?" Lar asked. "If she's home then maybe we can all go out to eat and if not we can bring carryout on the way back."

"Deal," Yo said. They drove past Alice's apartment. The lights weren't on in Alice's apartment, so they drove on.

When Alice got off the bus and started walking towards her apartment, Yo and Lar were less than one full block away headed in the opposite direction. "Now that's something you don't see every day, Mistress," Lar said with admiration in his voice.

"What's that, Edgar?" Yo said, completing the "Rocky and his friends Chauncy and Edgar" dialogue.

"A red Vet, not a Porsche, not a Beamer—a Vet," Lar said.

"You're right on that one, slave," Yo responded, initially wanting to express concern about the possible driver of the red Vet. Instead she engaged in the all-too-human magical belief that if something isn't talked about it won't exist, just as many couples in relationships won't bring up what is troubling them about the relationship for fear that the mention of the trouble makes it real and until it's mentioned it is only in their imagination. Lar was trying to suppress gooseflesh. He couldn't see a red Vet without it triggering some series of images, imaginings, and fears. He thought it would be silly to mention them—there were thousands of red Vets and the thought of freaking out every time he saw one was something he was trying to cure through repression.

The driver was in luck—the parking space he had vacated less than 30 minutes ago was still vacant, the first time that had happened since his surveillance began. He looked up towards her apartment just as the light came on. Fuck, the driver thought, away for a few minutes and then the bitch is in her apartment. He had a plan today. When he saw her emerge from the bus he would run towards her building wearing a disguise and ask her if she would let him into her building. He was wearing a green uniform with City Delivery on the shirt and cap. If she didn't run he would be able to get close enough to use his stun gun on her, then he could carry her to his car. Sure, there was some risk in carrying her across the street, but it was dark and if anybody saw him they would see that he was gingerly putting her in the passenger seat while he made hurt sounds about why did she always have to drink so much. Then it would be into an alley to secure her properly, then to a special place where he could have some fun and take some pictures. "Man, it's chilly out," he had been thinking. "I bet her nippies stand out even before I get her shirt off." But this plan was foiled—she was already inside. Carrying her completely out of the building was too risky so he would just have to go to plan B; it wouldn't be as noisy but he was sure he'd still have a good time. Make some money too. A man who loves his work never has to go on vacation because he's already having fun. That was his motto. It had served him well, and the pay was great.

Alice's building had a part-time door person whose primary job was less for security than to collect oversized packages and deliveries for the tenants. The driver waited 15 minutes, knowing that the doorperson would leave in 10. He waited a few more minutes, then walked up to the building and began pressing buttons at random, studiously avoiding that of his prey. The intercom hummed with a metallic, barely understandable voice. "Yeah?" a male voice queried.

"City Delivery," the driver answered.

"Who's it for?" the man asked, impatient.

"Motherfucker," the driver thought, "it's for you, dumb shit," but he didn't know who "you" was. He had pressed three buttons and he wasn't sure which one was responding.

"Yes," a female voice sputtered into the intercom.

"Shit," he thought, "now I have two of them." Then he realized that the odds had turned to his favor. Looking at the names beside the three buttons he had pressed, he realized that he had a two out of three chance of getting at least one of them right. He pressed the answer button. "City Delivery for Mann," he said in a businesslike manner, like a man who had been delivering all day and wanted to get home.

"Wrong apartment," he heard the male voice say as he heard the buzz of the lock being electronically opened. He was in and he already knew her apartment number.

Yo and Lar were quiet for a few minutes, then Lar said, "That Vet gave me the creeps."

"Me too," Yo responded.

Continuing to ignore protocol by not starting his sentence with the word "Mistress," Lar said, "How 'bout if we bag the dry cleaning and going to the hardware store for now and just go back and check on her?"

Ignoring Lar's breach of protocol, Yo said, "Let's get some carry-out first, that way we won't look like complete idiots when we show up and nothing's wrong."

Though Lar's gut told him that they should get back as quickly as possible, his first thought was that if he didn't act as if it was an emergency, it wouldn't be an emergency, and secondly, he did owe Yo a certain deference. "Good idea," he said. "She wasn't even home yet, anyway." He turned left so that he could stop at the Chinese take-out that was on the way back, the restaurant that never kept him waiting too long. He didn't know that even this brief delay would make his arrival too late.

Alice was booting her computer. Though her proposal was printed out, chances are there would be an inevitable typo to correct. She reached into her office carrying case that held the notebook, retrieved the thick pile of papers that was her proposal, and her disk. All work at the office had been done on her notebook and stored on floppy—she didn't trust Vicki or any of the other VP assholes. Alice was of the opinion that if they could get into her computer and take her proposal, most any one of them would gladly put their name on it and take the credit, leaving her out in the cold. She was right.

Her office computer had been used only for printing and now housed an outline which omitted the meat that made her proposal work. There was a knock at the door. What, no buzz? She looked through the peephole at a guy wearing a green uniform with City Delivery on the cap and jacket. Didn't the office use Reliable Delivery? City must be used by one of the potential buyers; just another way for the VPs to kiss ass, she supposed as she opened the door. The man was older than most delivery drivers; maybe he was a victim of some downsizing. Curious that he would wear alligator boots—I always thought they would be uncomfort…that was as far as Alice got with that train of thought. She saw a bright flash as if lightning had exploded, and her body felt as if she had been hit with a fist as large as she was.

They always lost bladder control, the delivery man mused as he pushed open the door, now being blocked by Alice's inert body. Some even lost control of their bowels. "Must hurt like a bitch," he said to no one in particular. Making sure the blinds were all drawn, he went to work. The first thing he needed to do was unplug the phone and secure her. Bitch must have all sorts of things he could use here, but at first glance all he could see was a chaos of papers and folders on every flat surface, even tables and chairs. The man without even a high school education but a natural sense for business, didn't understand how anyone could need this much mess to do their job. Then he realized it didn't matter…he only had a few minutes, so he had to find something fast. If he couldn't find something customized to hold a victim he had plenty of duct tape. He saw chrome and leather-strapped chairs by the table—one of those would do nicely.

The first thing he did was strip her by cutting the clothes off of her with a razor-sharp knife. Bitch had nearly ruined him 20 years ago and he didn't forget a debt. He knew how to take his time and when to pick his moments. After so many years of eking out a living as a picture-taking voyeur, his face deformed from fire and glass, he had pulled himself together again. He didn't come to the country much—way too hot, way too difficult to do his type of work. Overseas and in South America, in second and third world countries, there was unlimited talent for his productions. Plus, there were police who knew nothing of forensics and he had no fears of crack-addled boyfriends. He would come back, however, just to live it up in America, throw his money around or to do the occasional special project with an American girl when the price was right. One customer paid so much just to know that it had been done in the U.S. Each photo spread had to show something American, like a street lined with maybe a diner, McDonald's, and a telephone booth. There was even a bonus if the photo was accompanied by a newspaper article describing the murder. The photographer had toyed with the idea of just killing a white woman in another country and digitizing her into a few distinctly American prints, but that was unsporting. He did, after all, like his work and part of his work was the challenge.

The closest he had ever gotten to the police had been the day of the fire. Since then, as before, it had been all too easy, as his one-time dread of local police turned into a minor annoyance. His main fear in the States was the FBI; too many bodies and they would start thinking serial killer, and this would marshal their considerable resources of computers and interstate information-gathering. Local cops, though, like he always said, were dumb as shit. He had been wrong on one count though—big city cops were no better. He had no real evidence of this except that for the thrill years ago he had used a big-city girl, the results of which were the same as the girls in the towns—no problems from the police. Since then he tended to stick to the cities—more nightlife. The elaborate precautions he took in his youth, he decided, were mostly overkill, especially now that he only came into the country briefly. He never left the country from the city in which he had worked, so he knew their chances of finding him were nil. Years ago, he worried so when he transported his product to the post office; now he knew the realities: 1. Even if they saw him they wouldn't see the product. 2. If they saw the product he would call it movie stills. The photographer knew he was different from the rest. He got away with things.

This one. He had been thinking about this one for years, building a delusion that had no basis in reality but did serve as a convenient receptacle for any of life's difficulties for which he would prefer not to take responsibility. If she had been stripped in Tayler she wouldn't have put up such a fight, he thought. Women always fell apart if you stripped them against their will; the fight would leave them and all they would do is be helpless. He picked up a rag and stuffed it into Alice's mouth.

"If it hadn't been for you, Al's men would never have found me," he said as he wound the tape around her head—her mouth would be painfully open when she came to.

Yo and Lar were seated on a straight-backed wooden bench across from the cashier in the Chinese restaurant. Lar made his third trip up to the cashier in 10 minutes, following his fourth trip to the phone. "How much longer for our food, please? I mentioned we were in a hurry when we got here."

"I'll go check, one minute," the cashier said courteously as she took the check from some customers who were leaving. She recognized Lar as a regular and also as someone who usually wasn't this agitated. To Lar the cashier seemed to move in slow motion and the woman paying was intolerable. Why do so many woman go to a cashier as if they have no idea that they will be expected to produce either money or a credit card? The woman had waited until the check was rung up and the total announced before she even began her elaborate and ineffective ritual of retrieving her wallet from her purse. With the transaction completed the cashier started for the kitchen. Lar stopped her.

"I don't care if it's not completely finished, just bring what is ready. I don't want a refund—I just want to leave," Lar said desperately. His anxiety level was rising exponentially each minute. If he could just drive down the street and see that there was no red Vet he would be OK, but until he had that assurance, his anxiety would build. Already, food was the farthest thing from his mind, his stomach in knots. Yo did not so much feel anxiety as notice Lar's. Though she also had a feeling of alarm, she was starting to think they should have just made a U to check things out as soon as they saw the Vet; the toll this was taking on Lar was disquieting.

The photographer had Alice's arms secured. She was beside two sets of tall windows with heavy drawn blinds, next to the dining room table. He was about to do her legs when he had an inspiration for the series he was about to create. He pulled out his camera and flash—he had the first picture of his series, the not-yet-conscious victim. He knew that for his last picture he would open the blinds and turn off the lights inside so that the viewer would see the artist's handiwork against a distinctly American skyline with the Capitol Dome lighted in the distance. Between his first and last picture, he wasn't sure how, he knew that he would break this bitch and have her ready to kill herself rather than undergo any more of his ministrations. How he loved that game—giving them the one hope of release by taking their own life. They all opted for it eventually, but the photographer never let them complete the act; that was his privilege, one he would exercise much later, much to his model's chagrin. Now to set up a surprise. The photographer lit a cigarette, then took a length of duct tape, made it half-width, then put a band around Alice's forearm and fastened the cigarette in place by its filter. The cigarette would make a nice, slow long burn up her arm. If he was lucky she would flail those legs as her pain increased, providing the viewer with titillating views of her snatch, whetting their appetite for things to come. He flashed another picture and noticed that her eyes were fluttering. This was great—hopefully, he would be able to capture the look of surprise and pain as she woke up. He pointed his camera and held his breath anticipating the picture, his mind racing. He could do a cigarette series. This is why he made the big bucks, this was his art, these inspirations that came at just the right time in just the right place. Cigs on her nipples, stomach, and face, ought to get her moving. Then he would secure her legs so he could attach the cigarettes to the more tender places. He hoped he had enough; he could always zap her again, then go out for more cigs. They stayed out longer after you weakened them up some. Alice's eyes continued to flutter.

The waitress returned with a bag of carryout. "Fie mou min," she said.

Lar grabbed the bag in one arm, Yo's arm with his free hand, and left the restaurant. "I know I'm out of line," he said, out the door, "but I've got to get back."

Yo put up no objection and raced with him to the car. With Lar at the wheel they pulled out and drove the remaining eight blocks to Alice's street. One-half block from her door, a full block from her bus stop, was the red Vet. Lar looked up towards Alice's window and saw that the shades were drawn, however there was an unmistakable flash inside the window. Lar pulled the car to the

Loading and Unloading Zone in front of the building, opened the trunk and took out a tire iron. Yo reached for a piece of iron pipe that she kept under the driver's seat. Using his key Lar opened the front door; thankfully the elevator was open and they wouldn't have to run up 6 floors.

Alice was confused; as her mind cleared she was aware of a burning pain in her left forearm that was increasing at an alarming rate, the rate of her regaining consciousness. She noticed that she couldn't move her arms and that her mouth was opened painfully wide and she couldn't close it; she was almost drowning in her own spit. Her screams almost completely muffled, she opened her eyes with alarm and was blinded by a flashing light.

"Perfect," a male voice said enthusiastically.

Alice tried to blink the flash-blindness away. The locks on the door were opening and the photographer reached for his other stunner. This stunner shot electrodes 20 feet—it was silent and effective. An automatic with a silencer was beside it on the table, just in case. Alice's door opened only as far as the two door chains would allow. The photographer could see a woman's face; she was very pretty and looked rich. "She must have someone with her," he thought, "someone trying to get in the door."

Lar kicked at the door and it swung open. As soon as the door opened, a small dot spooling a spider web hit Yo, and she collapsed, writhing, on the floor. Another dot whizzed in front of Lar's face and struck the wall. Lar ducked and rolled himself in, quickly standing beside the door. Now he saw a man in a green uniform, his face scarred from old burns, reaching for a gun on the table. Only one chance—Lar threw the tire iron at the man, who momentarily ceased his grab for the gun to put his arms protectively up in front of him. The side of the iron hit him hard. The man who was reaching for the gun staggered toward what Lar now recognized as Alice, tied to a chair. He was reaching out his hands like claws, apparently intent on steadying himself at the expense of Alice's hair or face.

Seeing the door open, Alice used all of her strength to attempt to rock the chair forward so that she could support it with her legs. She succeeded only in slightly twisting the chair so that she was at a 45-degree angle from the windows. When she saw the man with the scarred face, the photographer, former big-hair asshole, staggering towards her she raised both legs and kicked hard. She felt her heels hit solidly into the man's groin and hips. The force of the kick knocked her chair backward so that the back of her head hit the carpeted floor; she saw stars.

Lar saw Alice preparing to kick; why did it look like there was smoke coming off of her left arm? She thrust both of her legs out powerfully and with focus. The man in the green suit was thrown back a step and that was all it took for him to shatter the window and fall out backwards, hands grasping at the air. Though Yo was lying in the hallway twitching and Alice was struggling feebly in an overturned chair, Lar could not escape the imperfection of his humanity. The first thing he did was run over to the window to take a look—he was not disappointed.

After only a brief glance Lar went over to Alice and began to work on her gag, then again he noticed the smoke. The son-of-a-bitch had taped a lit cigarette to Alice's arm. Grabbing at the tape and pinching the butt out with his fingers, he clawed it off of her arm then went back to work on her gag. Alice was in obvious distress and was having trouble breathing, a combination of being on her back, having a mouth full of spit and not being able to close her mouth to swallow. Lar righted her and Alice forced a stream of spittle through a small crack in the tape. Reaching the table he grabbed a knife and carefully slit the duct tape. He yanked the seam separating the bands, allowing Alice to open her mouth and ripping out a chunk of her hair. She winced but breathed easier. Then he freed her wrists and said breathlessly, "Are you OK for now? I want to check on Yo." Alice nodded, not yet able to speak.

Yo was still on the floor of the hallway; by now other doors had opened. "Has anyone called the police?" he asked. The faces, blank, just stared at him. "Please, someone call the police," then he remembered if you want something done in a group, don't ask the group—each member will assume someone else will do it. Lar looked at the face nearest his, directly into the woman's eyes. She flinched but returned his stare, cowering behind her partially-opened door. "Will you please call the police?" he said to her, then knelt to pick up Yo and take her inside.

Yo was already coming to, her eyes fluttering and arms moving, so he placed her on the floor and went back to minister to Alice, helping her remove the duct tape and going to her room to get clothing she could put on while she got her land legs.

Yo was standing. "Alice," she said, "we have to remove as many of your toys from here as possible—the cops are likely to think you're a whore who killed a John if they see all of your stuff."

Alice understood immediately. Her brand of sex was strange to many, therefore it was just lumped in with everything else that is strange, forbidden and loathed. It would be best to at least minimize police suspicions. "Lar, I'm still shaky—can you use the footlocker to...." Lar was already walking towards the bedroom. "We can't do anything about the wall fixtures but we can do our best."

"I'll get you a bathrobe," Yo offered.

Lar was in the bedroom; a wardrobe beside the bed was converted inside with pegs, coated with black velvet and a low-power yellow light. The wardrobe was filled with sex toys, whips, paddles, clamps, dildos, and harnesses. Lar had lowered a footlocker from the top of the closet, dumped the blankets, quilts and linens, and was filling it with sex toys. The saddle would just have to stay on top of the dresser—there was no room. Most of the toys, however, were locked up and the footlocker put back at the top of the closet, the wardrobe scattered with the footlocker's former contents.

By now the sound of the sirens was almost to the building. Lar was going to start on odds and ends in the closet then decided to check in. "What shall we tell them?" he asked.

"How 'bout the truth?" Yo answered. "We were coming here with carryout and stumbled on this."

"Oh," Lar said, the deception of Alice's wardrobe making him forget that there was nothing wrong with what they had done.

As Lar was about to go back into the bedroom the first police arrived. "Everyone stop what you're doing," the first cop said.

"These people saved me," Alice began.

"Not now please, maam," the cop said, businesslike. "There's a body below this window, so for the time being we're going to treat this as a crime scene."

"Well, it is that," Alice said again.

A man in a two-piece suit arrived. Obviously he was the one in charge. "What's that all over your arms and face, maam?" he said.

"The remains of duct tape," Alice replied.

"You and your boyfriend getting a little frisky?" The detective asked in a way that could be construed to be jovial or accusatory.

"Hell no! That creep tried to kill me!" Alice said.

"You mean..." the detective motioned toward the window.

Alice scratched at her arm and winced, the shock from recent events passing, allowing sensation to come back to her. "Son-of-a-bitch taped a cigarette to my arm," Alice said rolling up her sleeve showing the detective a nasty fresh burn on her arm.

"Oww," he said. "Do you need medical attention?"

"Well I'd like to clean it and put some Bacitracin on it," Alice said.

"If you don't have to use the bathroom could you leave the door open, please? We still need to treat this like a crime scene until we get this sorted out," the detective said.

A patrolman walked into the room. "No ID we could find without moving the body, but we did find these," he said, holding up a set of car keys on a ring from which a picture of a red Corvette Stingray dangled.

"See if they fit anything on the street," he said. "Start with the Vet up near the corner."

Turning to Alice he said, "Interesting decor." He was looking at the heavy polished boards attached to Alice's wall in the living room. Boards with wide metal rings attached, located about shoulder and ankle height.

"I thought it would be fun to go Goth for a while but didn't want to buy all new furniture, so I guess the apartment's a hodge-podge," Alice said.

"Mind if we look around a bit?" the detective asked.

"What's this all about?" Yo was indignant. "If we hadn't come in Alice would probably be dead from that creep. Can't you see that shit all over her hair? Look at her arm!"

"Your name please, maam," The detective had pulled out a small notebook.

"YoLynn Rebecca Johnson, JD," Yo answered, "My attorneys are the firm of Finch, Burns, Jackson and Green and I'm going to call them if you don't leave Alice alone—she was almost killed for god's sake."

"Ms. Johnson, please accept my apologies for our procedure. As your friend said she didn't need to go to the hospital, we are trying to clear up any loose ends that the DA might ask. As of now we would describe Alice as scared and all of you as cooperative. We can stop asking questions now but the DA will probably want the place searched. He'll have to get a warrant and we'll have to just stand around here not searching but making sure nothing's disturbed until someone can find a judge, then talk to the judge then get the paperwork to the judge...."

"I get the point," Alice said, her face getting pale. "Personally, I'm starting to feel awful." She got up and bolted from her chair, making a beeline for the bathroom when one of the cops got in her way.

"Where are you..." the cop said.

He didn't get any further—as soon as she was stopped, Alice threw up all over him.

"Jesus," the cop said.

"Never stand between a sex-crimes victim or a first-time perpetrator and the bathroom—just don't let them close the door," the detective said wearily. "Don't we have any females on this shift? Better get a crisis counselor here too," he said to no one in particular, though one of the uniformed policemen immediately began talking on his two-way. Looking at the policeman who had stopped Alice, he said, "Go get your uniform cleaned." Lar noticed that a cop in her bedroom was starting to lift the footlocker from its place in the top shelf of the closet.

Alice emerged from the bathroom, pale. Lar went to her and sat by her on the sofa. The uniformed policeman was again on his two-way: "Detective, I think you better come down to the Corvette," he said.

Curiosity was now getting the better of the patrolmen in the apartment; some were starting to file towards the door. This was just an apartment with some weird woodwork and furniture—someone had hit pay dirt outside. "Someone keep an eye on the witnesses while I go out to look," the detective said.

Yo headed for the door. "Where are you headed?" the detective asked.

"I'm going outside and I do not intend to be out of your sight," Yo answered evenly.

"Stay here. I'll be back," the detective said.

This is where Yo's moneyed upbringing became evident. Whereas Lar and Alice were quelled by the presence of the police, Yo was not. She had always had lawyers at her disposal who could negotiate the legal system for her, therefore the legal process going on in the room was not nearly as intimidating for her as it was for someone who wasn't accustomed to having a trusted lawyer on retainer. "If you are putting us under arrest let me know and I will call my attorney; otherwise I'm walking out that door. I will cooperate with you by staying in plain sight but if you don't allow me to come and go as I please, I'm calling my attorney now. We'll see what he has to say about the police putting the victim of a sex crime under arrest when she's fortunate enough to have overcome her attacker." Yo was 2 feet from the detective's face, looking him straight in the eye.

"Would you like to come too?" he said to Alice and Lar.

Lar looked at Alice; she was already looking better. She nodded her head. "Sure," Lar said.

"Please stay in sight," he said as he left the apartment.

"Christ," the detective said disgustedly after seeing the trunk's contents. Inside the trunk was a box with a small pile of glossy 5x7 and 8x10 pictures of rape, torture and murder. Most of the victims seemed to look Indonesian. There were passports from Indonesia, Venezuela and the US, each with a different name but containing the same picture. Beside the box were two cameras and a leather bag containing surgical equipment, hunting knives, and everyday tools, rubber gloves, elastic tape, duct tape, a plug-in battery charger, and two manila envelopes addressed to opposite ends of the country.

The detective closed the trunk lid and took off his latex gloves. Alice, Yo and Lar were standing about 10 feet behind him. "None of you is planning on leaving the city anytime soon?"

"No sir," they chorused.

He looked directly at Alice. "The sex crimes counselor will be here shortly. I suggest you speak with her. She'll have some suggestions for you too. It will cut down on your chances of getting PTSD. Sorry this happened to you—looks like you have some good friends and were real lucky," he said as they walked away.

They walked back to Alice's apartment and sat quietly for a few minutes. The police had left, removing Alice's attacker's belongings. Lar put plastic garbage bags around the window, secured them with duct tape and was gratified to see that Alice didn't cringe as he pulled tape from the roll. Then he sat beside Alice on the sofa; Yo was on a chair.

Alice got up, walked over to her briefcase and pulled out a floppy and with difficulty snapped it in half, then she retrieved a thick stack of papers. Taking a small, manageable group of papers in her hand, she proceeded to calmly rip the paper into 2-inch strips before returning to the pile to retrieve some more. Her face showed almost no expression.

"Alice, what are you tearing up?" Lar said, a little concerned.

"It's a mostly legal way to screw a lot of workers who are about to be laid off, losing a good chunk of their retirement, and to deduct medical insurance payments that they think have already been made, from their severance packages. Meanwhile the proposal lowers retirement and overall corporate benefits to all absorbed staff, except for senior absorbed staff and lets go all non-senior staff who are within 5 years of retirement, so that they will have to wait till they are 67 to receive reduced retirement benefits." Alice went on tearing up the papers. "This has been a big project; each employee had to be identified, and benefits calculated. Without this proposal on Corporate's desk by noon tomorrow they will not be able to screw everyone and," Alice paused for effect, "without this on Corporate's desk by tomorrow noon I am out of a job and so are my chances at a senior position anywhere for the foreseeable future. Screw-it, I'm not gonna do it, it's not worth it. Nothing like almost dying to let you know what's important." Alice continued to tear. She looked at Lar with an expression he had never seen on her—a mixture of fear and vulnerability.

"Lar, I want us to be together but I need to reevaluate my life. I don't want to be the type of person I was becoming. I need to simplify, maybe even move away from here. There will be some major changes in my standard of living and I'm not sure if you are ready for that. For one thing it would mean working full-time. I'm not going to be making as much money."

Looking at her, Lar was seeing Alice with new eyes. This was a woman who needed more than he had been giving. Even in his supportive role, he knew his deference had created a distance between a part of him and a part of Alice. He realized now that this was making Alice feel that part of her, an important part, was unneeded and unwanted. If he wanted to be able to stay with Alice he would have to pursue her and show his love for her as an equal partner pursuing something cherished, and not as he had done, as a passive slave who waited for her to make all their decisions and waited for her to make every move in the relationship. Lar understood that the next set of moves would have to be his, toward her.

Epilogue

The yellow light was thick as if it was a fluid. That is what it felt like. At first it was thin and so bright it hurt to see but the color darkened as it thickened, until it appeared that everything was under a sea of thick yellow water the color of the sun. It was there as before, but now the details were much more visible—it was huge, the head resembling a rectangular piece of stone the height of the rest of its body. The entire body seemed to be composed of slabs of brownish-gray stone that were imperfectly sized and imperfectly fitted together to make the huge head and the much thinner body with no discernible neck. The arms and legs were of equal length and width, each being wider than the central core body. There were no visible sense organs, just the body that looked like stacked rock slabs sitting on a great boulder with movements that made it appear to weigh no more than the light that surrounded its arms, appearing to float in the calming and peaceful light. This was the first time its body and head had actually turned fully in their direction, not just allowing interlopers a glimpse, but welcoming their presence with ever-increasing waves of calm and peace.

In the room, along with faint sounds of surf and sea gulls, the first light of dawn had begun to filter through an open window. The naked bodies on the bed were slick and glistening with sweat, the male spread-eagled on his back, tied tightly to the four corners. The woman's body was on top of the male's, mirroring his X. Both breathed in synchronous shallow, rapid gasps, bodies shuddering in time, the look in their eyes one of utter calm and peace. The male's body had been tested with a long, thin braided whip. The stripes on his back had been artistically applied with descending strokes from left shoulder to right buttock and right shoulder to left buttock. Where the stripes intersected they created a diamond pattern—except for the fifth stripe on the left. On the fifth stripe, the woman had erred, making a horizontal slash in his back, bisecting the diamonds into a double row of triangles across the base of his shoulderblades. "I couldn't do that again in a million years if I tried," she had said to herself after seeing the result of her mistake. He had been reduced to cries and grunts by the time the design was completed and she almost had to carry him to the bed, now covered with a sterile, rough canvas sheet. First he had been slowly and methodically secured, spread-eagled. Once secure, her climb on top of him had renewed his agony as the rough canvas further abraded his savaged back. From above, one can see her smooth naked back glistening with sweat, touched only by the breeze from the open window, shuddering in time with the body below her. Then there is a reddening on her back as welts burst open with raw angry skin. The welts start to form a diamond pattern, from her shoulderblades to her buttocks, except for the fifth stripe from the left which is horizontal, bisecting the diamonds into a double row of triangles across the base of her shoulderblades. Alice had made her mark and it was on both of them.

Beside the bed in the cramped efficiency is a small kitchen table. On the table is a small white cake with a single candle. The cake is less than a quarter eaten, but the words "Happy Anniversary" are clearly visible on an overturned card. There is a sound of early risers trying a locked door downstairs, but the early risers will have to leave—the owner-operated T-shirt shop won't be open for hours.

About the Author

The author is a psychologist at a psychiatric hospital and operates a KAP private practice. The writer also performed graduate research examining long-term relationships of people involved dominant/submissive lifestyles.

9 780595 162314